The Golden Pigeon

SHAHID SIDDIQUI grew up in the bylanes of Shahjahanabad, the walled city of Delhi, in an atmosphere of poetry, culture and creativity. He belongs to a family of illustrious journalists and writers. His father, Abdul Waheed Siddiqui, was a prominent leader in the freedom movement. He started writing in Urdu at the early age of twelve and translated many English classics into Urdu. He published the path-breaking fortnightly *Waqiat* in 1971 and went on to publish *Nai Duniya*, a weekly, in 1973, while he was still a student at Delhi University. Shahid did his master's in political science from Delhi University and taught there from 1974 to 1986. He has been a political activist since his school days and was in the forefront of the opposition to the Emergency in 1975. His activism brought him into politics and he was a member of the Rajya Sabha between 2002 and 2008. He has been writing in English, Urdu and Hindi for various newspapers and magazines over several decades. *The Golden Pigeon* is his first novel in English.

The Golden Pigeon

SHAHID SIDDIQUI

HarperCollins *Publishers* India

First published in India in 2014 by
HarperCollins *Publishers*
Building 10, Tower A, 4th Floor, DLF Cyber City, Phase II,
Gurugram Haryana – 122002, India
www.harpercollins.co.in

2 4 6 8 10 9 7 5 3 1

P-ISBN: 978-93-5136-992-9
E-ISBN: 978-93-5136-993-6

Typeset in 11/13.9 Garamond Premier Pro
by Jojy Philip, New Delhi 110 015

Printed and bound at
MicroPrints India

Prologue

I was shivering and so was my mother. Under the seat of the tonga in which we were hiding, we could hardly breathe. I wanted to cry but my mother had put her henna-coloured hand on my mouth. I used to love sucking her fingers but now she was virtually suffocating me. I could taste the pungent smell of fear emanating from her body, which normally smelled of roses and jasmine.

I could hear the rhythm of the tonga, taktaktak, tuktuktak. The beat of the horse's hooves used to be music to my ears when we rode in a tonga to the Qutb Minar for a picnic on the third day of Eid every year. All the girls in the family would be singing loudly, while I enjoyed the soft comfort of their laps. But today my mother and I were escaping from my father, with whom we had gone to Old Delhi railway station before sunrise. My father, Azizuddin Khan, had decided to migrate to Pakistan but my mother was opposed to it. She had resisted my father for two years. My mother, Hina Begum, loved the bylanes of Delhi. She could never imagine living in any city but Shahjahanabad, the city of her Mughal ancestors. My mother cried and cried, but failed to convince my father. When his jeweller's shop in Chandni Chowk was attacked and burnt down, Azizuddin said, enough is enough. He could not live in Delhi anymore. He was going with his beautiful wife Hina Kauser and his twin sons Aijaz and Shiraz to Pakistan, where he was told that every Muslim was safe.

'Lahore is as much the land of our ancestors as Delhi ever was. It was also built by Akbar, Jahangir and Shahjahan. You will not miss your beloved Delhi. Lahore is a carbon copy of Shahjahanabad,' argued Azizuddin Khan.

'But they speak Punjabi in Lahore, not Urdu, and how can you compare Dilli to Lahore.' Hina was scandalized. 'Lahore is the city of Noor Jahan, the conspirator princess from Persia, not the city of the Mughals. Our ancestors loved Delhi and Agra,' said my mother, trying to score some points in this argument, which she knew she was going to lose anyway.

We had our last dinner of Dilli ki nahari, a special spicy meat preparation invented by the Delhi of Shahjahan, on the evening of 30 March 1950. My Nani, Qudsia Begum, hugged us all for the last time. My mother was crying silently, tears rolling down from her golden-brown eyes and making Azizuddin miserable. My brother Aijaz and I were just two years old – though Aijaz was older than me by twenty-five minutes – and had no idea what all the fuss was about. The only thing we knew was that we were going to sit in a train, which we had only seen from a distance till then. Bundu Chacha, our family coachman, used to take us to the Old Delhi railway station in his tonga and show us the big black noisy engine. He was very good at copying the sounds of a train and we enjoyed sitting on his back while he crawled around the room on all fours, whistling like an engine. Tall and fair, with a handlebar moustache, Bundu Khan was a brave, proud man who claimed to be a descendant of the great horsemen of Samarqand. He plied his humble tonga through the crowded streets of Delhi with all the pride of a royal charioteer.

In the darkness of a cloudy Delhi morning, we took two tongas to the railway station. The city was burning. There had been riots all night in the walled city of Shahjahanabad. My father's house was in Kuncha Cheelan in Daryaganj. The rioters were still asleep, tired after a day of burning and looting. My father took advantage of this lull and asked Bundu Chacha to take us to the station to catch the morning train to Lahore. We reached the station safely. My father was carrying Aijaz while I slept in my mother's lap, unaware of the great drama taking place around me. My father settled Hina Begum on an empty bench and went to buy the tickets with Aijaz sleeping on his shoulder. My mother, clad in her black burqa, suddenly stood up and, holding me in her arms, ran out of the station. She would not go to this godforsaken place called Pakistan when the graves of her Mughal ancestors were all here in Delhi. She had gone blank with fear. She was not in control of herself, it was as though some jinn had possessed her. A woman who had never walked out of her door alone, a woman who had never spoken to a strange man, was running madly, not knowing where she was headed. Suddenly, she tripped and fell on the road, her burqa flying in all directions. I began crying at full volume. Someone picked me up, and then I was in the strong hands of Bundu Chacha. He helped my mother get up. When she told him to take her to my grandmother's house in Ballimaran, Bundu looked at her disapprovingly. Bundu was a follower of Maulana Azad and was entirely opposed to the idea of Pakistan, but he also knew that a woman's place was with her sartaj, her husband.

'Hina Begum, you must go back and be with your husband, wherever he may take you,' he admonished my mother in his gruff voice. But my mother was adamant she wanted to go to her mother's house. She could not leave her mother and all her memories here in her beloved Dilli.

❖

My mother had the stubbornness of her Mughal ancestors, and their fearlessness. Bundu had to surrender but he waited for fifteen minutes for my father to come out in search of her. It was daylight now. Bundu was afraid that with gangs of rioters on the rampage in the old city, it would be dangerous to pass Chandni Chowk with a burqa-clad woman sitting alone in his tonga. He removed the tonga seat and asked my mother to hide in the cramped empty space beneath. There was hardly any room but my mother was a thin, delicate woman and somehow managed to squeeze in, clutching me tightly to her bosom. Many gangs tried to stop us on the way but Bundu gave them all the slip, getting past the Company Garden and turning towards Ballimaran from the Town Hall and Clock Tower. The problem was that the Muslims had barricaded the entrance to Ballimaran with burning tyres and broken carts so that the Hindu rioters could not enter the area.

The Muslim hotheads refused to allow the tonga inside. A furious exchange of stones and burning rags took place between the two communities. Suddenly, my mother, clad in her torn burqa, stood up, removed the naqab from her face and shouted with all the strength at her command to let the tonga through. In the space of that tonga ride from the station, it seemed that she had become a very different woman. She stood tall on the seat of the tonga, looking fiercely at the stone-throwing ruffians. Taken by surprise by this angry but extremely beautiful woman, they meekly obeyed her command. The barricades were removed and we were in the safety of Ballimaran.

My grandmother lived in a huge house in Haveli Hissamuddin, one of the more famous localities of Delhi. She was a no-nonsense woman, tall and fair, with sharp aristocratic features. Her aquiline nose and big dark brown eyes were enough to cow down the strongest of men. She was always dressed as if going to a party. A direct descendant of the last Mughal emperor Bahadur Shah Zafar, she believed that she was the master of her universe, a woman in the real tradition of the Mughals, advising and even commanding men from time to time. She was shocked to see her daughter Hina on her doorstep. Just the evening before, Hina and Azizuddin had come to say goodbye, the last alvida. Qudsia Begum had been deeply unhappy. She hated this man called Jinnah. She told Azizuddin, 'What Pakistan? All the land of Allah is Pak. My Allah will protect me here, in my city, if he wants to. My Allah is not so weak that I have to run to Pakistan for my protection. Your Jinnah is not more powerful than my Allah.'

With tears in his eyes, Azizuddin had asked Qudsia Begum to forgive him. He knew that this two-nation theory was nonsense. But the atmosphere had changed. Muslims could not survive as equal citizens in independent India after this terrible Partition. Everyone had left and now even his shop had been burnt down. He wanted Qudsia Begum to come with them to Pakistan. How could she live alone here in Delhi? Who would look after her in her old age?

'I respect your courage, Qudsia Begum, but times have changed. You are not safe anymore in Delhi. Whether you like it or not, your place is in Pakistan. Neither Pandit Nehru nor Maulana Azad can protect you from the Sanghis and the Mahasabha,' Azizuddin said, trying desperately to convince his mother-in-law.

The old woman smiled. 'Who looked after me when my husband died and left me alone at the dargah of Hazrat Nizamuddin? Not your Jinnah but my Mehbub-e-Illahi and my Allah. How can I abandon my Khwaja now? Who will perform fatiha at the grave of Humayun every Thursday? No, I want to be buried in Nizamuddin, next to Amir Khusro and Mirza Ghalib. I cannot leave Delhi.'

Azizuddin, who came from a family of traders who had migrated 300 years ago from Iran, knew when he was defeated. He said his last tearful farewell to this old woman who had been a mother to him all these years.

'Where is Azizuddin?' she asked now, looking at her daughter in her torn burqa and with a wailing baby in her arms. She knew immediately that something was terribly wrong. When Hina told her that she had abandoned her husband and her son Aijaz at the railway station, Qudsia Begum smiled but admonished her for what she had done. 'Don't worry, Azizuddin will come back to take you and Shiraz, he cannot live without you.'

But Fate had a different game to play with Qudsia Begum and her daughter Hina.

◈

My earliest memory of my grandmother, whom we lovingly called Nani Amma, is of her introducing me to the king of jinns. I think I was three years old at the time and was in the habit of talking non-stop. One day, Nani Amma took me to the dargah of Hazrat Nizamuddin Aulia. It was a Thursday, the day Qudsia Begum went to the grave of Humayun to pray and light a few jasmine-scented agarbattis. She claimed that Humayun loved the smell of jasmine and his beloved wife Hamida Begum had lit jasmine agarbattis at his grave till the last day of her life.

After praying at the dargah and listening to the qawwalis for a while, she got up and we went to Humayun's Tomb to offer prayers at the graves of our ancestors. This was her routine every Thursday. She used to come to Nizamuddin with my mother, or all alone, in Bundu Chacha's tonga. Bundu was her bodyguard, driver, friend, advisor and all-purpose assistant. He was devoted to his horses and to Qudsia Begum.

This was my first visit to the mausoleum of the great saint and to the grand tomb of Humayun. Nani told me that her grandmother Kulsum Zamani Begum, the daughter of the last Mughal emperor, was also buried here. She had been the favourite daughter of the unfortunate emperor. The night Bahadur Shah

Zafar fled from Red Fort, he summoned his daughter and son-in-law, Mirza Ziauddin, and said, 'I am no more the emperor of my beloved Hindustan. You, my daughter, who has lived in the best tradition of the Mughal harem, will have to leave this palace and find refuge in a forest.' He kissed her on the forehead, handed her a casket of diamonds and gold chains and asked her to leave immediately. Mirza Ziauddin was not a brave man but he knew he could not leave his father-in-law to the mercy of invading armies, so he decided to stay back and sent his family away in the protection of his old servant Abbasi.

That same night, Kulsum Begum left for an unknown destination in a bullock cart, with just a few possessions, taking her one-and-a-half-year-old daughter Zainab with her. On the way, the party was attacked by some Gujjar villagers and all their precious jewellery and clothes were looted. The old and feeble Abbasi was no match for the attackers and was killed on the spot. Kulsum Begum and her daughter's lives were saved by a Thakur landlord and they were taken to the village of some Rajput Muslims, who gave them shelter. There they heard the news that the emperor had been taken prisoner, put in chains and sent to a secret destination. There was no news of her husband, Mirza Ziauddin, but it was assumed that he had been killed like other members of the family by the 'gori paltan', as the British sepoys were known. Kulsum Begum and the few family members who had accompanied her went into hiding and eventually reached Hyderabad, where some supporters of Bahadur Shah Zafar provided them with the means to travel to Mecca for the Haj. In Mecca, an old servant of their family, Abdul Qadir, who had been set free and had established a very successful business there, learned of their arrival. He immediately met them and offered them all his wealth, and promised to serve them with respect and love. My great-grandmother Zainab grew up in Mecca to be a very beautiful woman and was married to an Indian merchant from Delhi, who had come to Mecca for the Haj. The whole family came back to Delhi and settled down in Ballimaran, where my Nani was born and spent all her life.

So here I was, a three-year-old boy with all the weight of history on my shoulders, with my grandmother, at the beautiful tomb of Emperor Humayun, the second Mughal emperor, the son of Babur. It was getting dark and I saw giants and strange creatures behind every tree. But with Bundu carrying me in his strong arms, I was not afraid of anything in the world. At that point in my life, he was my hero, my Superman.

Nani took us behind the tomb to a secluded corner under a canopy where she spread a white bedsheet. She asked me to sit on it. She took out a copy of the Quran from her bag and a white paper, and told me to put the Quran on my head. She drew a few lines on the sheet of paper, wrote some Arabic verses on it and then told me to sit quietly and look at the paper.

After a few moments she asked me, 'Shiraz, what do you see before you?'

Today when I think about it, I am surprised. I hadn't even heard of television in those days. Now I can describe what I saw on the sheet of white paper like a scene playing out on the screen of a television. In it I saw four large black men emerge with an ornate golden chair, and there appeared a tall and handsome man with a beard, who looked like a king. He came and sat on the chair. What I saw I described to Nani.

'I can see four big black man and a Badshah, with a crown on his head, looking at me and smiling.'

'He is the king of jinns, my friend and protector. Offer your salaam to him.'

I did as I was told and heard him say, 'Walaikum assalaam.'

Nani told me to request him to show me where my father and

my brother Aijaz were. Suddenly, the scene changed and I saw my father sitting on a chair in a huge courtyard with a woman and my brother, who looked exactly like me, playing beside them. I became agitated when I saw my father and wanted to touch him. But everything vanished. We tried again but could not bring the king of the jinns back. Nani told me that only a child with an innocent and pure mind could see such a vision. She was angry because she was sure that my father had remarried in Lahore and the woman sitting next to him was his wife.

I was sick and had a high fever by the time we returned to our house. When my mother heard what had happened at Humayun's Tomb, she was livid. 'How dare you use my innocent child for your witchcraft? Don't ever do that again.' My mother, who had studied up to high school, considered herself a rationalist and refused to believe in jinns.

Qudsia Begum, on the other hand, had great faith in jinns. People said the king of jinns was in her control and would do anything to serve her. The story was that the king of jinns saw her when she was sixteen, in the garden of Humayun's Tomb, and fell in love with her. He wanted to take a human form and marry her, but before he could find the right vessel to do so, Qudsia Begum was married off to a powerful and rich contractor of Delhi. Though he could not marry her, the king of jinns remained her faithful servant for life.

In this ancient city of Delhi, people believed that there were jinns in every house, and as long as you did not disturb them, they did not interfere with you. But if they got angry with you for some reason, nobody could save you except the maulvi, who demanded a huge fee for fighting and throwing out the jinns from your house. Nani told us that there were jinns everywhere but we couldn't see them as they were made of fire and energy. There were good jinns and evil jinns. The good ones were our friends and helped us from time to time and the bad ones were up to mischief all the time. But these jinns could not perform any material task on their own. They had to possess a human body, a vessel, to communicate and perform physical tasks.

My childhood was full of these good and bad jinns.

PART ONE

Ballimaran: World of Magic

You were born with wings
Why prefer to crawl through life?

– Maulana Jalaluddin Rumi

1

The street of Ballimaran in Chandni Chowk, the world-famous bazaar built by Emperor Shahjahan, is a fascinating and magical place. I left the area fifty years ago but my spirit still dwells in that mohalla. All my dreams, even while making love to my English girlfriends, are located on the roofs and narrow bylanes of Chandni Chowk. In a way, I have carried that mohalla and all the characters who lived there and have long gone, on my shoulders. Sitting here in an old English country house near Cambridge, telling you this strange story of mine, I feel as though spiritually, I still dwell in that mohalla. The ghosts of Ballimaran never leave me alone. They have a habit of jumping out at me at any time, at any place, without any notice.

Last week I was travelling from New York to London, talking to an irritatingly polite air-hostess, when suddenly Masha-Allah Jaan, universal aunt and renowned rumour-monger of our mohalla, appeared before me and started narrating the latest gossip from Ballimaran. As for Nani, she doesn't care if I am talking to the President of the United States or the Queen of England, she accosts me whenever she chooses and starts admonishing me as if I were still a small boy. People think I am losing my mind, I am getting old, but that is not true. I have seen all these characters riding on my shoulders and interfering with my life since my childhood. Sometimes they turn my life into the Garden of

Paradise, my jannat, and at times they make me so miserable that I contemplate the most painful methods of committing suicide, just to get rid of them.

One night, sleeping on the big, uncomfortably soft bed in my English house, I saw my great ancestor, Babur, in a dream. The poet, conqueror and founder of the great Mughal empire was riding a white horse. He asked me to ride with him. In my dream I was just three years old but rode the black horse he gave me like an expert. Babur then requested me to sing for him. I sang a popular Hindi film song and the emperor really enjoyed it. I realized then that Bollywood had captured the minds of not only the people in this world but also of the ghosts of the great kings and queens of the past.

When I complained to Babur about the many peoplewho never left me alone and interfered with my life all the time, he smiled and told me he'd had the same disease. He used to carry all the characters from Farghana, his homeland, in his head wherever he went. They used to appear even on a battlefield and distract him, endangering his life more than once. How could you answer your grandmother when the enemy was attacking you with a blood-curdling war cry? How could you listen to your father's advice on the finer points of pigeon-racing while bargaining with your enemy to release your children, whom he wanted to keep as security? He was so fed up with them that he wanted to die or to kill them. But then he decided to transfer all the ghosts of his existence to the pages of a book: *Tuzk-e Babri*. He enslaved them and their ghosts for eternity inside his memoirs. He asked me to do the same.

'Words are chains, stronger than any man has created from steel, and they may give you freedom or enslave you forever. They are also double-edged swords – don't unsheathe them unless you intend to defeat an opponent or win a friend. And even then, chances are you may cut your own heart or spirit.'

I did not understand much of what Babur was telling me. He

had this irritating habit of saying the simplest things in a flowery and roundabout manner, as if he were a great philosopher and not a simple horseman and adventurer who had set out to capture a fistful of sky to claim as his kingdom. At any rate, the message was clear. If I wanted to get rid of the ghosts of my past, I had to write my life and enslave these annoying but loveable characters in the pages of my book. So here I am, writing my memoirs, as truthfully as possible, without wounding my loved ones, on the advice of the great Emperor Babur, poet and gossip-monger.

Many of you may have understood by now what a mohalla is, but let me explain nevertheless. Those who have lived in the Old Delhi of Shahjahanabad know all about a mohalla. A mohalla is not just a physical space but also a state of mind. It is a world within a world, a community of families living in a walled enclosure, where people share pain and pleasure, food and festivals. It is like a huge family living in different houses but sharing everything. We children could roam around freely within the mohalla, without any fear or restrictions. We entered any house at will as no doors were ever closed in the daytime. There were only heavy jute or oilcloth curtains on the door. Whichever house we entered, we were offered something to eat. I often used to find out who was cooking my favourite dish and eat there.

The lanes were paved with red stone slabs, which were washed every morning and evening by men who carried goat-skin bags known as mashaq, filled with water, on their shoulders. They were known as bhishtis, or dwellers of paradise, as they provided drinking water to every house, in the days before tap water arrived in our mohalla. I loved those polished red sandstone streets, especially after they had been washed clean in the hot summer afternoons; when cool water fell on them, the steam used to rise with a smell all its own. I used to follow the bhishtis around just to enjoy that smell.

Our mohalla was full of beautiful women, mostly Muslim Punjabis, who in reality did not come from Punjab but had migrated from the West and had very European features: blue eyes, golden hair and fair skin. In fact, after the Mutiny of 1857, the mohalla was raided by the British because of rumours that some British children kidnapped by the rebels were holed up there – in reality, these were the children of the Muslim Punjabis.

The menfolk were also handsome but they were busy making money. They used to leave for their shops early in the morning and return after ten at night. Even young boys, by the time they were seven or eight, were sent to the shops after they returned from school. The Shamsi, or the people of the sun, as these Punjabis were called, believed that real schooling took place in the shop, where the boys could learn the tricks of the trade. As a result, the mohalla was bereft of boys but full of girls, of every size and age, with nothing to do except eat, sleep and flirt. We non-Punjabi boys were the greatest beneficiaries of this, as we were showered with love, affection and food, whichever house we entered.

Ballimaran, the street on which my mohalla was situated, was one big bazaar, where many writers, poets, musicians and artists lived, including Mirza Ghalib, one of the greatest poets India has known. Bismillah Hotel in Ballimaran was their favourite haunt and they spent the whole day having innumerable cups of tea and seekh kebabs, discussing politics, poetry and everything else under the sun. Young poets like Gulzar and Sahir, still unknown, used to sit there listening to great poets like Josh and Hasrat Mohani. An artist with a long black beard used to spend hours drinking very sweet tea and sketching. Occasionally, he would give us children some of these sketches, which we used to paste in our school books without realizing that they were the work of a great painter. No one had heard of Maqbool Fida Husain in those days.

The atmosphere in that mohalla was such that while most other children were learning nursery rhymes, we knew the poetry of Ghalib and Mir by heart. I didn't understand what it meant but one of Ghalib's ghazals I used to sing was:

Aah ko chahiye ek umer asar hone tak
Kaun jeeta hai teri zulfksar hone tak

It takes a lifetime for a sigh to have an effect
I'll be long gone before you bestow your favours on me.

I may not have understood the meaning of this romantic poetry but I loved to play the whole day with girls, most of whom were a few years older than I was. There was one very beautiful and bubbly girl, Nasreen, maybe a year older than I was, who was fond of touching my 'phunnu', which is how the penis of a little boy was referred to. She was a fearless girl, fair and with light blue eyes, always giggling and jumping around. And she was fascinated by my penis. I was the only boy in that Muslim mohalla who had not been circumcised at birth and was therefore a target of curiosity for the other children.

There was a boy by the name of Javed, who had been circumcised at the late age of eleven. Something had gone wrong in the process and he used to lie on a bed the whole day, reading all sorts of books, from Leo Tolstoy to cheap pornographic literature. His house was also a centre for girls' education; his elder sister Nafisa was the first graduate girl in the mohalla. In the daytime we children were sent to her house to learn Urdu and cram mathematical tables and in the evening, all the girls of the mohalla used to gather there to be taught by Nafisa Baji.

Nafisa was a rebel in her own way. She had given up the hijab but dressed conservatively in white. She had sharp features and big bright brown eyes that shone with intelligence. When she walked on the streets of this very traditional mohalla, every eye was on her, but she never looked up. Nafisa had to prove at every step that even without purdah, she could be a woman of character. Every move of hers was watched by the elders of the mohalla, who were always on the look-out for something to criticize.

Women everywhere were opening their minds to the winds of change. My mother was encouraged by Nafisa Baji to appear for her high school exams privately and join a college for a Bachelor of Arts (BA) degree. Nani, an extraordinarily forward-thinking woman for her time, urged her to get a degree in English literature, as the time for Urdu was over; if Hina wanted to achieve something in life, she must study English. Nani believed that Mughal rule in India would have survived if only the Mughals had learnt English and dealt with the fair and just king of England directly. She whispered to me one day that even her jinns preferred to converse with her in English these days. I didn't believe her because I knew she was very good at making up all sorts of stories to prove her point.

Nafisa Baji's house was my first school. I was sent there by the time I was three or four, to learn to read and write. Nafisa's mother, a widow, was from a highly educated family of Bihar, who had settled in Delhi. Her brother was a well-known nationalist leader of the freedom struggle. Her husband, who helped write the Constitution of India, had died a few years after Independence. I spent a good part of my childhood in that house.

Javed, who was about fourteen when I went to learn the alphabet at their house, was my first real friend apart from Bundu Chacha. Because of the death of his father and his circumcision at a late age, he had become both psychologically and physically crippled. In a way he was our teacher; his mother, who was supposed to teach us, was busy cooking in the kitchen and it was Javed who would make us cram the maths tables loudly. I was still uncircumcised and was being constantly told that I would soon have to undergo the operation. Javed told me that I would become a cripple like him if I was circumcised at this age. In those days, and even now, circumcision in Muslim families was performed by a barber who had no training in surgery and used no anaesthesia. Usually, it was done a few days after the birth of a boy. Javed Bhai scared me so much that I decided to run away from home before any such torture could be inflicted on me. One day, I went with him to the Delhi railway station, which was not far from our house, to rehearse my escape from circumcision. The question was, where would I escape to?

Javed said, 'Shiraz, you run away to Bombay. I have the address of Dilip Kumar, you can go and stay there.' He had found the famous film star Dilip Kumar's address in some film magazine. I was barely five at this point but still had the sense to ask, 'Do you know Dilip Kumar? Why would he let me stay in his house?'

'He is a very good man and helps a lot of people.' Javed had read about his philanthropy in *Shama*, the most popular film magazine of those days.

So it was decided that I would board a train to Bombay and go and stay with Dilip Kumar, in order to escape the trauma of circumcision. When my mother told me that I would be shown the golden pigeon, *sone ka kabootar*, the next day, I knew what it meant. I had seen it happening to other boys. They would look up to catch a glimpse of the golden pigeon in the sky and the foreskin would be removed in a trice. I knew what was being planned for me but I couldn't gather up the courage to run away, as I had never set foot in a train till then. My mother bought new clothes and shoes for me. The whole mohalla was invited for lunch the following afternoon. I could not sleep the whole night, shivering with fear and anxiety. Bundu Chacha had told me, 'Shiraz mian, it is nothing, you look at the sky and you see a golden pigeon and before you realize it, the job is done. I was fifteen when I was circumcised but I never uttered a word. My parents were dead and I didn't want to die a kafir, so I went to the barber shop and got myself circumcised.'

I was not brave like Bundu Chacha. I developed a high fever in the night and rashes all over my body. Everyone was alarmed when they saw the big red rashes in the morning and the event was postponed. But it was a temporary relief. Nani used to brainwash me all the time that unless I was circumcised, I would not be recognized as a Muslim by the angels and when I died, they would take me for an infidel and throw me into hell instead of paradise, which was my rightful place as a Muslim and a descendant of the great Mughals. The belief was that infidels were the fodder of hell and all believers, however corrupt they were, would live forever in paradise, a place full of beautiful and pious houries.

By this time I had also realized that I would not be welcomed at the residence of Dilip Kumar, as he only liked pretty girls. At the age of eight, another attempt was made to circumcise me, but again the same thing happened and the rashes on my body saved me.

✧

In the hot summer afternoons, when everybody slept downstairs, we children had the free run of the terraces. In the Old Delhi mohallas, most of the roofs were connected and one could go from one roof to another.

One day, Nasreen took me and a few other boys to the roof

of a neighbour's house. She promised to show us a great drama. Through a small opening in the roof, she made us peep into the bedroom of a very rich businessman, Haji Phulle, who lived there with his children and his fat but very bubbly wife, Billu jaan. As I peeped through the small opening, I could see Billu lying naked on a bed and a thin young man, definitely not Haji Phulle, sitting beside her. Her watermelon-size breasts dangled on either side of her huge belly. The lady was a good friend of my mother and was in the habit of cuddling and kissing me whenever I came anywhere near her. She was now giggling and squeezing the man between her thighs. I felt nauseated as well as fascinated by what I saw. She opened her legs and put them over his shoulders. He had a phunnu the size of a banana. To my shock and amazement, Lady Billu took this huge banana into her mouth. I was terrified that she was going to bite it between her big square teeth. However, the thing was soon out of her drooling mouth and in one go vanished into her pee-hole, which was nothing less than a miracle to my young and innocent mind. Now she was kissing him desperately and writhing as if she was in great pain. Suddenly, I felt a hand on my phunnu and I realized that it had become as hard as a stick. When Nasreen saw my reaction, she started giggling. The couple below must have heard our voices, for the man jumped up, his glistening wet phunnu dangling. They were paralysed for a moment, not knowing who had caught them at it. Billu, with her huge watermelons hanging down to her ample belly, jumped up and, for the first time in my life, I saw the luscious figure of a naked woman. I often think my fascination for voluptuous women later in life was born in that moment.

We discovered later that the boy was a Rampuri lad working in a choti-making workshop, where they made beads and silk threads used by women to decorate their hair, in the basement of a house in the mohalla. There were a dozen young men, all tall handsome Pathans, working in this factory. Their hands and even faces were always coloured red, blue and green from the dyes they worked with. These young men were popular with the wives of the Punjabi shopkeepers, who had no time or inclination for sex. While the husbands were away in the shops, the young Pathans were often secretly invited in for passionate love-making sessions. Since we children were always playing on the roofs, we were witness to many such trysts. Nasreen, smart girl that she was, started blackmailing the men for ice cream and chocolates for our whole gang. Later, we became the go-betweens and brought messages for the men from the ladies and, in the process, gained power over these lovebirds.

Ultimately, at the age of ten, I was circumcised when an uncle of mine, Hakim Nasim, came from Kanpur. He was my favourite uncle and used to bring me toys. He took me to the red mosque of the mohalla, promising to show me a new toy. Bundu Chacha was already there with the barber and the Mir Mohalla, the chief of the mohalla, Mulla Idris, a colourful and jovial man. He had a huge belly and a big white beard and was always on the lookout for someone who had done anything un-Islamic to reprimand and lecture to. But we all knew that he used to watch films secretly in the nearby theatre.

They had all conspired with my Nani to quietly get me circumcised in the mosque. I was not given the opportunity to develop rashes and save myself. My mother was also kept in the dark because they knew she didn't have the heart to see me suffer. And so, at the ripe age of ten, I was shown the 'golden pigeon', my *musalmani* was performed, and I could stop worrying that the angels would not know me.

٢

My mother was a brave woman. She had the courage to take her own decisions in an age when women regarded their husbands as *majazi khuda*, gods on earth. The word of a husband was deemed to be the command of God and a woman was not supposed to hold any opinion of her own on any matter. Yet, my mother had abandoned my father at the railway station without even informing him, and decided to stay back in India. I was told later that it was the nationalist leader Maulana Azad, an associate of Mahatma Gandhi, who made thousands of Muslims change their minds and stay back in secular India, where people of all religions would have equal rights. His famous speech at Jama Masjid in Delhi became the inspiration for nationalist Muslims who rejected Jinnah's two-nation theory and stayed back in Nehru's India.

It was Nafisa Baji who gave moral support to my mother; otherwise all the women of the mohalla had ostracized her for defying her husband. Hina Begum was very much in love with Azizuddin Khan and now regretted her decision to stay back in India. She told us, 'Some jinn possessed me and made me escape from the railway station. I thought my husband would come searching for me but he went away to his bloody Pakistan, abandoning me and my child.' Ammi, like most people then, did not realize that Partition and the new borders were permanent.

You could not cross them at will. At that time there was no concept or understanding of a passport or visa. The enmity and legal rigidity between two countries born of the same womb like twins, came as a shock to most of us. Hina used to compare the birthing of her own boys on the night of 14 and 15 August 1947 to the birth of the two nations. My brother Aijaz was born ten minutes before midnight on 14 August, the day Pakistan came into existence and I was born fifteen minutes past midnight on 15 August, the day India got its freedom. We were truly the children of midnight, our fates intertwined with the fate of these two tragic nations. The day we were born, India and Pakistan were celebrating their independence, drowned in the blood of their own children. My brother Aijaz and I were the symbols of these two nations, permanently at war and constantly trying to embrace and love each other; Mostly, they didn't know when to love and how to hate. I envied Aijaz because he had my father, as surely as he hated me for getting all the love of my mother.

My mother resembled Nargis but, to me, she was much prettier than the film star, tall and beautiful, with the fine chiselled features of her Mughal ancestors. But it was her golden-brown eyes, long-lashed and full of mischief, that captivated everyone who looked at her. Nani always wondered where she had got them from.

After our separation, my mother and I waited for any news or a letter from my father. We expected him to come back to fetch us. Ammi cried all the time and missed Aijaz, her first-born. As for me, it was like someone had sliced me in two. Aijaz and I had been inseparable from the time we were born. We were carbon copies of each other, except that Aijaz had a mole under his left nipple. Except for my mother, everybody, including Nani, used to confuse one of us for the other. Being separated from Aijaz was physically hurtful and for months I vomited out everything I ate. I also had epileptic attacks every few months, which Nani declared were the attempts of the jinns to enter my soul but she, with the help of her good jinn, was able to keep them at bay.

❖

It was raining heavily. All the lanes had turned into waterways and I was making paper boats to float in our lane. Ammi was sitting on the rope swing that hung from the harsinghar tree in our courtyard and singing a song. Nani was making pakoras, a favourite during the monsoon. Suddenly, there was a knock on the door. Everyone was momentarily paralysed, as no one from the neighbourhood was in the habit of knocking before entering the courtyard, and who would come in this heavy rain? It had to be a stranger. Our servant girl, whom we called Bengali chuhiya, went out to enquire and came back all wet and grinning from ear to ear, with an envelope. Someone had just arrived from Lahore with a letter from my father.

Much later, one day, I discovered the letter in my mother's jewellery box and read it. It was in chaste and flowery Urdu with couplets by Mirza Ghalib.

Lahore, Pakistan

My beloved, queen of my heart, Hina,

I am writing this letter with an aching heart. I miss you and Shiraz with every pore of my existence. That fateful day, when I returned with the train tickets to the bench where I had left you and Shiraz, I found you missing. At first I thought you had gone to the toilet and I waited for you to return, but after fifteen minutes I started searching for both of you. I ran outside but found no one. One porter told me that he had seen a woman in a black burqa with a child similar to

Aijaz, boarding the train to Lahore. The train was about to leave, so I jumped on with Aijaz, under the impression that you were on the train. Throughout the day-long journey I searched frantically for you from one end of the jam-packed train to the other. People told me that I would find you when I reached Lahore.

At Lahore station I ran like a mad man, with Aijaz wailing on my shoulder, shouting your name. I made announcements over the loudspeaker. With a sinking heart I realized you were not on the train. Oh God, I had such horrible thoughts about you being kidnapped or killed by the rioters. For months I searched for you in every refugee camp, hospital, police station. I tried frantically to send telegrams to your mother but because of hostilities between the two countries on the Kashmir border, all communications were broken. It was only last month that a family from Delhi gave me the news that you and Shiraz were safe with your mother. It was then that I realized you had chosen your mother over me and Aijaz. Hina, I loved you from the first day I saw you from my roof while flying pigeons, and was bewitched by your dazzling smile and dancing eyes. I am not a poet or a writer. I don't belong to an esteemed family like yours but my family was rich and powerful. Your mother refused me because I had no khaandan or family pedigree and insulted my father as a newly rich shopkeeper. My father got dozens of proposals for me from the most beautiful girls of Delhi, who belonged to rich families. I told my father that if I ever married, it would be to my princess Hina. I was able to persuade my stubborn father and your arrogant and crazy mother to agree to our marriage. I thought I was the luckiest man on earth but today I regret the moment I fell in love with you. I realize that you love your Delhi, your mother, your Mughal ancestors more than your sartaj, your lover. I still love you deeply and will continue to do so until Angel Azrael takes me away on my last journey.

In Lahore I have been allotted a huge haveli, which belonged to a Hindu lala, close to the Badshahi mosque. My cousin Rehman Khan, who was a Muslim League leader in Delhi, is a powerful politician and an advisor to the prime minister of Pakistan. He is helping me get a few big building contracts. This country is full of opportunities and I am confident that I am going to do much better here than I did in Delhi. The best thing is, we are all Muslims helping each other build a new nation. You have chosen to be a slave in India but we are our own masters here in Pakistan. I am sure your Mughal ancestors would have chosen Pakistan over slavery in India, if they were alive today.

There is pressure on me from my cousins' family to marry their daughter Ayesha, who is convent-educated and very modern. I am resisting them as I believe that you will come to me as soon as you receive my letter. I will wait for your response for a few months and then take a decision. I can't look after little Aijaz forever, and he is missing you and Shiraz terribly. His health has deteriorated. If it were not for my aunt, mother of Ayesha, I wouldn't have been able to take care of Aijaz. I am sure you will reconsider and come to me in Lahore.

You may send the reply through the bearer of this letter. He will return to Lahore in a week's time.

My mother replied that she was coming with me as soon as she could get a Pakistani visa. Hina Kauser forgot all about Maulana Azad's sermons and her mother's pleas. She just thought of going to Lahore and being reunited with her son and her husband.

When I came home that afternoon, she had already started packing. For the next few weeks we talked about nothing but Lahore. Nani had been to Lahore once but, as usual, no other city in the world could compare with Delhi.

'Our Jama Masjid is like a pearl in an oyster and Lahore Qila is like a villager's house in comparison to Delhi's Lal Qila,' Nani told everyone loudly, although nobody seemed interested in her comparison of the two cities. I was so excited about meeting Abba and Aijaz, I didn't care if Lahore was a slum in comparison to Delhi. Ammi got a special sherwani tailored for my father. She herself made small kurtas for Aijaz with silver embroidery on the collars. Bundu Chacha was sad as he had become very fond of me, but he understood that a woman's place was with her husband, even if he had committed the crime of migrating to Pakistan.

Getting a visa for Pakistan was not difficult, but in our case it was taking a long time. Ammi went to the Pakistan high commission every day, but was told to come again the following day. Days turned into weeks, but the visa was not issued. We were told that there was much tension in Kashmir, and India and Pakistan, twins born of the same mother, had suddenly become enemies at war with each other. My young mind was too innocent to understand all this, but Bundu Chacha told me one day that, not long after I was born, Jinnah had sent his savage tribes into Kashmir and we had been at war with Pakistan ever since.

'Shiraz mian, they are killing children and women in the paradise of Kashmir,' Bundu told me. But it was impossible for me to comprehend this: for me, Pakistan meant my father and twin brother.

Ammi believed that Nani didn't want us to go to Lahore and had conspired with her jinns to make India and Pakistan fight with each other, so that we wouldn't get our visas. There was a big argument between her and Nani when Ammi confronted her with this accusation. Nani was livid. 'It is your Jinnah who has started the war and not my jinns. They are so peace-loving that they would not harm even a fly.' Nani was convinced that her beloved jinns were followers of Mahatma Gandhi and subscribed to his theory of non-violence. For a long time I too was convinced that Nani and her jinns were responsible for the hostilities between the two countries and the whole Kashmir issue had been raised to stop my mother and me from migrating to Pakistan.

One morning, when we were having our favourite breakfast of nahari and tandoori naan, there was a knock on the door. Someone from the neighbouring house had come to fetch my mother as there was an urgent phone call from London. In those days, there was only one phone in our mohalla and it belonged to Mr Baari, a journalist. Any phone call for anybody meant much excitement in the whole mohalla. Even before my mother was informed, half the mohalla knew about it and was bustling with anticipation. Ammi immediately rushed to the house, not even bothering to wear her burqa. Mr Baari and his family had gathered around the phone. No one had any concept of privacy as far as phone calls went.

Azizuddin's uncle, who lived in London, had called my mother to inform her that her husband had remarried, as he had lost all hope of my mother coming to Lahore. Hina heard the news calmly and thanked Uncle Baari, then she quietly walked back to our house. She went to her room and bolted it from inside. Nani rushed after her but Ammi refused to speak to anyone. She didn't open the door even for me. All the mohalla women streamed into our house, making excuses of one kind or another.

'Arrey, Qudsia Begum, where is your daughter Hina? I want her to read this English letter for me,' said the wife of Mulla Idris, looking all around for my mother. Nobody knew what the phone call had been about; all they could make out was that it was bad news. Some speculated that my father had died but Nani immediately understood that Azizuddin had remarried. Ammi didn't open the door for two days. It was only when I cried and cried and developed a very high fever that she relented. But the woman who walked out of that room was not my mother, she was her ghost. It took her months to become normal again. Nani went to every dargah to plead for my mother's health. Ultimately it was Nafisa Baji who made my mother understand that now she had to live for me. She had to resume her education, get a job and see that I got the best education.

My mother was an extraordinary woman. Once she gave up her burqa and joined Delhi College, she became the toast of the city. More than anything else, it was her intelligence, wit and fiercely independent nature that captivated people. However, she was reserved and did not allow anybody to come close to her. There was a very popular and handsome young poet who wrote hundreds of poems for her but she refused to even look at him. He then took to standing under her window every evening, until Nani had to inform the Mir Mohalla, who banned him from entering Haveli Hissamuddin ever again. We learned later that he drank himself to death because those molten chocolate brown eyes refused to recognize his existence even once.

۳

Bhagatji was a portly Brahmin whom we all loved. He lived next to Seth Chhunnumal's haveli in Katra Neel, a mohalla of rich Hindu lalas and Brahmins, just opposite Ballimaran. We used to wait for Saturday evening, when Bhagatji would come with his qawwali party and sing the whole night. Bhagatji was a fair man with big black eyes, long hair falling on both sides of his round face, a long red tilak on his forehead, and a paan perpetually tucked in his mouth, even when he was singing. He would shower everyone around him with red spit as he sang. Although he was a strict Brahmin, no Muslim in our mohalla had any problem with his paan spit. He was welcome in every house and no woman, young or old, ever covered her face before Bhagatji.

In those times of Hindu–Muslim hatred, immediately after Partition, there were strict border lines between the two communities. Chandni Chowk was the border, with Ballimaran and Kuncha Rehman, a Muslim enclave, on one side, and Katra Neel, Kuncha Ghasi Ram, Kinari bazaar, etc. on the other side. At one end of Chandni Chowk was Red Fort, the citadel of the Mughals, and at the other end was Masjid Fatehpuri, a mosque built by one of the wives of Shahjahan. In between was a world of magic and romance called Chandni Chowk, a bazaar which had no parallel in the world for its magnificence and colourful variety. I can say with confidence that if you hadn't seen Chandni Chowk, you hadn't seen Delhi. If I were to begin describing this bazaar, I wouldn't have space to write about anything else.

Apart from us children, there was another person in the mohalla who used to eagerly wait for these evenings when Bhagatji would arrive with his tabla and sarangiwala to sing his devotional natia qawwalis in praise of Prophet Mohammad. This was Maulvi Abu-Bakr, the muezzin of the red mosque, or lal masjid, as it was known. He was a thin tall man, with a long beard and a high cane cap on his head. He used to give the azaan, the call to prayer, five times a day, from the top of the minaret in the mosque. There were no loudspeakers then, but his melodious voice could be heard all around the mohalla. He was one of those who used to go into a trance listening to the qawwalis of Bhagatji. It used to be a comical sight with Bhagatji, a Brahmin, singing the same verse over and over again, and Maulvi Abu-Bakr dancing with raised hands for hours together. This was the state of 'haal' which people used to go into, captivated by the music. There was a strong belief that the same words had to be repeated again and again until the person collapsed on his own, otherwise he might either go mad or have a heart attack and die. Maulvi Abu-Bakr could continue with his dervish dance for hours, and poor Bhagatji had to sing non-stop to save him from dying. I used to wait with bated breath to see who gave up first.

Abu-Bakr's wife Masha Allah Jan was a strong-willed and pragmatic woman. She used to lock him up in the house whenever she had prior information about Bhagatji's arrival. But she herself was fond of qawwali and used to sit through all the performances. Once, when she locked her husband in the house and came to enjoy the qawwali, Maulvi Abu-Bakr jumped from his roof into the neighbouring courtyard. His neighbours, thought he was a thief and gave him a good thrashing before they realized that he was their respected neighbour. Abu-Bakr was so furious with his wife that he divorced her, but he in turn was thrown out of his house by his wife and daughter and had to sleep for the rest of his life in the lal mosque. Such was the impact of the qawwali of a Hindu Brahmin on this mohalla of devout Muslims, in those days after Partition, when Hindus and Muslims were supposedly at each others' throats. Nani, who hated Jinnah and his two-nation theory, and left no opportunity to debunk his justification for the creation of Pakistan, always used this example to tell us how silly the whole idea of Muslims being a separate nation was. Ironically, this pure-blooded Mughal, a descendant of Babur, who had come from Central Asia, she was more Indian than all the rest of us.

There was always a simmering undercurrent of religious hatred and suspicion between Hindus and Muslims. All Muslim children went to the Muslim school in the neighbourhood. I was the first boy to go to an English-medium school run by an Irish priest. We were about a dozen Muslim boys and girls in a school of more than a thousand children, most of them Hindus. From the first day, I was dubbed a Pakistani. Muslim boys were called mullahs and girls, mullihs. Even teachers used to bash us up for no reason, calling us bloody Pakistanis. But my ability to tell stories made me popular even among the bullies who regarded it as their patriotic duty to bash up Muslim boys and girls a few times a day. The whole class used to wait for break time to listen to the next episode in my stories

I had this habit of living in my fantasy world where I would experience all sorts of adventures. This world was my escape from the realities of those troubled times which my young mind failed to understand. I didn't know why my father lived in Pakistan, which was a hated word. I didn't understand why Hindus and Muslims claimed mutual hatred but still enjoyed each other's company so much. Why was I called a mullah in my school? Why did my teachers punish me for no fault of mine? Why did my mother hate my father so much, yet kiss his picture and cry at night when she thought I was asleep? Why was Lala Shamnath's wife Nani's best friend even though she told us all the time not to ever confide in a Hindu? Why did we love India but cheer the Pakistan cricket team? My young mind understood nothing but I felt a constant ache somewhere in my heart as I searched for the answers.

There was one boy in my class, Vinod, who understood my pain. He was the son of Lala Mukund Behari, an influential and rich jeweller of Chandni Chowk's Dariba Kalan, the famous jewellers' bazaar. Their family had been jewellers to Shahjahan and had been given prominent shops both in Meena Bazaar, inside Red Fort, and outside in the Dariba. Vinod had a huge haveli in Katra Neel. His uncle Lala Brij Behari, Mukund Behari's younger brother, had been a close friend of my father before he went to Pakistan.

Vinod and I were in the same class in school and used to travel together in the same bus. He was the only one who never called me a Pakistani or a mullah. Another reason for our friendship was that he loved cricket, like me, and was a very good all-rounder. Every Sunday morning we used to go to the sprawling ground in front of Red Fort to play cricket. There were Hindu teams and Muslim teams. However, there were a few of us who preferred to have a mixed team, to the dislike of our elders. I never understood it, but there was something fiercely tribal about cricket, which made even close friends think in terms of mohallas and communities whenever they played with each other. I was not a good player but Vinod was the best batsman in the area and insisted that both of us had to be selected together. Because of him, I was also given the opportunity to play my favourite sport.

Vinod was not allowed to visit my house by his mother, Naina Devi, who was afraid that he would eat some non-vegetarian food and lose his dharma. My mother, though, had no problem in my visiting his haveli to fly kites and look at his uncle's collection of pigeons. Brij Behari was famous for his pigeon-flying abilities and used to spend vast sums on buying 'kabootar' from all parts of India. I was told that some of his pigeons were the direct royal descendants of Babur's pigeons, which he had brought from Samarqand. On the roof of the haveli was a huge pigeon house with high bamboo and cane platforms for the pigeons to sit on. My father also loved pigeon-flying and had been both a rival and a friend of Brij Behari. They used to attend pigeon-racing competitions all over the country. Brij Behari used to guard his pigeons fiercely but because I was the son of Aziz Khan, I was allowed to see them. His collection of Shirazi pigeons was one of the best in India and he would jestingly call me his Shirazi pigeon.

Brij Behari was a peculiar man. He loved Urdu poetry and knew thousands of couplets by heart. He used to recite a couplet of Ghalib, Mir or Momin at the drop of a hat, to suit every occasion and situation. There was paan in his mouth all the time. Whenever he saw me, he loved to joke, 'How is my little Pakistani?' This infuriated me no end and I would shout back angrily, 'I am no Pakistani; I hate Pakistan.'

Lala Brij Behari used to laugh loudly and say, 'Shiraz mian, your father fled to Pakistan, leaving you behind.'

I hated him for saying this and would reply with tears in my eyes, 'I hate my father, my brother and all Pakistanis.'

'Don't say that, Shiraz beta, your father was a good man. We studied together at Delhi College and he knew more about pigeons than any other person I know.' Lala Brij Behari didn't like it when I criticized his friend but he was still angry with him. 'He gave his pigeons to a Muslim neighbour before going to Lahore. He should have given them to me and I would have paid him a good price,' he told me a hundred times. 'Now his pigeons are always creating problems for me and you, his son, know nothing about pigeons, what a shame.'

It was Brij Uncle who informed me that Shiraz was also the name of a famous homing pigeon. My father had a great collection of these Shirazi pigeons and had named me Shiraz because of his love for them. Ammi told me that he used to call me 'nanha kabootar', little pigeon. Shiraz is a famous city in Iran, built on the ruins of the great Persian city of Persepolis, which was burnt down by Alexander the Great. It is famous for this species of pigeon, which is prized by pigeon lovers all over the world. It is also known for one of the greatest poets of the East, Hafiz Shirazi. Nani loved Hafiz and used his Diwan, his collection of poems, to predict the future or find appropriate names for children. My mother's name Hina came from there, so did mine.

Vinod and I had no interest in pigeons but we loved to fly kites. Vinod's sister Anuradha, two years younger than him, had a natural talent for it. In those days, girls were not supposed to fly kites but Anu was so good that even her father, who was very conservative, never objected to it. I was ten when I met her for the first time and fell in love with her, instantly. I had no idea what love was but I remember feeling a warm glow somewhere inside my chest as soon as I saw her.

I knocked on Vinod's door one evening and a girl opened it. 'You are Vinod's Muslim friend?' she inquired with a smile and, without waiting for a reply, asked me to follow her. 'Vinod has gone to the market and will be back in five minutes.' Even at that age, she could captivate any man, young or old, with her large, innocent, smiling eyes. Her next question to me was, 'Do you like to fly kites?' Without waiting for a reply, she continued, 'I can defeat you at kite flying.' She led me to the terrace of her haveli, from where we could see all of Chandni Chowk. There were a dozen kites of all sizes lying on the terrace. She picked up a red-

and-blue kite and, with a flick of her fingers, sent it soaring up in the sky. I was angry with her for challenging me but I was also fascinated as I had never seen a girl flying a kite. I had never met a girl like her and never would again.

'You cannot defeat me,' I said confidently, as I had learnt kite-flying from Bundu Chacha. I picked up a yellow kite and searched for a good razor-sharp manjha, the cotton thread coated with egg yolk and small pieces of powdered glass, which could cut your fingers like a knife if you were not careful. Soon my kite was also in the air. Vinod had returned from the bazaar by then. 'Oh my god, she has trapped you into flying kites. Now you are finished, Shiraz, my friend,' he said, clapping and laughing. We had moved to opposite ends of the terrace for our duel in the air. Anuradha was short and thin, with delicate hands, but she manoeuvred the kite like an expert aviator. She was looking at my hands instead of the kite but I learnt this to my chagrin much later, when I had lost my kite to her. She was anticipating the movement of my kite from the movement of my hands. Like an eagle sweeping on its prey, her kite suddenly swung from left to right and before I knew what had happened, I could hear her shout, 'bo kata', and my yellow kite went swinging and dancing over the rooftops to my shame and anguish. Before I could react, she ran down the staircase, laughing and clapping.

Vinod said, 'Never accept a challenge from her, she is too good.' He patted me on the shoulder consolingly. 'No one in Chandni Chowk can beat her.'

'I will teach her one day what real kite-flying is,' I told Vinod without any conviction in my voice, I already knew I had no defence against her.

Since that day I had two obsessions: kite-flying and rushing to Lala Mukund Behari's haveli at any opportunity to see Anuradha. At that age I had no idea what this could lead to.

The lalas belong to a community also known as baniyas, a caste of Hindus that worships Lakshmi, the goddess of wealth. They regard money-making as an act of devotion to the goddess. During the Mughal period, they were the bankers to the empire and dealt in lakhs of rupees. Even the emperor and his family used to take loans from the lalas. During British rule too, they were busy making money. There were exceptions, of course, like Mahatma Gandhi, who belonged to from the same community but lived an austere life. The lalas of Delhi were the dominant community of Chandni Chowk, as it was the traders' bazaar.

Vinod's father and uncle were regarded as the richest and most influential lalas of Delhi, though Brij Behari, unlike his elder brother, was not interested in business; he only loved pigeon-flying. It was said that Lala Mukund Behari had a huge collection of Mughal jewellery which his ancestors had bought at throwaway prices from the marauding British soldiers who had looted the treasury at Red Fort after the failure of the Mutiny. It was hidden somewhere in his haveli.

The problem was that Vinod was interested in neither kite-flying nor pigeon-racing; he loved cricket and painting. Later, I learnt that more than anything else, he was interested in me. One evening, we were painting in his room on the first floor of his haveli. He had been gifted an imported paint-box on his tenth birthday. Anu had brought sweets and tea for us. She never missed an opportunity to be around us whenever I visited their house and Vinod had become jealous of my fondness for her. He pushed her out of the room and bolted the door. I thought he had done this to keep her out but he suddenly said, 'I want to see your phunnu.'

'Why?' I asked, taken aback.

'Please, just for a moment, I want to see what a circumcised penis looks like,' Vinod insisted. It was not an unusual curiosity.

Many boys in our class wanted to see if circumcision meant slicing off a portion of the cock or just removing the skin, but I had always refused to satisfy their curiosity.

'I'll give you my box of colours, I have another one,' said Vinod. It was an offer I couldn't refuse. Reluctantly, I opened the buttons of my fly. Vinod immediately put his hand on my cock. I felt a shiver like an electric shock go up my spine. I pushed his hand away but he said, 'Please, please let me kiss it.' He bent down to touch it with his pink tongue. I knew this was wrong, this was bad, but I didn't have the strength to push him away. There were a thousand flashes exploding in my brain. Suddenly, there was a knock on the door. Anu wanted to come in to take the empty tea cups. I pushed Vinod away and buttoned my shorts. Vinod opened the door. Anu was standing there with a hand on her hips, looking at us suspiciously. 'Why did you bolt the door?' she asked Vinod.

'So that you don't disturb us every five minutes,' Vinod replied. But I wanted Anu to stay. I didn't want to be alone with Vinod.

'Let's fly kites,' I told her.

'Can't you see it's raining outside? Why are you boys such idiots?' In other circumstances I wouldn't have allowed such a comment to go unchallenged but now I desperately wanted her to remain close to me. 'Okay, let's draw some kites then,' I said. Anu didn't need an excuse to play with us. Vinod was angry but he didn't say anything.

As soon as the rain stopped, I ran out. Vinod came after me with the paint-box, but I refused to take it and rushed back to the safety of my house in Ballimaran.

I didn't see Vinod for nearly a week. Then, one day, he came to our house on the pretext of inviting our family to a jagaran, a night of bhajan recitals in praise of Goddess Durga. Nani loved such get-togethers, although she was a devout Muslim. Vinod, with tears in his eyes, promised me that he would never touch me again if I didn't like it.

I was, in fact, more angry with myself for having liked it, and was afraid because I had been warned by Bundu Chacha, whose wisdom I trusted implicitly, never to allow any man to touch me there. I couldn't resist Vinod's pleas to forgive him. He was, after all, my best friend.

Lala Mukund Behari was a short, stocky man with big, round, bulging eyes like an owl's and a short, flat nose over thick red lips. He wore an achkan, a long black coat, and a black round cap throughout the year. Even in the hottest summer months, nobody saw him in any other attire. He was devoted to making money, with no time left over for his family. He was one of those lalas who experience bliss just by counting their money. He had no vices either, as that would have meant spending money.

His wife, Naina Devi, also belonged to a traditional Kayastha family of Bazaar Sita Ram. Her forefathers had been officers in the Mughal court and were scholars of the Persian language. She was a beautiful woman and I could see that Anu had got her features from her. She was tall for an Indian woman, with a sharp, straight nose and expressive kohl-filled eyes. My mother said she resembled Meena Kumari, the heroine of the Hindi film *Baiju Bawra*. She was a trained classical singer but her husband would not let her sing. Apart from Hindi and English, Naina Devi could read and write Persian. She was such a soft-spoken and graceful lady that even Nani had to be nice to her when she came to see my mother. Secretly, in our house, she loved to sing the ghazals of Ghalib in her melodious voice.

My mother said she had never heard such wonderful renderings and if she sang professionally, Naina Devi could be famous across the country. 'She is like a caged bird, I really feel sorry for Naina.' Hina, whose own life was far from easy, pitied this wife of one of the richest men in Delhi.

'Did you notice the sadness in her eyes as she sang?' Nani added.

'Her husband keeps her in strict purdah, otherwise we could involve her in our social work,' my mother said.

The best outcome of my mother's liking for Naina Devi was that she never stopped me from going to Vinod's house in Katra Neel. Naina Devi had also grown fond of me and never stopped me from playing with Anu and Vinod. In those days, there was hardly any socializing between Hindus and Muslims. A Muslim boy visiting the house of a lala, at any time of the day or night, was not something the neighbours approved of, but they could do nothing about it as I was virtually family now. Naina Devi loved to feed me because unlike Vinod, I appreciated all the vegetarian food she served. I hated the idea of killing animals for our culinary pleasure, but in my house there was hardly any vegetarian food, even the daal had meat in it.

Lala Brij Behari was the opposite of his elder brother in every way. He was tall with sharp features. It was said that he resembled his grandfather, who had played an active role in the plundering of Mughal households during the Mutiny. He loved the good things in life, including Western clothes, Urdu poetry and classical music. Unlike Mukund Behari, he was not a miser and had all the vices of a rich Dilliwala. He visited the kothas of the most expensive dancers every evening and spent a lot of money on his pigeons. He loved to eat paan and had the best Scotch whisky in the evening. He argued with his elder brother all the time, threatening to divide the property and walk away with his share, something that Lala Mukund Behari was not ready to allow at any cost.

One day I was flying kites with Anu on their terrace when an argument broke out between the two brothers. Hearing the commotion, we rushed down and, standing in the stairway, saw the elder lala sitting on a chair and the younger one standing tall over him, shouting and arguing.

'Let's divide the business once and for all,' Brij Uncle was shouting at his elder brother. 'You make huge profits and give me a few thousand rupees so that I keep my mouth shut. I will not tolerate it anymore.'

'You idiot, I am making this money for our family, not for you to waste it on your pigeons and prostitutes,' Lala Mukund Behari shouted back.

'What will you do with all this money? Will you light your funeral pyre with it?' Brij Uncle moved menacingly towards his elder brother as he spoke and Naina Devi had to come between them, to stop any scuffle from taking place.

'Bhabhi, don't come between us. This man has been cheating me of my inheritance all this while. I know where he has hidden the jewellery that our forefathers robbed from the Mughals. In fact, all the jewellery looted from Azizuddin's shop was bought by this thief. My friend had to leave India because of these thieves. I want everything to be divided between us here and now.'

'You call your ancestors robbers, *ullu ke patthe*. You have been robbing me blind for so many years. That jewellery is our heritage, it is not for sale.' The elder lala was now shouting at the top of his voice.

'This is my last warning, Mukund bhaiyya. Either you give me my share of the money every month or I'll teach you a lesson you will never forget.'

Their argument left a deep scar on my mind. These lalas were thriving on our treasures. Lala Mukund Behari had a hand in looting my father's shop, thus forcing him to leave Delhi and me. After that evening, I never felt the same about Vinod and his family, although my obsession with Anu remained.

۴

Sometimes I desperately wanted to see my father and brother. I had forgotten what they looked like, except for the black-and-white photograph my mother had kept in our bedroom. To me, my father existed more in black than in white, a one-dimensional figure hanging on the unplastered walls of my childhood memories. My twin brother I remembered only as a smell, without a face or a shape. My mother told me that he smelled different from me and that is how she could tell us apart, I smelling of roses and mint, and my brother of jasmine and green chilies. However, I remembered him as smelling of milk and urine.

I missed my father and used to fantasize about escaping to Pakistan and meeting him. I knew he had remarried in Lahore and had two daughters, my half-sisters. He was a rich businessman now with powerful political contacts. 'He can come to Delhi if he wants to see us,' Ammi used to tell me.

'Does he have a passport? Can he get a visa for India?' I asked.

'What is a visa for him – he is a big shot, close to Pakistan's new President, Ayub Khan, darling of the Pakistani military. He can fly to Delhi and go back the next day.' Pakistan International Airlines had recently started a bi-weekly flight from Delhi to Lahore and Karachi.

My mother had become bitter. Her beautiful golden-brown

eyes were full of sorrow. She was now teaching in a government school after completing her graduation and was very friendly with a young and pretty communist leader, Sarla Sharma. People had been astonished when this young and inexperienced girl won the municipal elections from the conservative Muslim locality of Ballimaran. We were told that even Prime Minister Jawaharlal Nehru was surprised and Home Minister Govind Ballabh Pant was worried that Muslims would turn communist in India and work to destabilize the still unstable nation; he had started looking for Chinese conspiracies behind this. The truth was that the efforts of my Nani and Nafisa Baji had made it possible for Sarla to win the elections.

My mother by now had begun to travel outside Delhi to attend conferences on women's rights. Many men had fallen for her beauty, grace and intelligence but were afraid to approach her directly. She still loved Aziz Khan and was averse to remarrying. In any case, she had not been divorced by her husband, so there was no question of her remarrying. Nani had sent a message to him to send a divorce to my mother so that she could be free of him, but he had not replied. Hina Begum kept track of Aziz Khan and had learnt that he had become a minister in Ayub Khan's military regime. She was not impressed; she was a democrat who hated any type of dictatorship. She used to say, 'They have decided to commit suicide, what can we do.'

Bundu had replaced my father as the man in my life. But he was more than a father; he was my friend, philosopher and guide. He took his role quite seriously, never hesitating to reprimand me if he felt I had gone wrong, or teach me what he thought I should know about life. He used to ply his tonga every day from

Chandni Chowk to Nizamuddin. One day, I was playing cricket in the narrow lane outside my house. Suddenly, my mother came out of the house, shouting my name. From her voice it was clear that there was bad news. 'Shiraz, come quickly. We have to go to Irwin hospital immediately.' This was the big hospital outside Delhi Gate, named after Viceroy Lord Irwin. I ran to my mother, worried that something had happened to my grandmother. 'What happened? Who is sick?'

Ammi pulled me on to a cycle-rickshaw and shouted at the rickshawalla, a thin, bearded old man, to get to the hospital as fast as he could.

'Who is in the hospital? What has happened to Nani?' I shouted at her.

'Bundu Chacha has had an accident. His tonga was hit by a truck. His condition is serious,' Ammi whispered, without looking at me.

'What?' I couldn't believe it. 'Is he dead?' I whispered back.

Ammi didn't reply. She was silently reciting a prayer.

Some friends of Bundu, who had brought him to the hospital, told us that his beloved horse, Genghis, was dead. Bundu himself was battling for life in the operation theatre.

Bundu was a popular figure among the tongawallas of Delhi. He was like their boss and guru. He used to win the famous tonga race from Nizamuddin to Qutb every year. Now all the tongawallas were gathering outside the hospital with tears in their eyes and prayers on their lips.

For three days, Bundu fought for his life. His lung was punctured, ribs broken, one leg crushed, but I knew he would not die. He would survive for me. He was like the North Star of my existence.

Ammi did not leave the hospital for three days. Bundu ended up having to stay in the hospital for nearly a month. I used to bring food for him every day and sit with him, listening to his stories. One day I asked him to tell me his own story. He had no family, no relatives; still my grandmother treated him with great respect. Who was he? Where did he come from?

In the past, everytime I asked him such questions, he had laughed and said, 'Shiraz mian, I am the son of a great jinn who came from a far-off planet.'

Lying on the hospital bed with his leg plastered and hanging from a pulley, and his chest covered with bandages, he was not in the mood to joke. That day he decided to tell me his story, the story of his forefathers, the legendary horsemen from the Golden Hordes of Genghis Khan.

'My real name is Bulund Iqbal Baig.' Bundu's voice showed no sign of pain. It was still strong and deep. 'I am a descendant of Mirza Moazzam Ali Baig, the great horseman, who was a childhood friend of Babur in Farghana. My ancestors were Mongols and we used to rear horses from the steppes of Mongolia for the armies of the Great Khan. Moazzam Ali wandered with Babur, searching for a place to sleep and a kingdom to bestow upon his children. Through the centuries, emperors came and went, but my family remained the keepers of their horses.

'We were the best horsemen in the empire. Akbar and Jahangir and their descendants had great faith in the ability of my family to rear, train and organize the horses for their armies and for personal use. My ancestors travelled all over Arabia and Turkey and the grasslands of Mongolia to get the best horses for them.'

Bundu was half sitting as he sipped sweet, strong tea from a large mug. My mother used to say that instead of blood, he had tea in his veins. It was his only weakness. He didn't smoke, drink or eat too much. Nani used to tease him that tea was the import of the angrez, the White Devils, designed to make Indians weak and subservient. But Bundu claimed that tea was brought to India from China by his ancestors when they travelled there to buy horses. They never traded in tea, but they always drank black kahwa tea with saffron.

Bundu thought he might not live much longer, so he wanted to tell me the story of his grandfather, who was hanged in 1857 by the victorious soldiers of the East India Company, at Khooni Darwaza, in front of Kotla Firozshah in Delhi.

'My grandfather Mirza Afroz Baig was a friend and advisor of the last Mughal emperor,, Bahadur Shah Zafar,' he said. 'We had a large haveli at Kashmiri Gate. My grandfather had the largest personal collection of horses in Delhi. When the Mutiny began, the Indian sepoys took away most of his horses. My grandfather advised Bahadur Shah not to associate himself with that motley group of undisciplined and unorganized mutineers. They went around looting and killing the British and did not spare even children and women. On the third day of the Mutiny, my father saw some sepoys looting the house of a British trader who had lived in Delhi for decades. His children were born in Delhi. My grandfather could not stand by and watch such injustice being done. When they tried to rape the mother and murder the children, he took out his sword and attacked the mutineers. They were taken aback by this unexpected assault and escaped with their booty. The English woman was severely injured and the children, a boy of six and a girl of three, were traumatized. Their father had been murdered. My grandfather brought them to our house, which was close by, and decided to hide them in a basement under the stables.' Bundu was telling the story as if he had been an eyewitness to it all, but of course he had heard it from his father, who had been nine years old at the time of the Mutiny.

A nurse came in to give Bundu an injection. The great Mongol warrior was terrified of needles and would have preferred to die than have this angrezi medicine injected into his body. However, all tied up, and with broken bones, he was in no position to resist.

It was time for me to go home, so the story-telling session came to an end for the day. I couldn't sleep the whole night, thinking of what had happened to the British family hidden under the stables of Mirza Afroz Baig's haveli. Next day I went to the hospital as soon as I finished lunch.

Bundu smiled and continued the story from where he had left off the previous day. 'The British woman died a few days after my grandfather rescued her. He kept the children hidden in the basement because the sepoys were searching for British families. Some of the mutineers were highly motivated but there was also a large group which was more interested in looting and raping than defending the city of Delhi. Grandfather was helping the mutineers to defend the city but he was also trying to stop them from killing and looting. This was not to the liking of some of the mutineers. They dubbed my grandfather a spy of the British. Our family fled from Kashmiri Gate to a house in the interiors of Old Delhi. My father, Mirza Altaf Baig, became very close to the two English children. The boy was called Emerson and the girl was Lucy. They wore Muslim dress, ate Indian food and had learnt to speak Hindustani. In the city of Delhi, the Mutiny began on 11 May 1857 and ended on 15 September, the day Bahadur Shah was arrested by Captain Hodson from Humayun's Tomb, though it continued in other parts of the country till June 1858. My grandfather was arrested for helping the mutineers. He pleaded that he had saved English families but he was charged with kidnapping English children and was hanged on 18 September 1857 at Khooni Darwaza, the bloody gate, named thus after it turned red with the blood of thousands of royal family members, including the sons of Bahadur Shah Zafar.'

'What happened to his family?' I asked.

Bundu was deep in thought. He didn't speak for some time and I thought that he had gone to sleep. Then he said in a whisper, 'My grandmother, who was still a beautiful young woman, was given to a Muslim Punjabi officer of the British army. He refused to take my father with him and sold him to a brute Sikh who took my father to a village near Amritsar. My father had been brought up in luxury. By the time he was nine, he could read and write many languages, including English. He was also an expert horse rider. But now he was made to live in a cattle barn and look after buffaloes. He was forced to work eighteen hours a day and was often beaten for no fault of his. The Sikh used to drink a lot and sodomize him every night. One night, my father could not take it anymore, and killed him with his kirpan and escaped from there. He went to Lahore and started working for a tongawalla. The tongawalla treated him like his own son. After his death, my father decided to come back to Delhi, the city of his ancestors. He became a chowkidar in the same haveli where he had spent his childhood and which was now occupied by a rich lala of Delhi. My father looked after the lala's buggy and became his coachman. He married very late, at the age of fifty-five, more to give shelter to an orphan Mughal princess, than to have a family. She was the granddaughter of Mirza Babur, the brother of the last Mughal emperor. My father always treated my mother like a queen and never allowed her to do any manual work, although he was himself a poor man. I was born a few years after the new Christian century began.'

Bundu's story opened my mind to what our ancestors had gone through. Here was a proud member of a family which had controlled all the horses in the kingdom, the son of a Mughal princess, but who, till recently, plied a tonga with a single horse. Bundu said that his horse had the blood of the Mongol horses and that's why he had named it Genghis. One could not find such horses in Delhi anymore, except at Rashtrapati Bhavan, where the British Viceroys had stabled some of the confiscated horses of the Mughal cavalry. Genghis had died very near the place on Bahadur Shah Zafar Road where Bundu's grandfather had been hanged.

'Shiraz, we are fortunate that we still live in the Dilli of our ancestors. We have a house to live in and food to share. Most of the Mughals were hanged, their women raped, their children taken away by brute sepoys of the British and turned into slaves. Many became beggars. My father told me the story of a Mughal prince who lost both his feet and used to drag himself around in the bazaars of Delhi, begging for alms. He was the grandson of Bahadur Shah. He had the fair handsome face of a Mughal but had to pull himself along by his elbows on the dirty streets of Delhi, which his great-grandfather Shahjahan had built as the most beautiful city in the world. There was a time when every citizen used to bow his head before him when he rode on his horse with a group of followers. But now he looked at every face silently, begging them to throw him a few pennies. He slept on the stairs of Jama Masjid, where many Mughal princes who had escaped hanging found refuge and survived by begging. Most of the Mughal princesses were kidnapped and died in villages around Delhi and in Punjab, their children not even aware of their royal blood and their ancestors, who had built one of the greatest empires in the world.'

Bundu was a great Sufi in his own way. He had seen how unpredictable life was. He had no desire or love for any worldly goods. He accepted the past glory and the brutal decline of the Mughals philosophically. 'Life is as wonderful as you want to make it or as horrible as you decide to live it,' he used to say. He had a great desire to pass on to me all the knowledge of our past, hoping that one day I would write these stories for the world to know. Unlike my teachers at school, he had an unshakeable faith in me and believed that one day I would make my Mughal ancestors proud.

'Shiraz, your Nani is a true Mughal princess. My father on his deathbed gave my mother and me into the care of your Nani's father. We were lucky to be in such a respected Mughal household. Now it is for you to keep the traditions of the Mughals alive and remember your ancestors.'

Bundu came back home and soon bought a pair of sturdy chestnut horses with the money that my Nani gave him. His tonga was once again the most popular vehicle on the roads of Delhi. He loved to wander around inside Red Fort. He knew secret passages to the fort and went in as he pleased. The superintendent in charge of Red Fort, Dr Bhattacharjee, was a family friend, who loved to talk to my mother and Bundu about their family history. Bundu would sometimes stay with him in his house inside the fort. But he did not tell him about the secret passages as he believed that it was only Mughal family members who could use this privilege.

One Sunday morning, Bundu took me to the Ring Road behind Red Fort. It was the month of December and Delhi was cold and foggy. It was early morning and still dark when we reached. There was an old grave made of red stone near the wall of the fort. He pushed aside some stones in the grave and then removed the heavy stone on top. There was an opening leading into a tunnel. Bundu slipped into the opening and asked me to follow him. I had more faith in Bundu than in any other human being I knew, but was still hesitant and afraid. Half bent, we moved into a tunnel which was hardly three feet high. After we had walked about a hundred feet, we came to a dead end. Bundu had a German torch in his hand. He brought out a long nail from his pocket and put it into a hole, moved it a few times and there opened another stone door in the wall. We were inside a large basement now. Bundu told me that there was a double basement under the hammams or bathing areas of the royal living quarters of the fort. These basements opened into other basements through many secret tunnels. They had been constructed by Aurangzeb with the help of a Chinese architect, who was then put to death to keep the secret. Bundu told me that when British forces surrounded the fort after the defeat of the rebels, Bahadur Shah used this passage to escape to Humayun's Tomb, from where he was finally arrested.

'Why are you showing me all this?' I asked Bundu.

'Because I am the only man alive who knows about these chambers and I am not certain how long I am going to live,' Bundu whispered into my ear as if he were bestowing a great treasure on me. 'I wanted to pass on this knowledge to a descendant of the Mughals before I die.'

Bundu and Nani were conspiring to put the burden of these secrets on my poor shoulders at an age when I hardly understood what it all meant. I was more interested in learning the secrets of kite-flying so I could defeat Anu. I was a bit disappointed as I had been hoping to learn some earth-shaking secrets of the emperors – these empty chambers and secret passages held no attraction for me. But I had to humour Bundu. We returned by the same secret route, Bundu explaining to me the complexities of the walls of Red Fort.

Lala Mukund Behari used to organize the grand Ram Lila of Delhi at the Ram Lila ground at Ajmeri Gate each year. The whole family would be involved in the preparations for this festival. Prime Minister Nehru would attend the last day of the festivities when Ravan, the demon king, exploded into a ball of fire to the sound of ear-shattering crackers.

It was the Ram Lila of 1961. Vinod was playing the role of Lakshman and Brij Behari was playing his favourite role of Hanuman. It was the final day; the prime minister and other dignitaries were expected to arrive any minute. Anu, who was now twelve, had worn a sari for the first time. She was rushing from one stall to the other, trying the chaat, the street food of Delhi. I was watching her antics from a distance. In spite of her superiority in flying kites, we had become good friends. Suddenly, she tripped on a rope near a tent and fell down. Her sari was torn and muddied. Her mother and brother could not leave the venue. I was the only person who could be spared, so I was asked to accompany Anu to her house so that she could change her clothes. I went with her in a rickshaw to Katra Neel. The sari made her look much older, and everyone on the street was looking at her. Escorting such a beautiful girl openly on an Old Delhi street was not something even a grown-up man would relish. Anu was a very confident girl even at that age. She was enjoying my discomfort and deliberately moved closer to me. 'Why are you so nervous, Shiraz?' she inquired innocently. 'Do you have a headache?' She touched my forehead to see if I had a fever. I was aware of the thousand eyes watching every move of ours on the street.

There was no one at home. Anu went to take a bath and change while I waited in the sitting room. Suddenly she came in, half dressed. 'Can you please help me wrap my sari? Ma helped me before, but since this is my first time, I can't do it alone.'

I didn't know how to wrap a sari or, for that matter, any female attire. Anu asked me to hold one end of the long Banarasi sari, while she tried to wrap herself in it. She was so close to me, I could taste her smell on the tip of my tongue. Her big honey-gold eyes looked at me, and without any warning, she kissed my neck. I stood there, paralysed.

She laughed. 'What happened, babuji? Did a snake bite you, or have you seen a ghost?'

I didn't know how to deal with this girl. She was mature beyond her years, but had such an innocent air about her.

We took a cycle-rickshaw back to the Ram Lila ground. This time, Anu covered her head and half her face with her sari pallu, not so much to save me from further embarrassment but to protect her hair from being blown about by the wind.

From that day we both knew that we were in love. I had known it since the age of ten, but now Anu too let me know she was attracted to me. Vinod was happy that I loved to spend so much time at his house. He was aware that I was interested in his sister and not him, but he never said anything. Brij Uncle, who was keen to turn me into a great pigeon-flyer like himself, could see that I was more interested in learning to fly kites with his niece, but he too kept quiet.

I was old enough to know my love was doomed. It was unthinkable: a Hindu girl from a prominent business family of Delhi falling for a Muslim boy whose father was a minister in Pakistan. But I must confess that from the moment I met her, Anu knew how to manipulate me and make me do her bidding without thinking of the consequences.

۵

It was my fifteenth birthday, 15 August 1962. We didn't celebrate birthdays in our family. Nani said it was the death anniversary which should be celebrated as that was the day people met their creator. Ammi said that since the entire nation celebrated my birthday, as Independence Day, there was no need for me to celebrate it. We would go instead to Red Fort to listen to Prime Minister Nehru make his Independence Day speech.

Every year. after listening to the prime minister's speech, we would form groups and visit different parts of the old city, singing patriotic songs. Each mohalla had its own flag-hoisting ceremony and the women would shower us with coins and flowers.

On that day, our group, which included boys and girls from the different lanes of Chandni Chowk, visited Bazaar Sita Ram. This was the mohalla of Pandit Nehru's wife Kamala Nehru and it was famous for its cultured Kashmiri Pandit families. Anu was the star singer of our group and people all over Old Delhi had started talking of her extraordinary beauty. I was enjoying the Kashmiri Wazwan with my friends, when my name was announced over the mike. Somebody was looking for me. It was my neighbour's son, Alladin. 'There are policemen at your house. They have surrounded your house. I came running to inform you. I knew you would be here.' Alladin looked scared.

'Did you find out what it's about?' I inquired.

'No, I was afraid to speak to them. I just ran to inform you.' Alladin, like most people, was terrified of policemen and tried to avoid them. Policemen coming to any house meant there was something terribly wrong.

My friends were also worried and wanted to come with me. But I told them to come later and ran back to my house. I was shocked to see dozens of policemen standing outside. The whole lane was being cleaned by an army of sweepers. What had happened? Had they come to arrest Ammi or Nani? I stormed into the house. 'What's wrong?' I shouted. Ammi was busy cleaning the house. Nani was laughing, 'Your Abba is coming to meet us.'

'Abba!' I exclaimed. 'But what are all these policemen doing here?'

'He's an important Pakistani minister now and is in Delhi to attend a conference. He's coming to meet you. The police are here to protect him,' Bundu explained.

'To protect him from his own family, from his wife and son?' I was still confused and in shock. I was going to see my father after all these years. It was unbelievable. I was wearing a khadi kurta pajama and a Gandhi cap. There was no time to change. I could hear the noise outside: he had arrived. I rushed out. The whole mohalla had come out to see their son-in-law returning as a Pakistani minister. The children of the mohalla, who had been too young when he left to remember him, wanted to see what he looked like. Some were curious to see a Pakistani at close quarters. Did he have two horns on his head?

Here he was, entering our very narrow lane, tall and handsome in his dark three-piece suit with a colourful tie. He had a black French beard and well-groomed wavy hair. He opened his hands wide, wanting me to come and hug him, but I stood like a statue, paralysed. He was a stranger, not the Abba who used to visit me in my dreams, not the one-dimensional black-and-white figure hanging on our bedroom wall. He was a different man, like a film star whom you could see but not touch. He came up to me and folded me in his arms. 'Shiraz, my lovely Shiraz. You look like an Indian leader. Have you joined politics?'

There were half a dozen people with him: officials, secretaries, and our Mir Mohalla and other prominent leaders of the area, who all wanted to be photographed with him. They sat in the big baithak, the men's sitting room at the entrance of the house. Very hesitantly, I took hold of Abba's hand and took him inside, to the huge courtyard where Nani, Ammi, and the other women of the household were waiting for him. Qudsia Begum embraced him. Abba looked at my mother. Hina Begum was looking down at her feet and not at him, her head covered with a colourful dupatta, like a newly married bride. She was afraid to look at him directly, as though she might be blinded by his presence.

She simply said 'Adaab', as if he were a complete stranger and not her husband. But even I could see that she was glowing and looked younger and more beautiful than I had seen her in a long time.

Azizuddin Khan looked at her, hesitated, and then very formally said, 'How are you, Hina Begum?'

Nani was angry. 'Why didn't you inform us earlier, I could have made your favourite bhindi gosht, now I've only made biryani and korma.'

Abba said, 'Amma, I have to leave in forty minutes for a meeting. I can't eat much. But I miss your bhindi gosht and nahari. I am leaving for Bombay this evening for a conference there, but I will be back after two days. I want Shiraz to come with me so that I may get to know him better.'

'Oh yes!' I burst out, jumping from my seat. 'We can meet Dilip Kumar there.'

Abba laughed. 'Not only Dilip Kumar, but Madhubala as well.'

Ammi looked at Abba with taunting eyes. 'You are still fond of Madhubala in your Pakistan?'

Abba smiled. 'Of course, there is no woman like Madhubala in the whole subcontinent.' And then Abba whispered in English, 'Except you, Hina Begum.'

Ammi smiled. 'You were always a bad liar, Aziz,' she said, but I could see that she was pleased.

I wanted my mother to take Abba into her bedroom and hug him. There was nothing in her demeanour to indicate this, but I knew she was dying to do just that. Suddenly I had an inspiration. 'Ammi, why don't you come to Bombay with us?' I looked at Abba.

He hesitated for a moment and then said, 'Yes, of course. If Hina Begum would like to come, I have no problem.'

'But I have a problem ...' She did not complete her sentence.

'You and Shiraz will be in a separate room and you will have a car to take you around as I will be busy with my conference,' Abba said, tucking into Nani's biryani.

'Ammi, please come, you don't have to sleep with Abba, you can sleep with me,' I offered a compromise. Everyone laughed, including my mother.

Abba asked one of his secretaries to bring a large suitcase inside. He had brought beautiful clothes for all of us. For my mother he had brought a red woollen coat from London. This touched my mother, that he had remembered her even while he was visiting London. There was an expensive striped suit for me, unlike anything I had ever seen anybody wearing in Delhi. He had brought a beautiful train set too, which had to be arranged on a table. He promised that when he returned from Bombay, he would do it for me. I was so excited that I jumped into his lap like a child, although I had turned fifteen that day.

He had brought a long coat for Nani and an overcoat for Bundu, who immediately tried it on over his kurta pajama and refused to take it off till he went to sleep although it was the hot, sultry month of August.

Nani took my mother inside and convinced her to go with us to Bombay. I think now that Ammi must have been more worried about her own feelings than of what others would say. She was too independent a woman to bother about the opinions of society.

Abba said, 'I will send a car in the evening to take you to the airport, where I will join you.'

There was a big crowd outside our house and everybody wanted to shake the hand of the Pakistani commerce minister, but there were many who had come to see their own Aziz mian, the son-in-law of Ballimaran. My father recognized many old friends and acquaintances. I told him about his old pigeon-flying friend, Lala Brij Behari. Abba laughed. 'Of course, Birju, our Hanuman, how is he? I would love to meet him.' But he had no time and the police were against his visiting a Hindu mohalla without proper security arrangements.

Abba had to go. As soon as he left, all the neighbours came to our house to find out what my father had brought for us from Pakistan and to gather all the gossip they could. The news that we were travelling to Bombay with him spread like wildfire. All my mother's friends asked her to get the autograph and, if possible, a strand of Dilip Kumar's hair for them to keep. In those days, after the release of *Mughal-e-Azam*, the great epic on the tussle between Emperor Akbar and his son Saleem, every woman from eight to eighty was in love with him. Every young man behaved like Prince Saleem, every woman like Anarkali, and every father like Shahanshah Akbar. Dilip Kumar, the king of tragedy, as he was known, had played the role of Prince Saleem in the movie.

Many girls had eloped to Bombay since, singing the song, '*Pyaar kiya to darna kya*' – don't be afraid if you are in love.

A car came to pick us up exactly at seven. Everyone was there to see us off at the gate of the mohalla, as if we were going on the Haj. In my excitement I had forgotten all about Vinod and Anu. I wanted to show them the train my father had brought for me from London. I wanted to show off my handsome father, who could speak English better than an angrez. But there was no way to inform them about my trip to Bombay.

I had dreamt of flying but had never even seen an airplane. Yet, here I was, sitting in an airplane with my father and mother and sipping a Coca-Cola. In just a few hours there had been so much adventure in my life that it was impossible for my young mind to absorb everything.

I was sitting between Azizuddin Khan and Hina Begum. They were still formal and courteous with each other. I was chattering away, telling my father about my school and friends. I told him all the good things. I didn't tell him that everyone teased me at school and called us Pakistani. I didn't tell him about my teacher, who used to slap me for no fault of mine except that I was a Muslim. I wanted to impress my father with everything in India, hoping that he would decide to return to Delhi, and not thinking that I could go with him to Lahore – the city Nani hated so much.

When I wanted to go to the toilet, I was escorted by a beautiful air-hostess. Standing close to her, I tried to inhale all the lovely smells she was exuding. When I returned to my seat, my mother was sitting next to my father, holding his hand. They had forgotten all about me. I knew enough about what goes on between a man and a woman, thanks to Nasreen, and I felt a pang of jealousy, looking at my parents holding hands.

In Bombay, we were taken to the great Taj Mahal Hotel near the Gateway of India. It was out of a storybook. I had never imagined that any place like this existed anywhere in the world. I felt like Alladin, who could get whatever he wanted with the help of his magic lamp. I could not decide whether my father was the magic lamp or the genie of the lamp. Right now he was behaving like Prince Saleem with his Anarkali; I was the unwanted intruder between the two lovebirds. My mother was staying with me in a separate room, but at night I realized that I was sleeping next to a pillow. She had quietly slipped away to the next room where my father was snoring contentedly.

Next morning, at the rooftop restaurant of the Taj, my parents were laughing and touching each other like a young couple on their honeymoon. I was not only jealous but embarrassed by their behaviour, and everyone was looking at us. Ammi, for the first time in my memory, was paying more attention to someone other than me. The sea looked beautiful from here. But she was not interested in Bombay and Abba had forgotten all about his meetings. Luckily, his secretary, an old Parsi gentleman from Lahore, came to remind him that he had to leave in fifteen minutes. Abba looked at me and said, 'Shiraz, take good care of your mother. There is a car which will take you around the city and in the evening I am giving you a big surprise.' Before I could interrogate him about the surprise, he was gone.

We had seen the beautiful city of Bombay only in black and white, on the cinema screen. But here we were, eating ice cream on Juhu beach and bhelpuri at Chowpatty. Ammi was running around like a young girl. I had not seen her so happy since that fateful morning when we escaped from Delhi railway station and saved ourselves from going to Pakistan.

'Sherry, aren't you happy? We will soon meet Aijaz, your brother and my son. I am dying to meet him,' said Ammi, shamelessly licking an ice-cream. In Delhi, no woman from a respectable family would have licked an ice-cream cone in full public view. But here, in Bombay, Hina Begum was enjoying her anonymity, to my embarrassment and irritation. She held out the cone to me, but I turned away sulkily.

'How come? Is he also coming to Delhi?' I asked.

'No, we will go to Pakistan very soon. Your father will buy a new bungalow for us on a beach like this in Karachi. We will live there, won't that be nice?' Ammi looked at me with a raised eyebrow, as if asking for my approval.

'Why should we leave Delhi and go to Karachi? Ammi, you know I hate Pakistan. Why can't Abba and Aijaz come and live in Delhi with us?'

'No, Shiraz, they can't. We'll have to go there. I want both my children with me.' Ammi tried to kiss my palm, but I pulled it away. For the first time in my life, I was angry with my mother. How could she take such a decision without consulting me?

'Have you told Nani about this?' I asked her with tears in my eyes.

'No, I'll tell her when we return to Delhi.'

There was some hope then. I knew that Nani would not let us go to Pakistan. 'I'll stay in Delhi with Nani,' I said stubbornly.

Now I understood the surprise Abba had been talking about. I hated him.

When we went back to the cool air-conditioned confines of the hotel, I sat in the balcony of our room, with its view of all the boats and big ships moving towards the harbour. My world was being turned upside down by my parents. My ship had no moorings, no harbour. I was drifting and angry with everybody around me, with Jinnah and Chacha Nehru and Maulana Azad and Nani and Bundu, who had taught me to so intensely dislike Pakistan. Above all, I hated my mother, who in just one night had changed and forgotten her anger towards my father and Pakistan. She had forgotten that Abba had married a woman called Ayesha in Lahore and had two children by her. How could my mother love this man called Azizuddin Khan, even if he was my father?

Ammi came and hugged me from behind. 'Sherry, don't be so angry. I love you more than anybody else in the world. We won't go to Karachi if you don't want to go.'

I started sobbing in her arms and eventually drifted off. I woke up to find Abba sitting next to my bed. It was dark outside. I had slept the whole afternoon, which was very unusual, as I never slept in the daytime. Abba informed me that we were going to a night club. I didn't know what a night club was and was not interested in finding out. But I had no choice and was made to wear a suit and a tie. Ammi, in her red sari with her hair up in a high jooda, looked like a film star. Who could be angry with such a beautiful woman? I once again fell in love with her. I could see my father becoming bewitched too, forgetting all about his Ayesha Begum in Lahore.

Bombay was glittering like a street prostitute waiting to barter her body for a few rupees, the only currency, I had heard people say, which this city understood. The club was next door, on the top floor of an old building. The entire stretch from the Taj to the Royal Night Club, a distance of barely hundred yards, was lined by half-naked beggars, women and children, trying to touch the rich and mighty of Bombay as they stepped out of their limousines. The beggars knew they could not only make them feel guilty but blackmail them into giving a few rupees as the price for not being touched and polluted by them. Inside, it was another world, glittering and shining, laughing and dancing.

For my mother and me, it was like the magic of Alibaba; we had never seen anything like it. Abba had been invited to the club by a very rich Parsi businessman and his French wife. Also present was a popular film star, R. Kumar. All the women there wanted to touch him and get his autograph. Abba introduced me to everyone and they shook my hand as if I was all grown up. Ammi was quite nervous; she had never been to a club before. Mr Modi, the Parsi gentleman, said, 'I thought you were a model or a film star, but now Aziz claims you are his wife. I don't believe it.' Ammi blushed and Abba laughed, his pride in his wife evident.

I was lost in this magical world, when the music started playing. Abba asked Mrs Modi for a dance; Mr Modi was already dancing with an Anglo-Indian girl. Suddenly, Abba came and pulled Ammi to the dance floor. Music drowned out the protests of my mother, who had never in her life thought of dancing before so many men. But she was soon taken up by the rhythm and began to enjoy herself. I was mesmerized by this dream world of lights and sounds. Except for the dance floor, the lights were dim in the room and then, in that darkness, under the table, a hand crept over my trouser front. I became aware of it only when it had opened my buttons and taken out my hard member. To my utter shock, I realized that it was the hand of Kumar, the film star. He was smiling at me and moving his hand up and down my very hard, adolescent cock. I wanted to push it away but at that moment, the music stopped and my parents returned to the table.

Kumar was still holding my cock in his soft fingers. Ammi was busy talking to Mr Modi, who wanted the next dance with her, and they were off again to the dance floor. Kumar's expert fingers were still moving up and down, sending electric shock waves to my brain. I had lost all my strength to the waves of pleasure that were emanating from my dick. I knew it was not right, it was unnatural, but I didn't have the willpower to stop him. Suddenly, something sticky splurged out of me. Kumar raised his hand to the table and discreetly wiped it with a napkin. I stood up, pushed my sticky member back into my trousers, and ran out of the club. I came out on to the street and blindly ran towards the hotel. The pavement was deserted. I entered the glittering Taj lobby and ran towards the lift. I thought everyone was looking at me and my wet, leaking trouser front. My shame was there for the world to see. I went straight to the bathroom, pulled off all my clothes and stood under the shower. I knew what an ejaculation was and had seen a couple of older boys ejaculating, but this was my first experience, and it shook me to the roots of my being. I changed into my pajamas and went to bed, trying to grasp all that had happened that night. After some time, Ammi came looking for me. I had spoiled her lovely evening. I told her I had a headache and she could go back to the club, but she seemed to be worried and sat there pressing my head until I went to sleep.

The sound of the waves and strong winds woke me up. It was raining outside, the kind of rain I had not seen in Delhi. It felt as though the waves would break into the hotel and sweep it into the Arabian Sea. More than me, Ammi was terrified. Abba had to go for his meetings, but we decided to remain in our rooms for the day. Around eleven, a waiter came with a letter from a guest staying at the hotel. He was British, and he wanted to meet us urgently. Ammi was intrigued, as we didn't know anyone from England. We invited him to our room and he arrived almost immediately.

'My name is James Hunter. My great-grandfather was a doctor who served the last Mughal Emperor, Bahadur Shah Zafar,' the gentleman said by way of introduction. He was around forty, a handsome man with brown hair and light grey eyes, tall and impressive looking, 'I'm sorry to bother you but I couldn't resist meeting you, when I learned from a waiter that you belonged to the family of the Mughals. To tell you the truth, I have come to India searching for my Mughal ancestors.'

'Aren't you English?' Ammi asked, surprised.

'Yes, I am English, but with some Mughal blood in my veins,' he replied with smile. 'It's a long story, but I would like to explain to you the history of my ancestors as briefly as possible.'

Ammi had been looking a bit uncomfortable and viewing the British gentleman with some suspicion. She had not even offered him a cup of tea. But now he had her full attention.

'I am told that your mother is a direct descendant of the last Mughal emperor. I would like to meet her.'

'I don't think she would agree to see a gora angrez, as she has a dislike for all foreigners,' Ammi said in a gruff voice.

'I understand her dislike for the British, but when she hears my story, she may agree to see me,' Dr Hunter replied.

'Tell me your story, I don't have much time.' Ammi, who had nothing else to do, was behaving as if she had a plane to catch.

'My great-grandfather, Dr Irving Hunter, was a physician in Delhi at the time of the Mutiny, and used to attend to the royal family frequently. He was very friendly with the family of Begum Zeenat Mahal, the youngest wife of the emperor. During the Mutiny, he tried to escape with his wife and young daughter. But they were captured by the rebel sepoys and brought to Red Fort to be killed. Begum Zeenat Mahal intervened on their behalf and saved their lives. She gave refuge to Dr Hunter's family in her haveli at Lal Kuan. The sepoys became suspicious of Begum Zeenat Mahal and accused her of being secretly in league with the British. By then, Dr Irving's wife Nancy had become very friendly with Saleema Begum, the sister of the last queen. As fate would have it, both Nancy and her daughter died of cholera as it spread through the city; there was no municipal authority to keep the city clean.

'The distraught doctor was sheltered by Saleema Begum's family despite the shortage of food and other essentials in the city, which was now under siege by the British army. The menfolk of the family were killed in the fighting. When the city was recaptured by the British and most of the members of the prominent Mughal families were butchered mercilessly, Dr Hunter's intervention saved the lives of Saleema Begum and her mother. He stayed in Delhi for nearly ten years and played an important part in saving a large number of Muslims and also served the injured and ill in the walled city of Shahjahanabad. His bungalow at Kashmiri Gate became a hospital and a refuge for the surviving citizens of the unfortunate city. Beautiful and strong-willed Saleema Begum became his assistant and served the people of Delhi with dedication and love. She never behaved like a Mughal princess but went from house to house in the narrow bylanes of Delhi, tending to the injured and ill with whatever little resources she and Dr Hunter had at their disposal. She became famous in the city by the name of Dawai Begum, the medicine lady.'

Dr Hunter was lost in narrating his story and we were totally engrossed in the description of those days when our family had lost everything in their beloved city of Shahjahanabad. Suddenly, a strong gust of wind pushed open one of the windows facing the sea. The window pane shattered into pieces and salty sea water rushed into the room. A piece of glass hit my mother on her forehead and she started bleeding.

I jumped from my chair and called the hotel staff. Ammi went into the bedroom of our two-room suite. Dr Hunter, himself a doctor, was deeply apologetic, as if he were responsible for my mother's injury. He said he would come back later, but my mother insisted he stay and complete his story. It was still raining heavily and we shifted to the adjoining room as the window pane was replaced in the room where we had been sitting. Ammi ordered lunch for all of us and Dr Hunter gracefully accepted. He seemed to be as eager to tell his story as we were keen to hear it.

'Dr Hunter had fallen in love with this graceful and compassionate lady who served the common people with such selfless devotion. Then, one day, when he was cleaning his gun, it went off accidentally and he was badly injured. Saleema took care of him day and night, and during this time they became so close that they decided to marry. Their marriage was looked down upon by the British and the Muslims alike, although they had both a nikah and a church ceremony. In the meantime, Irving Hunter's father died in London and, as the only son, he inherited all his property. As a result, he had to return to London. Saleema Begum decided to go with him in spite of her great love for her beloved Delhi.' Dr Hunter was silent, lost in his memories. Lunch had been served and we moved to the dining table.

'Dr Hunter and Saleema Begum had two sons and a daughter. I am the grandson of his second son William, who later came back to India and served as an advisor to Lord Curzon, the Viceroy. He knew Persian and from his mother had learned Urdu, which he could speak fluently. In fact, he wrote the story of his father and translated the diary of his mother Saleema Begum from Urdu into English. He also established a hospital in London in memory of his parents – it is one of the largest in England and I am now the chairman of the HS Trust, which runs the chain of hospitals. HS stands for Hunter and Saleema.'

'Why have you come to India now, looking for your Mughal ancestors?' Hina Begum whispered.

Dr Hunter looked at her with dreamy brooding eyes, as if he did not understand her question. 'Why I have come to India now, I don't know. I should have come earlier. I always wanted to. Since my childhood I dreamt of my Mughal ancestors. I regarded myself as more Mughal than English. I lived in my private fantasy world. Life, responsibilities, circumstances, fears, cowardice, everything kept me away. But last year, when my dear wife Anna and my son Irwin died in a car accident, I decided to fulfil my childhood dream.'

I could hear the pain in his voice. I was warming up to this stranger and so was Ammi. We felt somehow connected to this doctor from a far-off land who claimed to be one of us, who understood our pain and loss.

'I want to visit Delhi, the city my great-grandfather and Saleema Begum loved so much. I want to put some colour into the black-and-white dreams of my childhood. I want to visit the world of the Mughals, one of the most aesthetic and enlightened dynasties the world has ever seen. My great-grandfather described Shahjahanabad in those times as more beautiful than London or Paris. I want to see, smell and experience that eternal city with my own eyes, a city that rose from the ashes, time and again, a city of love, music, poetry and monuments.' Dr Hunter was back in the dream world of his childhood.

The shrill sound of the telephone broke the silence. Ammi picked up the receiver. It was Abba calling to tell us that he was on his way. Dr Hunter took our leave, promising to meet us in Delhi the following week. As he left, I looked at Ammi and saw that she was smiling.

'Why are you smiling?' I asked.

'Nothing, I was just thinking how fate works. This stranger from far away loves the Delhi of our ancestors, but those who dwell there have no love or regard for its past. They are destroying it with impunity. This Hunter seems to be a good and honest man. Your Nani will be pleased to meet him.'

Abba was concerned when he saw the bandage on Ammi's forehead. He also had bad news for us. He had been asked to return immediately by his President, Ayub Khan. He was to take the morning flight to Karachi and we were to fly back to Delhi on our own. Aziz Khan was worried. He said there could be war between India and China. The situation was fast deteriorating. Pakistan might also get involved. He had been asked to fly to Beijing with Mr Bhutto for consultations with the Chinese government.

'I want you to prepare to leave India immediately. I will make all arrangements. You just get your passports and be ready to fly to Karachi at a moment's notice. I have bought a bungalow facing the sea at Clifton. I am sure Shiraz and you will love these.'

'But you will be in Rawalpindi. Aijaz will also be there. Why can't we stay together?' I asked.

'Beta, you will be happy in Karachi. It's just like Bombay, a huge port city. Your Ammi will also love it.'

I knew my mother would not love it. She wanted to stay with him and Aijaz. But she kept quiet.

'Ammi doesn't like Bombay. It smells of stale fish and urine. Does Karachi also smell the same?' I tried to argue with my father. But he had made up his mind.

He laughed and said, 'No, Shiraz, Karachi smells of fresh roses and seekh kebabs. Don't worry, Aijaz will come and stay with you during the vacations and I will see you every weekend.'

I could see that Ammi was not happy. She wanted to live with him in Lahore or Rawalpindi. But she was aware that he had a second wife and Aijaz lived with her in Lahore. I could see she was ready to make any compromise to be with Abba and meet her other son.

Next morning, we said goodbye to Abba. Ammi was in tears. Abba said, 'Hina, you will very soon be in Pakistan. We will have a new life together.' He kissed me on my forehead. I was nearly as tall as he was.

✧

As our taxi entered Delhi Gate, I could smell my world, the colourful kites in the sky, the pigeons circling the minarets of Jama Masjid. I wanted to see Vinod and Anu right away and give them the sad news that we were going to Pakistan. Nani wanted to kiss me and embrace me forever, but I pushed her away and ran out. Getting out of Ballimaran, I ran towards Chandni Chowk, crossed the street, avoiding a few cars and any number of cycle-rickshaws, and entered Katra Neel. As luck would have it, there was no one at home except Anu. She was delighted to see me and hugged me close. Her soft breasts touched my chest as she kissed me all over. I took her face in my hands and kissed her on the lips. Anu closed the door and pulled me upstairs to her room. It was as though we had gone mad. We were kissing and touching each other as if there was no tomorrow. I wanted to break the news of my leaving, but she was in no mood to listen to anything I said.

'Everyone has gone to attend a marriage in Meerut. They will be back only late in the evening. I was unwell, so I stayed behind. In fact, I have been unwell since the day you suddenly left for Bombay with your father. Bhagwan has listened to my prayers. I was just sitting here thinking that if you came to meet me now, I would let you do whatever you liked to me. I will make love to you as my friend Asha does with her husband.'

Her friend had got married a month back and Anu had learned a few practical lessons about sex from her. Her hand was now on my cock, which was already on full alert. She unzipped my trousers and took it out. She was sitting on the bed, while

I stood before her like a fool, with my penis hanging out of my trousers. She licked the cap and tasted the wetness, then made a face. 'It's salty.' Before I could react, she had taken half of it into her mouth. I held her head, and tried to push the whole into her mouth. She was now sucking it like an experienced professional. And I was coming, the semen spurting into her hot, soft mouth. She gagged and pushed me away. It was over in a few minutes. She wiped her mouth with a handkerchief, a triumphant smile on her face. I pulled her to my chest and kissed her mouth. She kissed me back, pushing her pink, soft tongue into my mouth. Oh god, I realized to my horror that she was again holding my cock, which was once again ready to perform. She laughed and began stroking it. I pushed her away.

'I have to tell you something. I have to speak to you, Anu. I am going to Pakistan for good.'

'What?' She was shocked. 'What are you saying? How can you go to Pakistan, leaving all your friends behind?'

'I hate Pakistan, you know that. But my mother wants to be with my father; she loves him. And I want to meet my brother Aijaz.'

'What about me? Don't you love me?' She stood before me, one hand on her hip, eyes blazing. 'Shiraz Khan, what do you think of yourself? You can't suddenly announce that you will become a Pakistani overnight.'

'No, I can never be a Pakistani. I hate that country. But what can I do? I can't leave my mother. I have no choice. But I will come back one day to marry you.'

'Who wants to marry you, Shiraz mian? You will never come back. You know that.'

'All right, I'll tell my mother I'm not going to Karachi and anyway, who will look after Nani?' I said without much conviction.

'Chacha is right, we should never believe Muslims. They are

unreliable. You never know when they will migrate to Pakistan.' Anu was in no mood to listen to me. 'Go to hell, go to Pakistan, who cares.'

I walked back home, lost in my thoughts. I was being torn apart. On one side were my beloved Ammi, Abba, and my brother Aijaz and, on the other, my whole world: my Delhi, Nani, Bundu Chacha and, above all, Anu. I was just fifteen but I was already learning that life is all about choices. If you make the right choice at the right time, you may achieve your goals in life; otherwise, you will be thrown into the dustbin of oblivion.

My mother told Nani about Dr James Hunter and his great-grandmother Saleema Begum. Nani was aware of the story of Dawai Begum, the medicine woman, who had married a British doctor. Nani's Mughal ancestors and Saleema Begum were close blood relations; according to Nani's logic of extended family, Dr Hunter was indirectly related to us. She couldn't wait to meet this white Mughal.

Dr Hunter was staying at the Imperial Hotel and had already visited all the Mughal monuments of Delhi. He now wanted to meet Qudsia Begum, the only authentic Mughal princess still living in Delhi. Bundu was sent with his tonga to fetch him to Ballimaran.

Dr Hunter arrived, dressed in a dark suit and looking like a Hollywood star. Nani, who normally didn't like foreigners, soon warmed to this angrez. He had brought a copy of Saleema Begum's diary, which had been published in London in 1915. He asked Ammi to translate it for Nani, as the original diary in Urdu was lost. I could see that he had a special twinkle in his eyes whenever he looked at Ammi. Even Ammi had a smile on her face. Dr Hunter asked Nani if she knew of any direct blood relations of Saleema Begum who were still alive. Nani told him that Saleema's elder sister and the last queen of Delhi, Begum Zeenat Mahal, had been banished to Rangoon along with the emperor and had died there, leaving behind a son who later migrated to Calcutta. All the remaining relatives had either been killed during the Great Mutiny, or had migrated to other parts of the country. Dr Hunter now wanted to go to Calcutta and look for the descendants of Bahadur Shah Zafar.

'I feel I have a responsibility towards your family and the other Mughals,' he told Nani. 'Today I am a very rich man with half a dozen hospitals in England and huge properties all over Europe. It's my duty to help some of the unfortunate Mughal families.'

'No one can help those families,' Nani said with a sigh. 'Those who loved Hindustan and ruled it with such devotion and care were so brutally destroyed that today most of them are ashamed to reveal their identity. They survive as waiters, musicians and ordinary labourers. No one can help them now. We have reconciled to our fate, but we still love our Hindustan.'

The doctor had brought a picture of Saleema Begum. We were all surprised to see what an uncanny resemblance she had to Hina Begum. Ammi was quite embarrassed by his praise for her beauty and her resemblance to the great Mughal princess. We could all see that the British gentleman was quite taken by Hina Begum.

Dr Hunter invited us to his hotel the next day. Ammi declined his invitation, but I agreed to take him around Delhi in Bundu's tonga. I knew that Bundu could tell him more about the Mughals and their surviving descendants than all the books and historians put together. In fact, in spite of the language barrier, the two men became friends very soon. When Dr Hunter left for Calcutta, he requested Nani to let Bundu travel with him. The great Mughal horseman was to fly in an airplane for the first time and was probably more excited about that than his ancestors had ever been when they travelled from the land of Genghis Khan to Hindustan. I had never before seen Bundu so nervous and worried. But my mind was too preoccupied with my own problems to be of any help to either Bundu or Dr Hunter, although we had developed a liking for each other.

٦

Our passports were ready. Sardar Gadgaj Singh, the kotwal of Chandni Chowk, had sent a travel agent who was an expert in these matters to Nani's house, and the job was done in a trice. Sardar sahib was a great admirer of Nani, ever since she had saved his mother's life during the 1947 riots. The widowed Sardarni Kuljit Kaur lived in Farashkhana, a Muslim area, and Nani had kept her safe in her own house in Ballimaran for nearly two months until Sardar Gadgaj Singh, who was posted in Amritsar at the time, could come for her. After the sardarni passed away, Sardar sahib began to regard Nani as his own mother. He would discuss not only his personal problems but also take her advice on police cases that he was investigating. He used to say, 'Begum Sahib has the mind of a CID officer and would have made a better kotwal than me, if she was not a woman.'

Nani took him quite seriously and followed all the murder cases he was investigating. She claimed to have solved many murder and theft cases with the help of her jinns. We sometimes teased her by calling her 'Jinnati Thanedar', the police chief of the ghosts. Nani was by now reconciled to the idea of my mother migrating to Pakistan. She realized that Hina Begum loved Aziz Khan too much to be happy without him. Her efforts to get my mother remarried in India had also failed. So now she threw herself enthusiastically into preparations for our departure for

Karachi. She busied herself designing a whole new wardrobe for Ammi. Her jewellery was sent to Lala Mukund Behari, who was also our family jeweller, to be redesigned, as Ammi thought that it was too old-fashioned. She had two leather suitcases made as we could not board a plane with the tin boxes we had. I was the only person who was not the least bit excited about going to Pakistan. 'If you wanted to go to that godforsaken land, you should have done it before I grew up,' I shouted at Ammi one day. 'However hard you try, I can never become a Pakistani. My country is India and I will always sing *Jana gana mana*, even in your Pakistan.'

Anu was angry and had stopped talking to me since the day I told her that I was going to Pakistan. I tried to spend as much time as I could in her house, looking after Brij Uncle's pigeons, in the hope that I would get an opportunity to talk to her. But she avoided me and never came to the terrace as long as I was there. I was heartbroken. More than love, it was the memory of her kisses and the smell of her body that made me hang around near her house all the time. One day I was able to get hold of her on the dark, narrow staircase of her house. I pulled her close and kissed her roughly on the mouth, but she did not respond. She pushed me away and said, 'If you love me, don't go to Pakistan.'

'Will you marry me if I don't go to Pakistan?' I whispered.

'How can I marry you, you are Muslim,' she whispered back.

'But you want me to leave my parents for you?' I asked angrily.

'Can't you do this for your Nani? She loves you so much.'

'I can do this for you if you agree to marry me.'

'You are mad. I don't want riots in Delhi and people killed just because you want to marry me.' She pulled her hand away and went downstairs without looking back. I stood there on the staircase for a long time, hoping that she would come back. I was angry with her, with my father and mother, with Mountbatten,

Nehru, Jinnah and everyone who had divided my world into so-called independent countries, where one required a visa and a passport to love. My young world was collapsing around me. I had to choose between my love and my parents but I knew that I had no choice. I had to go with my mother.

Abba telephoned us virtually every day. He was fearful that there might be a war between India and China and wanted us to cross the border before that happened. Nani was confident that there would be no war: she had gone to a reception for the Chinese cultural delegation at the Imperial Hotel, where everybody shouted 'Hindi–Chini Bhai–bhai'. She said my father was making up the stories of war to get us into Pakistan before Ammi changed her mind once again.

But the unexpected happened and China attacked India two days before we were to leave for Pakistan. Flights to Karachi were cancelled. Abba told us to come by road via Wagah border, but Nani put her foot down, saying it was too risky. Tension between India and Pakistan was escalating and the borders were closed. We couldn't go to Pakistan until the war was over. There were rumours of the Chinese army entering India via Nepal and moving towards Delhi. Everyone was worried except me. I wanted the Chinese to take over Delhi. I was ready for anything except going to Pakistan.

Delhi became a city of rumours. We youngsters were put to work digging bunkers in every possible place. At night we used to roam the lanes of Chandni Chowk, taking over the job of the local police. Anu, Vinod and I were again working together but Anu was still cold towards me and avoided speaking to me most of the time.

If it got too late by the time we finished our voluntary duty, I would spend the night at Vinod's house as Nani and Ammi would have locked the doors at our place and gone to bed. One night, we got back to Vinod's house at 2 a.m. It was cold and I was dying to be in a warm, soft bed. Usually, when I stayed over, I would sleep with Vinod in his room but that day the room was already occupied by Brij Uncle and his friends. Vinod went down to sleep in his mother's room, and I was given the divan in a small alcove under the staircase. Anu brought a blanket for me. It was warm and smelt of her. She seemed to read my mind. 'It is mine, enjoy yourself and sleep with me,' she said. Before I could react, she was gone.

I was so exhausted that even before my head touched the pillow, I was fast asleep. I dreamt of making passionate love to Anu. As I was about to come, my eyes opened and there she was, her mouth on me. In the darkness I could not see her face but her silky hair was soft on my body. I thought I was still dreaming, but her nose pin scraped my cock and I knew that it was real. I didn't want to come. I wanted to enter her, make love to her, but she was bent upon making me come in her mouth. It was not just my semen but my brains that she sucked out of me that night. Before I had the strength to say anything, she wiped her mouth, gave me a hard kiss, and was gone. If it was not for my wet and sticky pajamas, I would have believed that it was just a dream.

I was thankful to the Chinese for giving my love back to me. If it was not for them, I would have been in Karachi by now. Everyone hated the Chinese except me. All over the country, Chinese shops were being burnt. In Calcutta they were easy targets but in Delhi it was difficult for the mob to find someone to vent their anger upon. They burnt the shop of Chhaina Ram Halwai, the famous sweetmaker, simply because he had long been known as China Ram, and the mob regarded this as a justifiable excuse to burn down his shop.

There was no contact with my father in Pakistan as all international telephone lines had been suspended. The nation blamed Prime Minister Nehru and Defence Minister Krishna

Menon for the fiasco but Nani blamed my father. It was Aziz Khan who had spoken of a war even before newspapers in India mentioned it. She regarded it as a Pak–Chinese conspiracy against India. Bundu, on the other hand, held Nani and her army of jinns responsible for the war. He was certain that it was a conspiracy hatched by her, with the help of the jinns, to stop us from leaving India. Ammi believed that it was her fate which had once again conspired with the Chinese to keep her from her husband and her firstborn. Only I knew that it was my love for Anu that had made God listen to me and send the Chinese so that we did not have to go to Pakistan. I even went to the dargah of Hazrat Nizamuddin Auliya with Bundu to give thanks to God for listening to my prayers.

My mother did not speak again of going to Pakistan, nor did my father ever contact us again. Little did I know that the Pakistan I hated so much would be my refuge one day.

Nasreen, the girl who had introduced me to the complexities of life and the realities of sex, eloped one day with a neighbourhood Hindu boy, and this led to a communal riot in Delhi. She had grown up to be a beautiful young lady and had been made to give up her tomboyish ways and stay in purdah at home. But Nasreen was not to be confined to the four walls of her home for long. Her house was on the fringes of the mohalla and the neighbouring roof was that of a Hindu Punjabi family. Nasreen was friendly with Anjala, the daughter of that house. They used to exchange recipes and discuss the film released that week and their favourite film stars. Nasreen's father had put up a barbed-wire fence on their side of the roof, which was sometimes jokingly referred to as the India–Pakistan border. The girls used to stand on either side of the 'border' and talk for hours. Even Nasreen's mother sometimes exchanged favourite dishes with Anjala's mother across the barbed wire. Every Eid, a big bowl of sewain was sent for Anjala's father across this border. Many Muslim and Hindu neighbours even played Holi, the Hindu festival of colours, across such barriers. No one really resented these exchanges, as there were no young men in these houses. Anjala had a brother, Akshay, who was studying in Bombay and lived there with his uncle.

Therefore, when Nasreen eloped with Akshay, it was a shock for all of us. I had met her on a few occasions after she had been confined to purdah, and had once confided to her about my relationship with Anu. Everybody in the mohalla suspected I had helped her, but the truth was that she didn't ever give me the slightest hint that she was on talking terms with Akshay. Even when he came to Delhi, he never came to the roof. I had seen him only once. He was a few years older than me, a handsome Punjabi boy with dreams of becoming a Bollywood hero someday.

Within hours of the news getting out, politicians had entered the fray on both sides. A report of kidnapping a minor, innocent Muslim girl was registered at the Chandni Chowk police station. Stories did the rounds that Hindu Mahasabha leaders had a hand in the incident and it was part of a planned strategy to kidnap all Muslim girls and convert them to Hinduism. I had no doubt that this 'innocent Muslim girl' had coaxed Akshay to agree to elope with her. She used to dream of making it to Bollywood and must have seen Akshay as the only possible gateway to that dream.

Their elopement led to riots in the city. A poor beggar was stabbed by someone in a bylane of Ballimaran. He was actually a drug addict and no one knew whether he was a Hindu or a Muslim. But Hindu leaders spread the rumour that a sadhu had been murdered by Muslim fanatics. In retaliation, a Muslim rickshaw-puller was stabbed and some pieces of meat, suspected to be pork, were thrown into the Moti Masjid in Chandni Chowk. Rumours spread like wildfire. One of them was that Nasreen's nude and mutilated body had been found near Yamuna Bridge. Mullah Idris vowed that he had seen the body with his own eyes. She had been raped by Hindu fanatics and the police had cremated her in order to hide the truth. This rumour had the desired effect and the riots spread to Daryaganj, Ajmeri Gate and Hindu refugee colonies across the Yamuna. Dozens of poor Hindus and Muslims, who had no idea why they were being killed, were sacrificed to the flames of mutual hatred and suspicion. In no time, the religious tolerance Shahjahanabad was known for had evaporated and the city was divided into Hindu and Muslim fortresses. Curfew was clamped in the Walled City. I could not cross Chandni Chowk to reach Anu's house in Katra Neel. Doors were closed to Bhagatji, the Hindu qawwal so popular in every Muslim home. Even telephone lines went dead as the authorities blamed them for the spread of rumours.

Nani, a nationalist and a liberal, warned me not to see Vinod and Anu anymore. Ammi, who already suspected that there was something between Anu and me, told me to forget her and concentrate on my studies. But how could I concentrate on anything with houses and shops burning, and people throwing burning rags on each other? Loud slogans of Har Har Mahadev and Allahu Akbar were raised through the night. Nani said that if Mahatma Gandhi had been alive, he would have controlled the riots in no time. He would have gone to Hindu mohallas and Muslim areas to sing his bhajan, '*Ishwar Allah tero naam, sab ko sammati de bhagwan.*'

The situation eased a bit when Nasreen and Akshay made a call from some unknown destination, to say that they were fine and no one should worry about them. Nasreen told her parents that Akshay had converted to Islam and they had performed nikah.

Akshay told his parents that they had married according to Arya Samaj rites, which allowed them to get married without any fuss, unlike the long and complicated Sanatani Hindu marriage rituals. Both sides were made to believe that they may have lost a son or a daughter, but their religion and honour were safe and intact. Sardar Gadgaj Singh went to Bombay in search of the couple, but could find no clues to their whereabouts. Although the riots were controlled in a few days, an air of mutual suspicion prevailed over the city of Delhi, like a thick blanket of poisonous smog.

∠

Like his ancestors, Bundu was a great expert on horses. People believed that he could talk to them, and I knew this was true. He had a telepathic communication with horses. He used to go to the Delhi Race Course club every Monday. All the horse breeders wanted his services and were ready to pay any amount to get him, but he loved his freedom, his Old Delhi, and our family. He preferred to serve Qudsia Begum than a rich Marwari businessman who liked nothing better than to make money by any means.

Bundu had never married; people said that he had once fallen in love with Munni Jaan, the famous tawaif of Chawri Bazaar. She was the most sought-after tawaif of Delhi. Traditionally, a tawaif was not simply a singer–dancer who performed for men and bestowed her favours on them in return for money and jewels; she was a highly cultured woman of taste to whom young men of rich families were sent to learn manners, culture, poetry, the right pronunciation and the finer points of music. In the early 1930s, when movies had still not become the craze that they are today, people were ready to give their right hand to be allowed to attend one of the mehfils or sittings at the kotha of Munni Jaan. The richest lalas and the most powerful nawabs were regular clients at her kotha. Gold coins were showered on her every evening, but no one was ever allowed to enter her bedroom. The richest men of Delhi and north India offered her all the wealth she might desire for the privilege of being her lovers, but she loved only one man and refused to be persuaded by any of them. That young man was Bundu Khan. Bundu was twenty-five at the time, tall and handsome, with a sharp straight nose, long black hair and a moustache that could put any Pathan to shame. He owned a stable of the finest horses in Delhi, which he rented to the nawabs and lalas for marriages and other celebrations.

Munni Jaan was madly in love with him and he spent all his evenings at her kotha. He wanted to marry her but she was a free bird like him. She gave him her heart and her bed but was not ready to sacrifice her freedom for love. Nani tried to persuade him to marry a respectable Muslim girl and have a family but Bundu was intoxicated by Munni's voice and her beauty.

My friend Javed told me the story of how one of Munni's admirers, a powerful nawab from Rampur, tried to get Bundu killed. On a winter night, when Bundu was sleeping with his horses in his large stable at Ajmeri Gate, someone sprinkled kerosene around it and set it on fire. In trying to save his horses, Bundu was badly burnt. All his beloved horses died. But the nawab's plan misfired, as Munni Jaan came closer to Bundu after this incident. As soon as she learnt of it, she rushed to Irwin Hospital to be with him. It was said that for seven days and nights she sat at his bedside, refusing to eat or rest. Once he had recovered, he moved into Munni's large kotha, a well-appointed haveli. She gave up dancing and sang only for Bundu. The nawab offered to marry her and make her one of his begums, but Munni rejected his offer with disdain.

Bundu, who was a great supporter of Mahatma Gandhi and Maulana Azad, took a lot of interest in the national movement. Munni also encouraged him to participate in the activities of the Indian National Congress. She was as opposed to the politics of the

Muslim League as Bundu was. In 1935, there was a demonstration in Chandni Chowk and Bundu was arrested and sent to jail for six months. Nani used all her influence and contacts to get him released, but this time even her jinns failed to help her.

When Bundu was finally released from Central Jail, which was located in front of Khooni Darwaza at Delhi Gate, he went straight to Munni's kotha. He was shocked to find no trace of her. Her kotha had been sold to a rich lala of Chawri Bazaar. No one knew where she had gone. Bundu searched for her everywhere, but in vain. There were rumours that she had been kidnapped by the nawab and was in his custody. But the nawab had died in an accident a few months before Munni disappeared. It was obvious that she had gone away on her own, after selling all her possessions. But no one knew why and where. Bundu would have gone mad if not for Nani, the only person he listened to.

Bundu was not the same man after Munni's disappearance, but he still had his old knack of communicating with horses. He took to plying a tonga around the city. He had no regrets in life, except not being able to help Munni when she needed him the most. He still believed that Munni had been taken against her will and was alive somewhere in the clutches of some nawab or rich lala.

After their sojourn in Calcutta, the friendship between Bundu and Dr Hunter deepened. Bundu had found a soulmate, someone who loved the Mughal past as much as he himself did. After a long time, he began taking a real interest in life. He wanted to live not just for the present but also the future. The doctor had returned from England after a few months and now wanted to stay in Delhi for a while. He rented a bungalow in Sunder Nagar; from its roof one could see Humayun's Tomb. In this palatial eight-bedroom house, he lived alone. One room was reserved for Bundu, who began to spend more and more time there. He even started a small stud farm behind Humayun's Tomb. One weekend, all of us went to the house to spend some time with Bundu's horses. I could see that Ammi had started enjoying Dr Hunter's company. He now organized free medical camps in the poor localities of Delhi and Ammi loved to assist him in this work. I think it was his genuine love for Delhi and its people that attracted her to this stranger. There was something childlike and positive about his attitude that made us all like him.

In the evening we all went to the dargah of Hazrat Nizamuddin to listen to the qawwali. Dr Hunter was wearing a kurta pajama that Bundu had given him. With a Lucknowi cap on his head, he looked like a real nawab. Ammi was wearing a white salwar kurta with delicate lace work. She had fresh white jasmine flowers in her hair. Nani, however, preferred to don her black chador even on this warm evening. We sat together in the open courtyard in front of the tomb of Hazrat Amir Khusro.

'Amir Khusro was an advisor and a minister to several kings, a very powerful man of his time, yet he preferred to live like a poor dervish and wrote poetry, sang songs, danced and created music. I wonder why.' Dr Hunter seemed to be talking to himself.

'He realized that fulfilment lies in self-realization and not in material achievements,' Ammi said softly.

'But what is self-realization? Don't we deceive ourselves by abdicating our responsibilities to society and becoming a dervish or a Sufi?'

'Yes, for some of us that may be true, but Amir Khusro was unlike any other Sufi. He lived life to the full but could still detach himself from his material success and devote himself to his beloved pir, Khwaja Hazrat Nizamuddin Auliya,' Ammi responded. Sitting on the cold marble floor, playing with the red roses and jasmine flowers we had brought for the Sufi saints, I listened with rapt attention to the conversation between Dr Hunter and my mother. Nani was nowhere to be seen. She had gone to meet some of her jinns who, according to her, assembled every evening in large numbers to listen to the qawwali. They were all great devotees of the Khwaja.

'How does one become a Sufi? Is there a ritual one has to perform?' Dr Hunter asked Ammi

'No, all rituals are within one's own heart. In a way, a Sufi rises above all rituals to be one with his beloved. You have to fall in love with everything around you to be a Sufi.'

The qawwals were reciting Amir Khusro's famous poem, '*Khusro dariya prem ka ulti wa ki dhar; Jo ubhra so doob gaya jo dooba, so par.*' Hina explained the meaning to Dr Hunter: 'Khusro says, the river of love flows in the opposite direction; he who floats will drown, he who drowns will get across.'

'What is love? I have tried but failed to understand this peculiar emotion,' said Dr Hunter.

'You have never been able to detach yourself from your own existence, that's why. Love is to give without expecting anything in return. Success is not everything; sometimes you win by losing. As Khusro says, sometimes you get across by drowning, not necessarily by swimming. You, in the West, would find this contradictory, or even silly. For you, winning is everything and every emotion, every act is a barter, a quid pro quo. For you, life is a business. For a Sufi, life is love, life is devotion without expectation.'

The qawwali had stopped and most of the devotees had left. It had become quite dark but Dr Hunter and Hina Kauser continued to sit there silently. I was thinking of my beloved Anu. Was my love without any expectation or was it an emotional barter? I realized that I expected a great deal in return from her. Sex was always on my mind when I was with her. I was not a Sufi, nor did I want to be one. At that moment, I wanted so much from life, most of it material. However, I could see that Dr Hunter had fallen in love with the spiritual side of my mother, and she was discovering a friend in him, to whom she could speak as an equal.

Nani returned with Bundu, carrying a tray full of fresh tandoori naan and gaajar ka halwa. We ate, sitting in the courtyard of the dargah. Nani was very popular there, virtually everyone knew her, not as the great-granddaughter of the last Mughal emperor but as the lady who had befriended the jinns and was therefore to be dreaded and respected. They gathered around her now, and wanted her to pray for them at the mazar of Hazrat Nizamuddin.

I joked with Nani, 'Why don't you become a pir and open a shop in Nizamuddin? We could all get very rich.'

Nani laughed. 'My son, one has to rise above any greed to come close to the Sufis and the jinns.'

'All these pirs and khadims around the dargah fleece the innocent devotees day and night but are still regarded as great Sufis. Yet, your jinns take no action against them,' I retorted.

'To get to pure honey, one has to bear with the bees. Similarly, to reach the great pir, you have to go through the maze of these cheats.' As usual, Nani had her own logic for everything.

٨

The house that Dr Hunter had rented in Sunder Nagar was next to the newly established Delhi zoo. All through the night, one could hear the animals. I imagined that I was in a wild jungle, living on a tree top. Early morning was beautiful and filled with birdsong. One could see parakeets from the windows of the bedroom on the first floor. Nani said she couldn't sleep the whole night for fear that one of the lions would jump the walls of the zoo and enter her room.

'You should leave this house immediately. I don't want you to become breakfast for one of those lions or tigers,' Ammi advised Dr Hunter.

We all laughed. I said, 'No lion will be able to digest Uncle James; he is too tough for both tigers and jinns.'

We were having nahari for breakfast that morning. It was a foggy winter morning, but Bundu Chacha had got up at 4 a.m. and gone to Turkman Gate to get the nahari and naan. Ammi explained to Hunter that this was a dish peculiar to Delhi. It had its origins in the time when thousands of construction workers were building the city of Shahjahanabad. Big pieces of mutton and leg bones were cooked with very special herbs, the whole night long, in huge pots called degh. These pots were buried in the ground and heated on a slow fire that was lit underneath. Nahari means 'very early in the morning' and the food was eaten by the working class very early on winter mornings, before they went to work. It gave them strength and they didn't require lunch in the afternoon as it took a long time to digest.

Dr Hunter loved the nahari in spite of the strong spices and ate with gusto. He told us that he was planning to establish a hospital near Nizamuddin for the poor and the needy. 'I want you to be the president of the society that will run the hospital. I want it to be called the Dawai Begum Hospital in memory of my great-grandmother.'

'But where will we get the doctors from? There is such a shortage of doctors in Delhi,' Ammi said, though she seemed to be quite taken with the idea.

'I could send some doctors from England to begin with and I'll spend some time here too. Hina Begum, I want you to run this hospital. Our society, which I propose to call Bahadur Shah Zafar Charitable Society, will pay for your services.'

'No, you don't have to pay me. This is a project I have always dreamt about. I've been providing free education to women in Old Delhi's mohallas all these years. I'll work for the hospital,' Hina Begum said with a smile.

'Running a hospital is a very expensive business.' Nani, as always, looked at the practical side of things.

'That won't be a problem. Our foundation already runs several charitable hospitals and we have enough money. In fact, we'll buy the land next week and the construction can begin soon. Bundu, my friend, will be in charge of all the construction work. He is also going to rear some of the best horses and we are going to make a lot of money selling them. I have not come across another man who understands horses better. It's amazing, the way he talks to them. He's wasting his talent as a tongawala.' Dr Hunter was in full flow. He said he even wanted to take Bundu to London to see the royal horses at Buckingham Palace, as he was a great friend of the royal family.

That morning, over our breakfast of nahari, we were all excited about a new beginning, a new life, about fulfilling many of our dreams. For Nani, Dr Hunter was like the son she never had. She wanted to teach him not only Hindustani but all the ways of the great Mughals. Dr Hunter saw in her the grandmother he had fantasized about since his childhood. For the first time after my father had left her, I could see a smile on my mother's face. I could tell that she was attracted to the doctor, who was a dreamer like her and far from the pragmatic politician and businessman my father was.

We all went to look at the horses Bundu Chacha was rearing in an open space behind Humayun's Tomb. I loved to visit the tomb. Nani believed that it was the finest work of Mughal architecture, and if not for the white marble, it would have given the Taj Mahal a run for its money. Ammi loved it because it was the tribute of a woman to her beloved husband. Hamida Begum had initially hated Humayun and was in love with his younger brother Kamran, but once married, she stood by him with such devotion that few women in history could match her. She not only acted as the dowager queen to Akbar, who was just thirteen when he was crowned, and moulded him into one of the finest rulers of India, but also personally supervised the construction of Humayun's Tomb. People talk about the love of Shahjahan for Mumtaz Mahal and the Taj Mahal he built for her, but forget about Hamida's tribute to her beloved Humayun. Ammi often said there was no comparable example in the whole world of a woman's love for her Sartaj.

Next to the dargah was a vacant plot of land, an old graveyard, which Bundu had taken over for his horses. All his life he had wanted to rear the best race horses and not just ordinary tonga horses. Dr Hunter had provided him with the money to indulge his passion. The best thing was that Dr Hunter also loved horses. Bundu had purchased some beautiful colts from the stable of the maharaja of Jaipur and was training them. He had named one of them, a one-year-old chestnut colt, Shiraz, and was confident that one day it would turn out to be a fine race horse. I fell in love with it as soon as I saw it and was dying to show the beautiful creature to Anu and Vinod.

By now, the atmosphere of hate and suspicion had evaporated like the fog that envelops Delhi in winter. Hindus and Muslims were intermingling again. Bhagatji was rendering his qawwalis in Muslim homes and Nani was enjoying her bhajan get-togethers at the purdah bagh. This love-hate relationship between Hindus and Muslims was like a tiff between lovers. When they fought, they vowed never to talk with each other again, but a few days of separation made them pine madly for each other. I was once again spending time with Anu and Vinod. Bundu promised me that the following Sunday he would bring them both in his tonga to Nizamuddin to see the horses.

'Shiraz mian, you know why I have named this colt after you?' asked Bundu.

'Tell us, tell us,' Ammi said. She was enjoying the outing more than any of us.

'Look at its face, doesn't it resemble Shiraz?' Everybody laughed, except the horse and I.

Dr Hunter's house became our second home. Bundu Chacha now virtually lived there. Nani loved it as it was next to her beloved Nizamuddin Dargah and Humayun's Tomb. She could stay late at the dargah and listen to the qawwali, and spend the night at Sunder Nagar. But it was my mother who eagerly waited to get there every weekend. Construction of the charitable hospital in Nizamuddin had begun, and she dreamt of turning it into one of the best hospitals in Delhi. Even when Dr Hunter travelled to London, she spent most of her time in his house. It was I who was having a difficult time, as staying there meant staying away from Anu. But now that our high school exams were approaching, I had the excuse of home study with Vinod. His parents didn't mind my staying over, as I was a decent student and they thought I was a good influence on their son. They didn't realize what a bad influence Anu and I were on each other. She loved to distract me from my studies all the time and, in any case, she, and not the exam, was the real reason I stayed there. Vinod knew what was happening between Anu and me, but it didn't bother him at all. He liked my company even if he had to use his sister as a bait to have it.

Vinod and I appeared for our high school exams in 1964. That summer, Brij Uncle decided to take us both to Calcutta. There was a pigeon-flying contest there and Brij Uncle, as a top kabuterbaaz, had to participate. In Calcutta, there still lived some of the best pigeon-fliers of the country, who had migrated there with Wajid Ali Shah, the last nawab of Awadh. The excitement of going to this famous city, the first capital of British India, made me forget my worry about Anu. She was busy with the marriage of one of her friends, whose parents had arranged a match for her though she was only fifteen, as was the custom among the lalas of Delhi. I was beginning to worry that Anu's parents would get her married too, now that she was nearly sixteen, and had started fantasizing about eloping with her.

The trip to Calcutta was like a powder run for me. Brij Uncle said that if you wanted to know the real India, you must travel in a train, that too in the third class. He was right. I realized that it was true what people said, that the railways were the greatest gift the British had bestowed on India. There was no caste, no class, no religion; all barriers came down in the third-class compartment.

In no time, Brij Uncle was playing cards with an uneducated villager from Bihar, without bothering to know his caste. We befriended a Bengali boy, Pradeep Chatterjee, who was travelling with his father, who was a clerk in some government department in Delhi. His mother lived in Calcutta and he travelled every month from Delhi to meet her. He was a fair boy, slightly effeminate, with big black spectacles and a permanent smile on his lips. I could see that Vinod had fallen for him. I felt a little jealous but also relieved that I would no longer be the focus of my friend's amorous attention. Soon the three of us were chatting away like old friends. Pradeep lived in Ballygunje, an area not far from Park Street, where we were going to stay with a rich Marwari friend of Brij Uncle. In his soft melodious voice, he told us about Calcutta and promised to show us around the city. He was clearly attracted to Vinod; they were already touching each other.

After dinner, Vinod and Pradeep lay under one sheet on the upper berth, whispering to each other. Pradeep's father was sleeping on another berth, Brij Uncle was lost in his game of cards and I was dreaming about travelling with Anu and enjoying the rocking rhythm of the train. It was only when I travelled in European trains much later that I realized what beautiful music Indian steam trains made. It was a mesmerizing sound that took you into a world of daydreams. In my old age, one of the things I miss most is the sound of that big brute rail engine and the whistle that sent shivers down my spine.

Soon we were all asleep, in whatever cramped space we could find. Every train in India is a big family, where people share everything from food, blankets and the most intimate thoughts with total strangers. Nani said the railway was the biggest mistake of the British. It brought Indians closer, turning them into one nation, which they never were, nor could have been, without its help.

Next morning, we arrived at Howrah station, which is situated on the west bank of the Hooghly. We were used to crowds in Delhi but were not prepared for the stream of people, moving continuously like an ever-flowing river, on the streets of Calcutta. I fell in love with the city the moment I set foot on its soil. It was a strange place where one moment you saw something that captivated your heart and the next you encountered something most ugly. Delhi had its share of social and economic contrasts, but Calcutta, it seemed to me, had only two shades: black and white, ugly and beautiful, rich and poor. Here I saw some of the most beautiful girls, happy and carefree, and some of the saddest faces I would come across in my life.

Vinod was eager to visit Pradeep's house in Ballygunje. We took a tram, reliving our childhood memories, of a time when we used to travel from one end of Chandni Chowk to the other in trams. Calcutta was the only city in India where you still had this slow-moving form of transport. Pradeep's ancestral house was an old crumbling villa that had seen much better days. His mother was a charming woman, who chattered non-stop to us in Bangla without bothering to know whether we understood a word of what she said.

We also met Pradeep's elder sister, Pronoti. She did her best to make us comfortable and soon, the four of us had became close friends. If I was not deeply in love with Anu, I would have definitely fallen for Pronoti. Tall, fair and beautiful, she was always dressed in a simple cotton sari and had an aura of joy around her. Unlike her brother, she was mischievous and outgoing. I could see that Bengali women were much more smart and confident then women in our part of the country. Pronoti was a few years older than me, but treated me as an equal. In the next few days, she took us to all four corners of the city, from a boat ride on the Hooghly to the eateries of Matia Burj. I was pleasantly surprised to find a street in Calcutta nicknamed Chandni Chowk, with wonderful Mughal food which could give the Jama Masjid of Delhi a run for its money. I was told that some of the best Awadhi and Mughal cooks had migrated to Calcutta after the decline of Lucknow and Delhi. One night, we went to eat at a restaurant called Shiraz, to the amusement of Pronoti.

'How come you were named after a Calcutta restaurant, Shiraz?' Pronoti teased me.

'No, you are mistaken, the restaurant was named after me.'

'Oh, I didn't know you are a hundred years old. This Shiraz was established in the last century. Do you come from a family of traditional cooks?' Pronoti mocked me with a big smile on her face.

Vinod was scandalized. 'Don't make fun of him. He is the direct descendant of the last Mughal emperor. His Nani is a princess whom even Pandit Nehru respects.'

Pronoti took this as a joke and started laughing. 'Shiraz, you Mughal tandoori, I will eat with roti puri.'

'Shiraz is a famous city in Iran and my father's family came from there, hence the name Shiraz,' I tried to explain to her.

We enjoyed the famous chops and firni of Shiraz, but Pronoti was stuck on the idea of my being a Mughlai chicken tandoori and started calling me by that name. By the time we returned to Ballygunje, if we had not heard the news that paralysed the whole country, I would have either hit Pronoti in anger or fallen in love with her.

I was saved from doing anything foolish by the news of Prime Minister Nehru's death. For a moment, I felt as though my own father had died. I knew Nani would be devastated. She used to say, 'So long as Nehru is alive, India will remain a secular state.' She believed that her Pandit Nehru was immortal and would never die. Nehru, too, had great affection for my Nani and treated her with the respect due to a Mughal princess. He had even honoured her in a public ceremony organized at Red Fort to celebrate the hundredth anniversary of the revolt of 1857. In 1957, I was only ten years old but I vividly remembered Qudsia Begum sitting beside the prime minister on the stage and being presented a silver plate to commemorate the historic day. I also remembered that he shook my hand with a big smile on his face and said, 'Shiraz, my dear friend, you are the future of India, I want to see you as the next prime minister of the country.'

Nani said, 'Panditji, your shadow will always be there on our heads, you will always remain the prime minister of Hindustan.'

Nehru laughed. 'Qudsia Begum, you and I are both going to leave soon and then these children will build the India of our dreams.'

Now Chacha Nehru was gone and, with him, a part of Nani's dream of a secular, democratic India had died. After the defeat of 1962 at the hands of the Chinese, Nani used to pray every day for Nehru's long life. She used to say, 'Panditji has been stabbed in the back by these Chinese and their friend Krishna Menon.'

Ammi didn't agree with her. She had become a communist under the influence of Sarla Gupta and claimed that Nehru and his conservative home minister, Govind Ballabh Pant, were responsible for the war. 'This war was brought on our heads by the Americans, who want to use India to checkmate and surround the Chinese,' she would say.

Sitting in Calcutta, I wept as much for my grandmother as for Pandit Nehru. Pronoti's family were also sad but they were surprised at the depth of my reaction. On hearing the news, we immediately returned to Park Street. Next morning, we left for Delhi, saying goodbye to our friends and promising to meet them in Delhi someday.

Life changed after the death of Nehru. Delhi became a difficult city to live in for everyone, but for Muslims it became hell. There were long queues everywhere, for everything from wheat to sugar to kerosene. We felt as if we had been woken from a long sleep. The harsh realities of independent India dawned on us and people started thinking back to the good old days of the British Raj. Lal Bahadur Shastri, the new prime minister, was popular with the Hindu upper castes. The Rashtriya Swayamsevak Sangh, the militant Hindu organization, looked upon him as the first Hindu Brahmin prime minister, but Muslims were suspicious of his intentions. Nani said that he spoke the same language as the Hindu Mahasabha. Ammi, as usual, disagreed with Nani and said that the poor man had been handed a bankrupt economy, a government in disarray, and a Congress party unwilling to cooperate with him. I was not interested in politics but knew that we were in deep trouble as it was I who had to stand in long queues for everything from morning till midnight. I had no time either for Anu or for kite-flying.

I finished school and was admitted to the famous Delhi College at Ajmeri Gate, where I studied English literature, like my mother had before me. Vinod went to Hindu College in the university campus. Now I hardly had the time or opportunity to meet Anu. Life was changing very fast. India was also changing: defeat at the hands of the Chinese and the death of its founder prime minister had brought the nation to a place from which it was finding it difficult to extricate itself. Ammi was worried. She was doing a lot of voluntary work for the poor with the help of Dr Hunter. One day, some RSS men got after her, calling her a foreign agent and an enemy of the country. Hina Begum was a strong woman, she did not care about those communal idiots, but Dr Hunter was furious and got into a fight with some of them. He was beaten up and had to be hospitalized.

While the common people regarded my mother as a messiah of the poor, some of political elements resented the voluntary medical assistance to the poor. One very nasty character called Jai Veer Singh of the Hindu Mahasabha talked of the nexus between the Muslims and the British to once again enslave India. For him, my mother represented all that was evil in Islam and Dr Hunter all that was bad in Christianity and the British. They attacked the dispensary and looted most of the medicines. If it was not for the courage shown by some of the slum dwellers, they would have burnt the place down. This incident shook my mother more than anything she had seen at the time of Partition.

Nani was a strong woman too, but even she was anxious these days because of the communally charged atmosphere. One day, some boys clad in the khaki shorts of the RSS – we called them knickerwalas – confronted her in Chandni Chowk. In those days, it was common practice for Muslim women to be asked to reveal themselves to make sure that they were not Pakistani spies hiding behind burqas. There were rumours that Pakistan had air-dropped paratroopers or saboteurs, who were moving around the city in burqas.

Qudsia Begum was surrounded by the RSS boys, who carried lathis in their hands and behaved like supercops. But my grandmother was not one to be easily intimidated. She caught one of them by his shirt collar and tore it with a sharp tug.

'First you take off your knickers to show me that you are not a woman disguised as a man,' she shouted at him. Her slap on the face of another RSS hoodlum made them run for cover. But since that day, Nani, who had fought all her life against the idea of Pakistan, was hated by the RSS men, who whistled at her and taunted her as a Pakistani agent whenever she passed through Chandni Chowk.

The atmosphere in Delhi was volatile. There were strong rumours of war with Pakistan. Ayub Khan, Pakistan's President, thought this was the moment to strike, as India was weakened after its defeat at the hands of the Chinese. The sudden death of Pandit Nehru had further destabilized the country and left it leaderless. His aggressive foreign minister, Zulfikar Ali Bhutto, was conspiring with the Chinese to encircle India. My father, a close advisor to Ayub, became a hated man in India.

One day, we were flying kites on the terrace of Vinod's house, when he suddenly asked me, 'Shiraz, if there is a war with Pakistan, whom will you support?'

The question, coming from my closest friend, was like a resounding slap on my face. I was stunned for a moment and didn't know what to say. Anu came to my rescue and rebuked Vinod. 'How dare you ask such a silly question of Shiraz, you know that he will support India.'

'No, Anu, he is right to ask the question. If there is a war with Pakistan, would I support India?' I was so perturbed that I didn't realize my kite had not only been cut but captured by the lads on the neighbouring roof, who were jumping around and doing a victory jig to taunt us. Anu was furious.

'Look what you've done. Our champion has been defeated by those next-door idiots. How will he fight the Pakistanis?'

'Sorry, Shiraz, I didn't mean to upset you. I know how patriotic your family is. In fact, it is I who am not sure whether I want to see a war with Pakistan.' Vinod tried to hug me.

I pushed him away and said, 'No, you are right. I must prepare myself to hate Pakistan enough, to fight it and go to war with it.'

'Why should we go to war with Pakistan? If the Kashmiri people want to join Pakistan, let them do it. After all, Nehru believed in the right to self-determination for all the people of the world,' Vinod said, parroting the arguments of his leftist teachers at Hindu College. He had fallen in love with his young and handsome history professor, a committed Marxist. The problem was that Professor Anand was openly flirting with a beautiful colleague, who unfortunately was the daughter of a rich industrialist and hated Marxists.

I said, 'Vinod, as an Indian Muslim, I believe that Kashmir has to remain with India, whatever the cost. If Kashmir goes, India will not remain a secular country. That's right, now I know why I have to fight Pakistan. Not because I hate it, but because Kashmir must remain with India, if we do not want another bloodbath in the subcontinent. Secular Kashmir is essential for the existence of secular India.'

Anu was getting bored by all this talk of war. She said, 'Neither of you will go to war with Pakistan. You are both cowards who cannot even fight the neighbourhood idiots who have taken our kite and are mocking us. I am going to get some pakoras and tea for you both.' She left us to our argument, in which we were now joined by Brij Uncle, who had come to the terrace to feed his pigeons.

'Look boys, both the countries will be destroyed if they go to war. We can't even feed ourselves, how can we go to war? Prime Minister Shastri is asking us to fast one day every week to overcome the food crisis. Doesn't he know that most Indians fast every day of their lives and have hardly enough to eat?' Brij Behari, one of the richest men in Delhi, was also getting influenced by the leftist rhetoric.

'Brij Uncle, it is Pakistan that wants a war with India. What can we do?' argued Vinod.

Brij Uncle laughed and said, 'Our Shiraz can stop the war. His father and my wonderful friend Aziz is an influential minister in

Pakistan. Let's send Shiraz to Pakistan to convince his father that war is in nobody's interest.'

I knew that Brij Uncle was joking, but the idea fascinated me. Could I go to Pakistan and stop this hullaballoo of war? Could I influence Ayub Khan, the Pakistani dictator, to give up Kashmir? I went into my world of fantasies and colourful dreams. It was Anu who broke the spell with her spicy pakoras and hot tea. Soon we had all forgotten about the impending war and were laughing and joking with Brij Uncle. We convinced him to give us fifty rupees so that the three of us could go to Connaught Place, watch a movie at the Regal and have coffee at Gaylord restaurant. In those days, fifty rupees was a princely sum.

९

Dark, thick war clouds were gathering over the horizon. Pakistan had sent its 'mujahidin' into Kashmir. Rumours that Pakistan had dropped its paratroopers into Indian territory flew thick and fast. Every Indian Muslim had become suspect. Even Dr Zakir Hussain, the first Muslim President of India and a leader who had fought against the very idea of Pakistan, was suspected of being a spy and sending messages to Pakistan. In my college, a teacher sympathetic to RSS ideology told me that an intelligence officer had informed him that a transmitter had been found in the President's house. If the President of India was a suspect in the eyes of the common man, no Muslim could be above suspicion. Those who knew that I was the son of a Pakistani minister treated me as a potential threat to the nation. I, who had chosen India as my country over my father, my mother who had sacrificed her lover for the love of her motherland, my Nani who had donated most of her jewellery to the cause of the freedom movement and Bundu, who had physically fought the Muslim League supporters, were all suspects in their eyes.

The kotwal of Chandni Chowk, Sardar Gadgaj Singh, came to meet Nani early one morning. It was still dark and he was in plain clothes so that nobody could recognize him as he entered our house. It was obvious that he was disturbed. He declined the cup of tea offered by my mother, took Nani inside her bedroom, closed the door and spoke to her in hushed tones. Then he left immediately, as though fearing for his life.

Nani refused to tell us anything, but I had never seen her so fearful and worried. She called Bundu Chacha and whispered into his ear. Now he seemed to be as worried as Nani. I was told to stay at home and not go anywhere. I had planned to participate in a pigeon-flying competition with Brij Uncle that evening. Brij Uncle never tired of telling me that my ancestors were great pigeon-flyers and therefore it was my duty to assist him and take care of his pigeons. He believed that, as the son of Azizuddin Khan, pigeon-flying was in my blood. It was a fact that his pigeons seemed to like me and would come and sit on my head and shoulders, whenever they landed after a long flight. 'Shiraz, pigeons can smell your father in you, especially my great Mughal pigeons, Akbar and Shahjahan,' he would say.

I told Nani that I was going with Brij Uncle, unless they explained to me what all the fuss was about and why everyone was looking at me with such fearful eyes.

Nani relented and took my mother and me into her bedroom. Now I was really worried, because Nani was never secretive about anything. She embraced me and kissed me on my forehead. 'Look Shiraz, my child, the police have been informed by some people that you are spying for Pakistan, that you and your father are exchanging messages with the help of homing pigeons. Higher police officers have asked Gadgaj Singh to investigate and keep an eye on you.'

I was shocked to hear this. 'How can anybody believe such foolish talk? We have no pigeons at home. All the pigeons belong to Lala Brij Behari. Do people suspect him also of being a Pakistani spy?'

'No, the thanedar knows that it's utter nonsense. But he fears for you and wants you to stay at home as long as the atmosphere is tense and there is this silly talk of war,' Nani explained.

I didn't know what to say or do. How long could I be a prisoner in my own house for no sin of mine? I went up to the terrace of my house to look at my beloved Delhi from there. I felt like going to Anu and Vinod's house and asking them whether they too thought I was a Pakistani spy. I wanted to hide my face in Anu's bosom and cry. I wanted to wash away the smell of hatred and suspicion with the fragrance of love and faith. I knew that she would understand my pain, she was the most reasonable and positive person I had come across in my life. I wished I had Nani's power over the jinns, so that I could ask them to turn me into a kite and fly with the birds. Strangely, I always wanted to be a kite; I never dreamt of flying like a pigeon.

In the evening, Ammi decided to take me to Dr Hunter's house in Sunder Nagar. She wanted me to stay with him till the dust had settled. College was closed for the summer vacations. It was decided that I would assist Dr Hunter in the hospital and stay away from Chandni Chowk for the time being.

I didn't mind staying in Sunder Nagar, for I loved the company of Dr Hunter. There was never a dull moment with him; one moment he would be serious and philosophical, the next moment he would be laughing and pacing about like a mad man. Every morning, he got up at four to watch the parrots in the wilderness behind Humayun's Tomb. He loved to play golf on Saturdays and cricket on Sundays, and enjoyed singing and playing the guitar. He was as comfortable with poor slum dwellers as with the stiff-upper-lip brown sahibs who believed that India was still ruled by the British. The best thing was that he treated me as an equal and shared all his thoughts with me.

Bundu accompanied my mother to Sunder Nagar every day from Ballimaran, and we went together to the charitable hospital. I was surprised to see the devotion and patience with which Ammi handled the poor patients who, sometimes, instead of being thankful to her, were quite nasty. It was also obvious to me that Dr Hunter and my mother were in love with each other but were afraid to accept it.

One evening, I was sitting with Dr Hunter on the balcony of his house, watching the sunset and sipping lemonade. Suddenly, he said, 'Shiraz, are you in love with Anu?'

I was taken aback. I had thought my love for Anu was a secret I had successfully hidden from everyone else. For a moment I didn't know how to respond, whether to accept or deny the truth. But the smile on his face encouraged me to open up. 'Who told you about my friendship with Anu?' I decided to ask a counter question.

Hunter laughed and said, 'I knew it even before your mother told me. It's written all over your face, my boy.'

'My mother? Does she know too?' I was incredulous.

'Mothers know everything. You can't hide anything from them.'

'But she never said anything to me.'

'Your mother is worried about you, Shiraz. She knows that an affair between a Muslim boy and a Hindu girl can go nowhere. It will only cause trouble for everyone. You are already being targeted for being the son of a Pakistani minister.'

I was suddenly angry. 'Is it my fault that I am the son of a Pakistani whom I hardly know? Is it my fault that I was born into a Muslim family? Did I have a choice? Did Allah ask me where I wanted to be born?' I was now virtually shouting at Dr Hunter, who was taken aback by my reaction.

He remained silent for a few moments and then came forward to embrace me. 'Shiraz, my boy, I understand your dilemma, but life is not a game of cricket. There are no fair rules here. Life tosses you around unless you learn to take it by the horns and force it to obey your commands.'

'I don't care about your philosophy of life. I know only one thing, that I am in love with Anu and don't care whether she is a Hindu or a Sikh.' I knew I was being rude, but at that moment I didn't care about his feelings.

We sat silently, listening to the sound of crickets, lost in our own thoughts.

Then I turned to him. 'Are you in love with my mother?'

It was his turn to be shocked.

'I ... I ... yes, but ...' He didn't know how to answer my query. He must have realized that he had to be careful with the young son of the woman he was in love with.

'Shiraz, you want to know the truth? I have never loved another human being as I love Hina Begum. I know that she will never marry me, but I am able to share her company through our work, and that is good enough for me. I know I can't ask for more.' Dr Hunter had a habit of chewing his lower lip when he was worried.

'Why not? Are you afraid of rejection?' I was now talking to him as an adult, man to man.

'More than that, I know she is devoted to you and your Nani. She doesn't want to share her love for her son with anyone else. I respect her feelings and don't want to hurt her in any way.'

'But more than me, she needs a loving, caring man. How long is she going to live on the memories of my father, who never really loved her?' I knew I was stepping beyond my age and experience, but I wanted to have my say once and for all. 'Uncle James, she is in love with you but is afraid to admit it. I want my mother to be happy. She has devoted her life to me but I don't want to bear the weight of her sacrifice all my life. I want her to live for herself and not for me. Why don't you admit your love to her?'

Hunter laughed. 'Do you think I have not already done so?'

'Then what are you waiting for? Marry her and take her to England, far away from all these problems,' I whispered.

'You and your mother have similar ideas.' Dr Hunter was smiling and looking at me with affection. 'She asked me to take you to England, far away from Anu and all these troubles.'

It had started drizzling outside. We could hear the thick drops of water falling on the leaves to create a wonderful orchestra. The cook had brought steaming hot cups of coffee for us. Sipping the coffee and listening to the gently falling rain, we sat lost in our thoughts.

Dr Hunter broke the silence. 'Are you ready to come with me to England? There may be a war sooner than expected and it would be better for me to stay in England till things settle down in India. I am planning to leave next month. Come with me, Shiraz, you'll love it. Visit our universities. You could even study there and, if you want, you can come back to India later.'

'I have another idea. Why don't you marry my mother and we can all go to England and later return to run the hospital in Delhi?'

'I would love to do that, but I know it cannot happen.'

'Why not, has my mother said no?' I was taken with the idea of Ammi marrying this Englishman, who was more Mughal than we Mughals. He knew more about us than we did ourselves; he had a great collection of books on Mughal history and culture and was spending huge amounts of money on buying Mughal artifacts from around the world. Above all, I loved him because he understood my feelings better than anyone else and was an enlightened and compassionate soul. Ammi believed that in his past life he had been a Mughal prince.

'Your Nani will never allow her daughter to marry an Englishman. She hates us for all that we did to your ancestors and I don't blame her. She has already warned Hina against the machinations of the British. She has told her that what the British can't get by force, they acquire by diplomacy. She regards my love for Hina as a ploy to win over what remains of the Mughals.'

'Maybe she is right. You want to take the remaining treasure of the Mughals back to England and a Mughal princess like my mother would be the most colourful feather in your cap.' I couldn't resist teasing him a bit.

'You know me better than that, my boy. I want to preserve what remains of Mughal art and culture. I have no ulterior motives. What appalls me is the lack of respect for the past among Indians. Even Muslims have no love or regard for their heritage.'

'I'll try to persuade Nani. I know that your intentions are noble and I would love to have you as a father more than Azizuddin Khan, who doesn't give a damn for his past or heritage,' I said. I was confident that I would be able to win over my Nani, who I knew was fond of the doctor despite his British origins.

That night I encountered Babur again. Strangely, he was driving a white Ambassador instead of his usual white horse. In my dream, I found nothing amiss in this, since all the VIPs in Delhi were fond of driving around thus. We drove to India Gate, where we had a choco-bar each. Taking a big bite of the ice cream, Babur said, 'Don't you worry, Shiraz, the war between India and Pakistan, like a cricket Test match, will end in a miserable and lacklustre draw.'

'A Test match ends in five days, but a war may go on for months or even years.'

Babur laughed, spitting ice cream on his royal clothes, and said, 'How many wars have you fought? Indians never fight wars for months; they prefer a Test match war, preferably one that ends in a draw.'

'But the Pakistanis may want a longer war,' I argued.

'Pakistanis are more Indian than Indians, in every sphere of life. Where did they come from, from Paradise? They are another version of Hindustanis, worse at everything except making tandoori kebab.' Babur was anything but a democrat and wouldn't allow anybody to contradict him.

'But what should I do? Shall I go to England or stay back in Delhi?'

There was a loud honking behind us. I turned around to see who was disturbing our discussion but standing over my bed was the cook with a cup of tea and orders from Dr Hunter to get ready quickly as we were going to Ballimaran to meet Nani before we planned our trip to London.

Before any decision could be taken, however, war was upon us. Officially, it began on 6 September 1965 and ended, not in five days, as Babur had predicted in my dream, but in five weeks, in a miserable draw, to the chagrin of both the nations, as they had been fed on myths about the great superiority of their respective armies, religions and 'manhood'.

Dr Hunter returned to England. In the present atmosphere, no decision could be taken, either about his marriage to Hina Begum or my education in England. The charitable hospital was closed down, the Sunder Nagar house was locked up, I returned to my house in Chandni Chowk, but nothing was normal anymore. Nani had a heart attack but refused to be treated with English medicine. My mother was angry and frustrated by the closure of her dream hospital. She was also missing Dr Hunter more then she had ever missed my father.

In those days, there was a shortage of everything and my duty was to stand in long queues every day to procure whatever I could for the family. Bundu was busy looking after his horses in Nizamuddin. I hardly had the time to meet Anu, who was annoyed with me for no fault of mine. Brij Uncle had lost some of his best pigeons, as they could not fly during the worst days of blackouts and aerial bombardments. He also took out his anger on me for not being able to travel to Pakistan and convince my father that, instead of a war, we should have organized a cricket match to decide the fate of Kashmir.

Prime Minister Shastri died of a heart attack or, as people said, of his vegetarian diet in the extreme cold of Tashkent, where he had gone to discuss the ceasefire with the vodka-drinking President Ayub Khan of Pakistan. We no longer had to go hungry every Monday, as Shastri had desired, and had the freedom to be hungry throughout the week. Of course, most Indians had enjoyed this great freedom even under the dictatorial rule of Aurangzeb and the East India Company.

Shastri's death brought Indira Gandhi to the helm, to the great happiness of my Nani. She believed that only fair-skinned people like the Mughals, the British and the Nehru family had the right to rule India. My mother, who was a strong believer in equal rights for women, was pleased for a different reason. She thought that Indira Gandhi's emergence was a major victory for the women of Asia. Now, women would get their due in Indian society and no one would be able to treat them as an inferior species.

10

Anu was studying for her high school exams and was not allowed to fly kites with us. The only opportunity for us to meet came when she went for tuitions to the house of a classmate in Kashmiri Gate, and we would sometimes meet briefly either at Khyber restaurant or at Ritz cinema.

The Ritz was a favourite rendezvous of young lovers, as it had what was known as a family box, where couples went to indulge in kissing and petting rather than to see a movie. *Guide,* starring the debonair Dev Anand, was showing at the Ritz. On one of the afternoons when Anu came for her tuitions, I bought four tickets for ten rupees, half my month's pocket money. A box had four seats, and we wanted the whole box to ourselves. In no time, Anu and I were kissing and touching each other.

'What are you waiting for,' Anu whispered. 'I don't want to waste all that money.' Without waiting for a response from me, she unzipped my trousers. I was numb with pleasure, my mind blank and shocks of excitement rising from my groin and slowly spreading to every pore of my body as her hot, soft lips performed their task to her satisfaction, and mine as well. Suddenly, the door opened and torchlight flashed on our faces. For a moment we were paralysed. A harsh voice came out of the darkness, 'What is happening here, get up, you two.' It was a burly policeman. I pushed Anu away from me and tried to zip my fly.

The policeman took us to the manager's room. We stood with our heads bowed, praying for the earth to open and swallow us. The policeman, a burly Jat, was thoroughly enjoying his moment of triumph, a greasy smirk on his face. 'I can put you behind bars for attempting to rape this innocent girl,' he said.

The manager, who was a portly middle-aged man with a huge belly and a Charlie Chaplin moustache said, 'Let's call your parents and see what they want to do about this.'

'We didn't do anything, sir, we were just watching the movie,' I whispered unconvincingly.

'That we will see when your parents arrive. Give me the phone number and I'll call them.'

'There is no phone in our house,' Anu said.

'Same with me, sir. There is no phone connection in the whole area.' In those days, phone connections were still rare.

'In that case, you two will come to the police station with me and then we will see if somebody has a phone connection in your family or not,' the policeman said, still smiling.

We knew that if our families learnt about this, we would be separated forever. It was one thing to fly kites and play together in one's own house, but it was unforgiveable to be caught in the box of a cinema hall. No respectable family could face such humiliation. My mind went numb with fear. I was more worried about Anu: this would destroy her reputation.

Then Anu spoke up. 'All right. Call my father Lala Mukund Behari and tell him that I am in your custody.'

'What? You are the daughter of Lalaji?' the policeman said in a shocked voice, the smirk vanishing from his face. Everyone in Old Delhi knew Lalaji.

The manager looked alarmed. 'Lalaji, Lala Mukund Behariji?' With a gesture of his hand, he asked the policeman to follow him out of the room.

I looked at Anu; she was a brave girl and much more in command of the situation than I was. 'How could you have told them about your family? Now they will inform your father.'

'No, they won't. They know that my father, before punishing me, will punish them for bringing such shame to his family.' Anu spoke confidently, with a smile on her lips. She was right. The manager came back alone, wiping his face with a dirty handkerchief.

'Beta, please sit. You children belong to such respectable families. You go back and watch the movie. I will send some Coca-Cola for you,' he said with a sheepish smile, his moustache dancing like a butterfly over his thick lips.

We were in no mood to watch the movie anymore. We left the theatre for our respective homes, swearing to never watch a movie there again. Later, I learned from my college friends that it was a trick played by the manager quite often. The local police constable and he were in league to fleece young couples. Many had to give up their expensive watches or gold jewellery to be rid of them.

After this incident I used to fantasize about making love to Anu all the time, but there was no opportunity to turn my dreams into reality. When the opportunity did come, though, it came in abundance. I had a college friend, Rajinder, whose younger sister was a classmate of Anu's. Her parents had got her engaged at a very young age and she was now to be married. It was common for friends to stay together for a few nights before a girl got married. Anu went to stay at Rajinder's house in Daryaganj and we had the opportunity to meet each other in the evening, when everyone was busy with the marriage rituals. Again, it was Anu's daring that led us into an undesirable situation.

The mehendi function had been organized in a small hall near the bride-to-be's house. Everyone had gathered there, leaving her house vacant. We boys had arranged a few bottles of beer and were sitting in a separate room, as we were not supposed to mingle with girls during the function. Suddenly, I saw Anu outside the window, motioning for me to come out. I knew my friends would pull my leg about it later, but Anu was making faces and signs for me to come out immediately and I had no option. She told me that her sandal had snapped and I was to go with her to her friend's house to get a new pair. I knew she was lying, but went with her quietly, to avoid further embarrassment.

There was no one in the house; even the servants were attending the function. Anu's room was on the terrace floor. She asked me to come up with her. All alone in that room, with a few glasses of beer inside me, it was not difficult for her to seduce me, even against my better judgement. Anu had been talking to her friend about what happened on the first night, the suhaag raat, and was in a mood to experiment. She raised her sari and petticoat and removed her panty. She wanted me to go all the way. I tried clumsily to force myself between her legs. Anu was giggling, more out of fear than pleasure. She lay on the edge of the big bed, all wet and sticky, while I knelt on the floor. Suddenly, we heard sounds: someone was coming downstairs. I sat up quickly and pulled up my zip. Anu was irritated. 'You are such a coward, Sherry. No one is coming. Do it, we won't get an opportunity like this again.'

Next day, again, Anu found an excuse to take me to the empty house. This time she was determined to do 'it' and see how it felt. She had learned from her married friends that it was better to use some oil to ease the entry. That night we not only achieved our goal but had sex three times in succession. Anu did not mind the pain and bleeding as she had made up her mind to do it before she got busy with her high school exams. I'm not sure we enjoyed the sex, but it was a sign that we had become truly adult.

After this, we both got busy with our exams. She had her preparatory leave and was not going to school. After the war with Pakistan, and the talk of my being a spy, I was no longer welcome in Anu's house. We had no opportunity to meet, although every evening I used to stand for hours in the lane in front of her house, hoping to get a glimpse of her.

A day before the festival of Holi, Anu called. 'Sherry, will you come to play Holi with us tomorrow?' she said.

'How can I come, Anu? Your father won't like it.' I had played Holi with Vinod and Anu every year throughout our childhood, but now things had changed.

'Come in the afternoon, when Father and Brij Uncle are busy playing Holi with their friends and drinking bhang.'

Vinod had started playing Holi with his gay friends in the university hostel, so I didn't have any excuse to go to his house. I knew that if I wanted to be with Anu, I would have to go there secretly. Anu said she would leave the front door open and I could go up the stairs to the terrace.

In the morning, I played Holi with some of my friends in Ballimaran. In those days we normally used red gulal, the natural colour made from herbs. I never liked bhang but that day my friends forced a thandai, a drink made from milk and ground dry fruits, mixed with bhang, on me. I drank it thinking it would give me the courage for my afternoon mission.

As Anu had promised, the huge front door of her haveli was unlocked. I peeped into the courtyard. It was empty. Since childhood I had come to this house hundreds of times, but today I was entering it like a thief. As silently as I could, I went up the stairs to the terrace, which was empty except for Brij Uncle's hundred-odd pigeons. Today the pigeons had not been let out to fly and were eating bajra in their large cage, which occupied nearly half the terrace. I went out onto the terrace, hoping that Anu was aware of my arrival. Before I realized what was going on, Anu had poured a bucket full of coloured water over my head. She had been hiding behind a door, waiting to take me by surprise. I was drenched in red colour. I ran after her into her room and in a moment we were kissing passionately. The girl was shameless and full of mischief. I was now over six foot tall, a powerful young man with broad shoulders and a confident personality, but with Anu I became an innocent adolescent. In our games, she always took the initiative. Looking back, all my life I have been lucky to be surrounded by free-spirited women like her, far ahead of their age and time.

Anu pushed me into a chair and ran out to get some sweets and thandai. I lay there quietly, my eyes closed, savouring the taste of her lips on my tongue. I don't know how long she was gone, I must have dozed off under the influence of the bhang. Suddenly, I heard the loud sound of something falling. I rushed out and saw that Brij Uncle was lying on the terrace, near the pigeons' cage. It was obvious that he had had too many glasses of bhang and was not in his senses. He was drenched in colour, his hair a dark, thick red. I tried to lift him but to no avail. I realized then that what I had thought was colour was, in fact, blood oozing out of a wound on his head. There was blood all over my hands and shirt. Before I could react, there was shouting and the sound of footsteps on the staircase. A number of people had come up to the terrace and everyone was shouting. Somebody caught hold of me and shouted, 'How did this Muslim boy get here?'

I realized that it was dangerous for me to stay there any longer. I pushed the man away and ran down the stairs. I could hear the shouts of 'thief, murderer, catch him' behind me. I ran onto the road where hundreds were dancing and singing in the spirit of Holi, and hiding amongst them, I managed to reach my house.

I went straight up to the roof, trying to make sense of what had happened. At that moment I didn't realize the gravity of the incident and how it could change my life. I didn't know then that Lala Brij Behari was dead, that he had been murdered.

The rumour spread fast in the city that Lala Brij Behari had been killed by a Muslim. By the evening some Hindu organizations had jumped into the fray with their wild theories of Muslims planning to kill all the prominent Hindus of Delhi at the behest of Pakistan.

After taking a bath and changing my clothes, I went to sleep, tired and groggy from the bhang I had drunk in the morning. I was shaken awake by Bundu and my mother. They told me that I was being held responsible for the murder and there were eyewitnesses who had seen me escaping from the haveli immediately after Brij Behari's body had been discovered. The rioters were already trying to enter Ballimaran. There were rumours of many Muslims and Hindus having been stabbed in different parts of Delhi. Ammi had already prepared a bag for me with a few clothes. Nani gave me a few hundred rupees and I was told to go with Bundu to the house of a family friend, Pir Sahib, in Nizamuddin. I was to remain underground till things were sorted out.

'Tell me what happened at the lala's house. Did you see anybody attacking Lala Brij Behari?' Ammi asked.

I lied to her that I had gone there to play Holi with Vinod. Since he was not there, Anu asked me to go to the terrace with her. I was waiting there while she went to fetch some sweets for us, when I heard something falling and discovered Brij Uncle lying on the floor near the pigeons' cage. I didn't see anybody attacking him or running away.

'You fool, your life is in danger now. Everybody believes that you murdered the lala. It's so convenient for them to believe that.' Ammi was sobbing now.

Nani, who had seen so many upheavals in her life, was not worried. 'Don't you worry, Hina, he will be all right. I have already spoken to Sardar Gadgaj Singh, and he has asked me to hide Shiraz for some time till they find the real murderer. He will be safe in Pir Nizami's house, under the protection of Khwaja Nizamuddin; no one will dare touch him there.'

I was in a daze, not knowing what was happening. Like a robot, I prepared to leave the house, little knowing that I would not walk through its doors again for a long time to come.

Curfew had already been imposed in the walled city. We took the bylanes to cross Hauz Qazi and reach New Delhi railway station in Paharganj. Bundu knew the timings of a couple of trains which stopped at Nizamuddin railway station.

Sitting in the dirty third-class compartment of the local train, Bundu told me to stay away from Anu and Vinod.

'Blood is thicker than friendship. Don't let anybody know where you are. Your friends may betray you.'

'How can you say that? Anu would never betray me. She knows I haven't done anything wrong.' I desperately wanted to get in touch with Anu. She was witness to my innocence. In fact, Brij Uncle loved me more than he loved Vinod, and I regarded him as a father figure. Anu and Vinod both knew this. They would vouch for my innocence.

My room was in the attic of Pir Sahib's large house. I could see both the dargah of Hazrat Nizamuddin and Humayun's Tomb from there. Pir Sahib was one of Nani's many admirers. With a big saffron pagri on his head and a long thin Chinese-style beard, he resembled a snake charmer more than a Sufi. He had known me from childhood and I had visited his house many times with Nani. He had three daughters who lived in purdah but were never asked to cover their faces before me. They called me Shiraz Bhai, but as is common in Muslim households, this 'brotherhood' did not rule out the possibility of a liaison between us, as marriage between cousins was the norm. They were quite happy to have me in the house and it was obvious that all three were competing for my attention. I, however, was not in any frame of mind to flirt with them, even playfully.

A few days passed and things calmed down a bit, but there was still a strong demand for the immediate arrest of Lala Brij Behari's murderer. I was the obvious perpetrator of the heinous crime. The whole city was talking of how unreliable Muslims were. It was a great lesson for all those who thought that Muslims could ever be regarded as true friends. 'Look how much Brij loved this Muslim boy and how he betrayed his trust by robbing and killing him.' The neighbours told anyone and everyone who would listen that they had constantly warned the lala not to allow me into his house, and now he had paid for disregarding their advice.

The kotwal came to search our house and reluctantly interrogate Nani and Ammi. There was pressure on him to arrest me. Lala Mukund Behari had told the police that I had robbed him of some precious jewellery. Lala Brij Behari had caught me red-handed, he told them, whereupon I had attacked him with an iron rod and killed him. A blood-smeared iron rod was discovered in the elder lala's bedroom, and the tijori, the strongbox in which the family jewels were kept, was found open. Lala Mukund Behari claimed that some pieces were missing.

I was shocked by this statement coming from Anu's father. I urgently wanted to talk to her and Vinod. I was sure that they did not believe the crime had been committed by me. I was also worried that they may have discovered that it was Anu who took me into the haveli. I tried to call her but the telephone in her house didn't seem to be working.

A week after the murder, Kotwal Gadgaj Singh was transferred from Chandni Chowk to Paharganj police station, under pressure from some political leaders who believed that he was sympathetic to my family and was deliberately not arresting me. The new police chief was aggressive and tried to intimidate Nani and Ammi.

Qudsia Begum came to the dargah at Nizamuddin on Thursday, as had been her routine for decades. I went to meet her behind Humayun's Tomb in the small mausoleum where she used to meet her jinns and other celestial friends. She looked old and broken. For the first time in my life, I saw real fear in her eyes.

'Beta, tell me honestly, did you kill the lala?' she asked in a very tired voice.

'Nani, how can you even ask such a question? You know I loved Brij Uncle and I am not a thief.'

'But Shiraz, all the evidence is against you. Even Inspector Gadgaj Singh, who is a friend of our family, believes that you committed the crime,' Bundu said in a hoarse voice. 'He thinks that if you are arrested, you will go to the gallows. He wants you to escape; otherwise, he believes, the best of lawyers can't save you.'

'You must escape to Pakistan, to your father, only he will be able to save you,' Nani said, sitting cross-legged on the floor.

'No, no, Nani, never! How can I flee to Pakistan when I have committed no crime? Then everyone will believe that I did murder the lala.' I was now really upset.

'You can come back when the real culprit is caught. Who do you think killed Brij?' Nani was feeding me biryani with her own hands as she spoke, as if I were a child. I was not hungry but ate to please her, for she had made the biryani especially for me.

'He had been asking Lala Mukund Behari for his share of the property and they used to fight a lot, but I don't believe he could kill his younger brother,' I replied. 'Nani, I would prefer to go to England and stay with Uncle James. I have spoken to him on the phone; he wants me to come to London.'

'Shiraz, you don't understand. There are arrest warrants for you. You can't use your passport, you will be arrested. I have already spoken to Hunter Sahib. You have to cross the border illegally. Don't worry, we are making arrangements with the help of our Sikh friends in Amritsar. We will go to Amritsar and, from there, they will help you cross the border and reach Lahore. They do it every day,' Bundu said, trying to explain the situation to me.

I quietly ate the biryani and listened to the twittering of parrots. I didn't want to take refuge in Pakistan. I didn't want to go to my father and my brother as a fugitive, escaping from the law in India. But there seemed to be no option. Suddenly, we saw Rehana, Pir Sahib's youngest daughter, coming towards us. She was wearing a burqa and seemed to be in a hurry.

'Nani, the police have come searching for Shiraz. Abba sent me to warn you, please don't return to our house, otherwise they will arrest Shiraz.' She was speaking in great agitation and fear.

I didn't know what to do. Nani said she knew a safe place in Humayun's Tomb where I could hide. The tomb was in a huge garden, with waterways and fountains all around, enclosed by high walls. Hardly anyone visited the tomb at that time of the evening. A couple of caretakers were supposed to be on guard but they used to go home, locking the main gate, afraid of the ghosts of Humayun and other Mughal kings who were known to freely roam the place as soon as the sun went down. It was rumoured that on every full moon night, Babur held a durbar, with all the Mughal kings who had ruled this vast empire for 400 years standing respectfully before him. It was said that they didn't want outsiders to be present there after dusk.

Bundu had his apprehensions. 'Won't the spirits of our great ancestors be angry with his presence here? Even Bahadur Shah Zafar couldn't hide for long and was arrested by the British when he took refuge here after the failure of the Mutiny.'

Nani was composed by now. The old, confident Qudsia Begum took control of the situation that was threatening the very existence of the last few Mughal descendants.

'My great-grandfather was arrested before he could use the powers of escape bestowed upon us by our ancestors. Those powers can only be summoned by one of the direct descendants of the Mughals on the night of the full moon. Unfortunately, when Zafar came here to hide, the full moon was still seven days away. You are lucky, Shiraz. Full moon night will be upon us tomorrow.' Qudsia Begum spoke in a monotone, as if in a trance.

Nani claimed to know a place under the tomb, where no one could find me. She told Rehana to return immediately to her house. Then she took Bundu and me to the right of the main tomb, which was as large and grand as the Taj Mahal. Through an opening in the ground, we entered a catacomb of old graves. Many Mughal princes and princesses were buried here. It was a maze which the bravest and most experienced were afraid to enter. Nani walked slowly, with Bundu using a small torch to show her the way. Then, abruptly, she stopped between two large graves and waved to us to sit down on the cold dusty floor. I could smell the stale, cold air. My heart was fluttering with anxiety and anticipation. Nani sat quietly, looking at our fearful faces with bright burning eyes, as though trying to enter our souls.

'I am going to tell you a secret known only to a chosen few in our family. We Mughals pass this secret on only to a few very senior and important members of the family. Today, I am the only one alive who carries this secret in my heart. I wanted to pass it on to the right person before I died. I think the time has come to pass it on to you two, the most trusted descendants of Babur, our great ancestor.' Nani was breathing hard, as if finding it difficult to inhale. She held our hands and kissed them. In the silence, I could feel the darkness enveloping me like a thick blanket.

'Vow in the name of Allah and all our great ancestors that you will not reveal this secret to anybody, even at the cost of your lives.'

From the pocket of her gown, Nani took out an old copy of the Quran, which she claimed had been handwritten by Aurangzeb and handed down from generation to generation. She gave it to me, asked me to kiss it and touch it to my eyes. She asked Bundu to close his eyes and look the other way. Then she murmured some Arabic verses, which I didn't recognize as being part of the Quran. She moved her hand from one end of the grave to the other. It was an unusual grave, very long and with no sign on it. She now touched her hands to my head and moved them slowly, all over, from head to toe. Every pore of my body tingled with some unknown fear. Nani then placed her hand in a small opening under the grave and pulled some lever. The tombstone slowly started moving to one side and we could see an opening in the grave, with stairs going down. Nani asked Bundu to show us the light and, still murmuring the unfamiliar verses, walked into the narrow opening. I was not surprised by these developments as I had seen Bundu doing the same at Red Fort, when he had shown me the secret passages of the Mughal rulers. The Mughals had developed this science of underground tunnels into a fine art as their lives depended to a great extent on a quick getaway from their enemies, and sometimes from their own family members.

Soon we were in a small chamber that was surprisingly dry and full of fresh air. Nani spread her shawl on the floor and gestured to us to sit down.

'Shiraz, I can only show you the path. After this, you are on your own. Beyond are the spirits who supported Emperor Humayun in the wilderness, when he was defeated and all alone, and helped him regain his empire. The spirits of the great Sufis, with the help of the jinns at their command, helped establish the empire of the Mughals. Aurangzeb, in his puritanical fervour, rejected and defied these spirits and the Sufi saints, and relied on his mullahs. That's what led to the downfall of our empire.' Nani was now breathing hard. Her voice seemed to be coming from somewhere far off.

'Today, in this hour of crisis, I am handing you over to these holy saints and to the spirits of our ancestors. Insha'Allah they will save you, I have no idea how. Beyond this chamber is another chamber, which you will enter alone tomorrow, the night of the full moon. There you will find a box with some instructions. Follow them to summon the spirits to help and protect you.'

Nani took me to a niche in the wall, which had some Arabic verses carved on it. She brought out a crescent-shaped piece of steel from her bag and placed it in a gap between the verses. It fit perfectly.

'Tomorrow night, you will put your hand on this crescent and read these verses.' She handed her copy of the tiny Quran to me. 'You will do it all alone, after midnight, and remember, follow the instructions you are given faithfully. God willing, you will be helped by the pure and holy spirits of the Sufi saints.'

Nani got up to leave, giving me her shawl and a small torch. She said Bundu would come back with food, blankets and a stronger torch, to help me stay there for the next twenty-four hours. The rest of the path I would have to discover and follow on my own. I was terrified and wanted to go back to the safety of our house in Ballimaran. When Nani embraced me, I held on to her like a little boy terrified of his own shadow.

Bundu came back after an hour. I couldn't eat the food he had brought for me from some eatery in Nizamuddin, but drank tea from the large flask that he carried. He had decided to keep me company till the hour of my ordeal, which I would have to face alone. We talked of my childhood, my father, and of the great Mughals. Not once did we discuss what lay ahead of me the following night, when I would have to summon the powerful spirits of the Sufis. I had a thousand and one doubts but didn't know how to voice them. I don't know when I fell into a tired, dreamless slumber.

Bundu woke me up. He wanted us to go out and wash before dawn. There was a well near the back wall of the tomb. We washed and I changed into clean white clothes, as I had to pray the whole day and keep myself pure and clean.

I was nervous and would have escaped from there, back to my mother, but for Bundu, who didn't leave me alone for a moment. I missed Ammi's soothing voice, her soft bosom and her smell, which always gave me strength in moments of doubt and fear. It was the longest day of my life. What could the spirits do after all? Make me invisible? I knew that I would have to travel to Amritsar and from there, cross over to Lahore, to save myself from the police. Bundu had already spoken to some of his reliable Sikh friends to help me cross the border. He said that once I had the blessings of the saints, we would leave for Amritsar, dressed as Sikhs. I had not shaved for the last few weeks and had grown a small but respectable beard in preparation. I wanted to leave immediately but did not want to disappoint Nani by not waiting for the blessings of the spirits in whom she had such faith. I didn't want to defy them and suffer the consequences as Emperor Aurangzeb had done.

Bundu Chacha hugged me lovingly before he left me alone in that dark space with the spirits and the jinns. He promised to wait for me outside the main gate, at the tomb of Isa Khan, as Nani had instructed him to do. As soon as I came out, we could go to the railway station.

I was nineteen, but the events of the last few weeks had turned me into an adult. I closed my mind to all fears and doubts. I stopped thinking of Anu and my mother. I just prayed and asked Allah and all the spirits of the saints to deliver me from this misfortune. Sitting there alone and praying, a strange thought came to my mind. If I could be a pigeon, a Shirazi pigeon, as my father and Brij Uncle had lovingly called me, I could fly unseen all over Delhi and Lahore. I smiled at the thought. Childhood memories of my mother pointing to the imaginary golden pigeon in the sky came to mind. I sat there quietly, reading the Quran and waiting for the midnight hour to arrive.

At midnight, I stood up and went to the niche in the corner. As I put the steel crescent in the space and read the Quranic verses with the help of the powerful torch Bundu had brought for me, I thought of Uncle James, who used to tell me that one could overcome any adversity in life if one had faith in oneself.

My thoughts were interrupted by the sound of a heavy stone moving. A small space had opened in the wall, allowing me to step into another chamber. I moved my torch around, afraid of having something or somebody jump on me. Now I understood how deep the terror of the unknown could be, and to what lengths one might go to overcome one's fears.

As I threw the torch light around, I could see that this was an ornate chamber. Persian blue ceramic tiles covered the walls, with the ninety-nine names of Allah carved on them. There was a white marble grave in the middle. I saw nothing else in the room to guide me, no treasures, no path, no guide, no instructions. I didn't know what to do next. I searched for a gap beneath the grave as Nani had done with the grave upstairs. I found a small iron ring, which I pulled with all the strength left in my body, and was rewarded with an opening at the top of the grave. In that opening was a golden box with Quranic verses engraved on it. I picked it up and opened it; it was unlocked. I had closed my heart and mind to all fears and was moving as if in a trance. Like pain, one becomes immune to fear as it increases beyond the threshold of tolerance.

The box was empty except for a crumbling yellow paper. On it was written something illegible in Persian or Turkish. I didn't know what to do. I only wanted to get out of this place at the earliest and go back to the real world of my mother, far away from this spirit land. I picked up the box, which seemed to be made of solid gold, and walked out of the chamber. I went up the narrow stairs and into the garden. Under the soft golden light of the full moon, Humayun's Tomb floated like a weightless ship moving on the surface of a calm and serene sea. I was suddenly overcome by exhaustion. I sat down on a red stone bench facing the tomb. Without realizing it, I fell into a deep sleep, entirely unaware of my surroundings.

In a foggy, moonlit dream that followed, I saw the smiling figure of Babur moving towards me. He sat down on the bench and put my head on his lap. 'Shiraz, my dear boy, what are you going to do now? Will you escape like a criminal to Pakistan?'

'What else can I do? They all say that if I am arrested, I will go to the gallows.'

'Yes, fly from the city of Hazrat Nizamuddin to Lahore, the city of Hazrat Daata Ganj Baksh, and he will protect you,' Babur said with a hand on my head.

'How can I fly, I am not a pigeon or an eagle. I wish I were.' I was at peace after a long time with my head on my great ancestor's lap.

'What would you like to be, an eagle or a dove?' Babur asked with a smile.

'A dove, a Shirazi pigeon, as my father Azizuddin Khan wanted me to be,' I replied.

'Pigeons are more powerful than eagles. They can fly faster, they have more endurance, greater stamina. Their vision is as strong as that of an eagle, but they can never be the kings and masters,' Babur said, as if he were weighing my options. 'Eagles are hunters and pigeons are romantic lovers. What would you like to be, my dear Shiraz?'

'I am not a killer; I cannot be an eagle. I am a romantic lover like you and would prefer to be a pigeon.'

Babur's laughter shattered the silence of the full moon night. 'You consider me a pigeon and not an eagle, a romantic lover and not a ruthless conqueror and empire-builder. Have you not read your history, my dear boy?'

'I have read your heart; it is that of a dove, not an eagle.'

Babur laughed again. 'You are the first person to say that in the last 400 years. My father was a great pigeon-flyer and always wanted me to be a dove. His death and the betrayal of those I loved turned me into an eagle, but you are the first to understand that I always remained a pigeon in the garb of an eagle. Something I myself realized only after my death. I fought wars like an eagle, killed and maimed people like a hawk, but cried at night like a lover and a poet. After every victory, I felt defeated; with every territory gained, I lost a part of myself. Every conqueror has to pay the price of victory,' he said thoughtfully.

'I have to go now. Bundu is waiting for me outside,' I said, fearing that Babur was in the mood to philosophize the whole night long.

'Let him wait. You have to fly alone. He is a horseman; he can never be a pigeon. My father died while flying his beloved pigeons. Everyone believed that he had turned into a pigeon and flown away. He escaped the betrayal of the people around him. Today, you will also escape as a pigeon, as your great-grandfather Bahadur Shah Zafar could not. Shiraz, in you I see the heart of a dove and the determination of an eagle. I was the same at your age. I will let you fly for now but, unlike my father, you have to come down to earth one day. You will go to the grave of the great pir and Sufi, Daata Sahib, in Lahore, and there you will find the solution to all your problems.' Saying this, Babur stood up and pointed towards the moon, which was hanging like a magic lantern in the sky over the white marble dome of Humayun's Tomb.

Then, slowly, he turned to point his finger at me. A strange shudder went down my spine. I felt as if I were losing myself, as though I had somehow shrunk. I could not see myself but realized suddenly, to my horror, that I had turned into a pigeon. Babur had meant it literally when he told me to fly to Lahore.

I didn't know whether I was the Shirazi pigeon my father always wanted me to be, or the pigeon that Babur's father had turned into that fateful evening in Farghana, when people thought that he had died. But here I was, flying around the white marble dome of the tomb and looking at the charbagh, the garden of paradise, laid out by Queen Hamida Bano with such love and care. Babur had vanished, but I could see Bundu sitting outside the main gate of the tomb, waiting for me. It was still dark, but in the moonlight I could see the silver line of the Yamuna behind Humayun's Tomb. I was enjoying this very strange feeling of floating in the air and looking at the world below me with literally a bird's-eye view. I flew down and sat near Bundu, trying to tell him that I could not escape with him to Lahore. He looked towards me and threw a few pieces of bread in my direction.

Everything had changed. I realized that I could see everyone but nobody could see me, except as a pigeon. There were no more barriers for me: no walls, no doors, and no policemen with arrest warrants.

PART TWO

The Flight

For once you have tasted flight
You will walk the earth
With your eyes turned skywards,
For there you have been,
And there you will long to return.

– Leonardo da Vinci

11

Growing up in Ballimaran, I used to dream of flying into the sky and looking at the city of Delhi from above. In my dreams I had invented a personal flying machine, which allowed me to fly and land on any roof at will. Sometimes I imagined myself as a kite, soaring into the sky. Now here I was, a pigeon, flying over the dome of Humayun's Tomb.

In the soft morning light I could see India Gate and the minarets of Jama Masjid at a distance. I rose up in the sky from where I could see the twin cities of Old and New Delhi stretching in all their glory for miles and miles. I flew along the Yamuna towards Red Fort. I could see hundreds of pigeons flying very high in the sky. Pigeons love to touch great heights, but I was still afraid to leave the earth. Moreover, I was enjoying this view of my beloved city. I could see the ruins of the old fort, where Humayun died, and the zoo, where I had spent innumerable evenings with Uncle James. I wished he were here to guide me in this new world of clouds and winds. I tried to find the house where he used to live in Sunder Nagar. Suddenly, there was a strong gust of wind and I lost control. I came crashing down to the ground. The first lesson I learned as a pigeon was that you can't reflect while navigating. Luckily, I didn't injure myself and landed on soft grass in the lawn of a bungalow. Before I could rise into the air again, a huge black dog sitting on the lawn jumped up and caught me in its large canines. I was afraid that my flight was over even before it had begun. I was going to die even before I had the chance to look upon my house in Ballimaran.

The next thing I knew, Babur was standing there shouting at the dog. It dropped me on the grass and ran for its life, as if it had seen a ghost. Babur picked me up and said, 'Shiraz mian, learn to fly like a pigeon, you have to go very far. I can't help you anymore. Luckily, not much damage has been done this time.' Saying this, he threw me up in the air. I tested my wings; I could still fly. Babur had saved me once again.

As a pigeon, I could fly straight up like a helicopter, unlike other birds. I flew over Delhi Gate and looked down at the congested streets of Daryaganj. Red Fort looked beautiful, with its gardens and palaces, and Jama Masjid rising in front of it like a jewel in the crown of Delhi. Now I saw hundreds of pigeons, mostly rock doves, flying all around and trying to distract me from my path. In front of Red Fort I could see Chandni Chowk, where I had spent all my life till now.

My pigeon's heart beat fast at the thought of seeing my mother after so many days. But, even in the body of a pigeon, I was a man in love. Before I flew to my house I wanted to have a peek at Anu, my darling girl, and inhale her fragrance. I flew over Lala Mukund Behari's haveli and perched on the roof of the pigeons' cage on the terrace. I thought of Brij Uncle and how he would have loved to see me as a pigeon. I wanted to cry then, but realized to my dismay that pigeons can't cry.

Anu was probably still asleep. All the pigeons Brij Uncle had loved to fly were locked up in their cages. If he had been alive, he would have come early in the morning to feed them and let them out to fly. He used to say, 'Pigeons in the air are like fish in the water. They never tire of flying; they can fly hundreds of miles every day without resting.'

I could see the huge mirror on the wall of Anu's room on the terrace. She used to comb her long hair for hours, sitting before that mirror, or look at herself while flying kites, to check how sexy her breasts looked with her hands up in the air, holding the kite. I was overcome by an urge to look at myself as a pigeon. I hopped in through the window of the room, which was empty. I flew to the mirror and saw my reflection for the first time. I was both shocked and pleased to see that I had turned into the famous Shirazi species of homing pigeon, which my father valued so much. I preened and pranced before the mirror, admiring myself in all my glory. I had white and golden-brown feathers. There was a broad strip of golden feathers on my head, and it extended down my back, up to my tail. I had long shiny wings. As a matter of fact, I had never seen such a beautiful golden pigeon. If Brij Uncle had not been murdered, he would have given his right hand to possess me.

The door to the room opened and Anu stood before me, rubbing her eyes and raising her hands to yawn and shake off her early morning lethargy. How beautiful she looked, just like a princess. I wanted to hug and kiss her but had no option but to just look at her. Her eyes fell on me and she laughed, clapping her hands in delight.

'Oh, what a lovely Shirazi, where did you come from?' She moved towards me to catch me. To her astonishment, I flew up and sat on her shoulder. She took me in her soft delicate hands. I was dismayed to find that she did not look particularly unhappy, and seemed to be in good spirits, happy to find this strange golden pigeon on her terrace. Hadn't she missed me, her Shiraz?

'You golden pigeon, where have you come from? I have never seen a golden Shirazi before,' she said.

I wanted to tell her that I was her love, her Shiraz. I tried to speak, but to no avail. I bobbed my head and looked into her eyes, trying to tell her who I was.

Anu smiled and, as though she could read my eyes, said, 'Are you my darling Shiraz? Have you turned into a pigeon to come and kiss me?' She laughed at her own joke and kissed me on the beak.

I wanted to tell her that she was right, I was her Shiraz. I was so happy to find that she still thought of me as her beloved Shiraz, not as a thief and a murderer.

Anu released me and, opening a box, threw a handful of pearl maize at me. I became conscious that I had not eaten anything since I had turned into a pigeon. I was famished. I became so engrossed in eating that I didn't notice when Anu went down the stairs and vanished. I was now dying to see my mother and find out how she was doing. I flew off towards Ballimaran. These two mohallas of Hindus and Muslims were culturally worlds apart but flying over them, I could see how close they were to each other. With a few movements of my wings I was flying over the roof of my house. I could see my colourful kites still lying on the roof with nobody to fly them. I flew down to the courtyard, where Nani was reciting the Quran aloud. Ammi sat on a chair beside her, with a cup of tea, reading the newspaper. I landed softly near her, wanting her to touch me. But she was absorbed in reading and paid no heed to me.

Through the open door I entered my bedroom and perched on my favourite chair. The room smelled of me. Nothing had changed. On the wall was a photograph of me with Bundu and his horses. There was one taken in Bombay with my parents at Juhu beach. Since I was supposed to be flying to Lahore, to my father, I looked carefully at his face. I had almost forgotten what he looked like. How would I recognize his house when I had never been there before? I didn't know how pigeons sought out a particular address. But that was the least of my problems at the moment. Suddenly, I wanted to change into a human being once again and lie on my bed with my head on my mother's lap while she sang softly to me in her melodious voice. I cursed the moment when Babur had transformed me into a pigeon. What was the purpose of saving my life if I didn't exist for my loved ones?

I flew out and tried to get the attention of Nani and Ammi. Nani was praying loudly to Allah for my safe journey to Lahore. Ammi joined her, her hands raised in prayer, tears in her eyes. I so wanted to embrace her at that moment and tell her not to worry. I was right there, safe and sound, sitting next to her, but she had decided not to notice her Shiraz. Ammi, unlike Abba, was never interested in pigeons. I flew up and sat on the empty cup of tea, so that she had no option but to notice me.

'How beautiful, where did this pigeon come from?' she said, finishing her prayers.

'Must be from the flock of Master Nasir, he is spending all his wealth on buying these exotic pigeons,' Nani said.

'Why is it hovering over me? I have never seen any pigeon doing that in the past.' Saying this, Ammi caught me in her soft, beautiful hands. I felt her fingers on my feathers, ruffling them as she used to ruffle my hair. I wanted her to put me in a cage near her and never let me fly anywhere again.

The front door opened and there was Bundu, saying a loud 'Salam alaikum' to register his arrival. Ammi immediately let me go and focused all her attention on him.

'Shiraz has vanished. I left him in the underground chamber last night, as you had instructed me, but in the morning I couldn't find any trace of him. How could he go anywhere without telling me? Shiraz is not so irresponsible.' Bundu was clearly agitated.

Hearing this, Ammi started crying but Nani remained calm. 'Don't worry, he is in the safe hands of our ancestors. The spirits of Babur and Humayun will protect him.'

Ammi turned on her angrily. 'What nonsense! I want to see my boy. Where have you hidden him away? No spirit is going to protect him. Bundu, why did you leave him alone in that dark, horrible chamber? He is still a child and I know how terrified he is of the darkness.'

I wanted to hug my mother and wipe her tears away. My delicate pigeon's heart was on the verge of bursting. I had never felt so helpless in my life. I hated myself for allowing Babur to turn me into a pigeon, without giving me the ability to turn back into a human being.

Nani hugged Hina Begum and said gently, 'Believe me, Hina, he is safe. Our Shiraz has gone all alone to Lahore. He has been helped by Hazrat Nizamuddin and the magic of our Mughal ancestors. I have no idea how and where, but I am confident that he is safe in hiding somewhere.'

I watched as they embraced each other, unable to do anything to reassure them. At that moment I decided to do as Babur had asked me to: I would fly to Lahore at the earliest and find the solution to my problems at the shrine of Daata Sahib.

I looked at them one last time and flew up into the sky.

There were all sorts of birds flying in the sky but none except eagles and falcons could soar into the heavens as we pigeons could. I felt safe as I saw no falcons in the sky. Two pigeons were flying alongside me in the north-westerly direction. One was a Kabuli and the other a white Laqa. They began communicating with me. I learnt that they were also flying to Lahore, and had flown on that route frequently. It seemed that all the holy spirits and the ghosts of my ancestors were conspiring to help me. The Kabuli told me that it was easy to fly over the Grand Trunk Road towards Lahore. The Laqa was more talkative and chattered non-stop. The

Kabuli was keeping an eye out for any danger. We landed in a green field of wheat to have our fill and restore our strength.

Suddenly, a shadow fell over my head and before I knew what was happening, I was in the strong talons of a falcon, the biggest threat to pigeons in this part of the world. I thought my escape to Lahore was over; I was destined, instead, to become a falcon's meal. The bird of prey was trying to attack my head with its sharp beak. The next moment, though, a strong gust of wind caused it to lose its balance and I fell from its talons. I came crashing down on a mango tree whose branches saved me. But I realized that my left wing was broken.

The Kabuli was angry. 'Didn't you hear the falcon coming?' he shouted. 'Didn't your mother teach you how to protect yourself from a falcon? You are the biggest Shirazi I have ever seen and that's why the falcon couldn't hold you properly, but you seem to have no brains.'

How could I tell him that I had no mother? I was the creation of Babur's imagination. My two companions could not help and had to leave before it became dark. They advised me to hide in the mango tree for a few days until my wing healed and I could fly again.

I would not have flown ever again if it was not for the Sikh boy who came up the mango tree to steal some mangoes. He found me hiding there and immediately took me to his grandfather, a very old Sikh who loved pigeons.

He looked at my injuries and said, 'Puttar, we need to set its broken wing, otherwise it will not fly again.'

I was lucky to be in his experienced hands and soon had my wing reset and bound. The old man looked at me with wonder and said to his grandson, 'Amrit puttar, this is a special pigeon, I have never seen a golden Shirazi. It is also larger than most pigeons. Take good care of it.'

In a few days, I could fly normally again. I didn't want to leave that family of Sikh farmers but I had to reach Lahore. I flew off towards Amritsar. From the sky the Golden Temple looked amazing. The golden dome of Harminder Sahib, surrounded by water and white marble walkways, was the purest form of architecture I had ever seen. I could see hundreds of pigeons flying all around the temple complex and perched on the dome. I struck up a friendship with a couple of young pigeons. They told me that they flew to Lahore regularly. In fact, they spent their mornings at the Golden Temple and afternoons in Lahore at the Daata Durbar. Partition had not stopped them from eating prasad at the temple in Amritsar and bajra at the Badshahi mosque of Lahore. There were no borders, no passports or visas for pigeons, and no hatred. We could enjoy both the gurbani and the azaan without losing our faith. It was only humans who lost their faith and senses at the slightest provocation.

I befriended another Shirazi, a bachelor who was not bound by the responsibilities of a household, and persuaded him to fly with me to Lahore. Pigeons remain loyal to their partners all their lives and share the responsibility of rearing the young ones. It is not easy to find a singleton among them, but my friend Pinku had just reached adulthood and was still searching for a suitable partner to spend the rest of his life with. He was born in Lahore and knew the city well. He agreed to be my guide. We reached Lahore in an hour's time and went straight to the huge mausoleum of Daata Ganj Baksh.

At the dargah, pigeons were served special laddoos made with pure ghee. Nobody went hungry from this durbar – human, animal or bird. As we flew over Lahore, I remembered my father saying that it was a pastiche of Delhi. The Badshahi mosque, the fort, the Shalimar garden, the houses and the mohallas – if any city in the world came anywhere near Delhi, it was Lahore. I fell in love with it at first sight.

I had dreamt often of coming to Lahore to meet my father and brother. But now I didn't know how to go about finding them. I knew Azizuddin Khan lived in Model Town, a locality in new Lahore. He also had a bungalow in Islamabad, the new capital of Pakistan, and a house on the beach in Karachi.

Emperor Babur had promised that I would find the solution to my problems at the shrine of Daata Ganj Baksh. Now here I was at the dargah, but I had no clue how to turn back into a human being. My friend Pinku had found a partner and the lovebirds were having a passionate honeymoon. My problem was the long queue of female pigeons falling all over me. They said they had not seen another golden pigeon as handsome as I was. The pigeons had no shame. Once they decided on a partner, they got busy mating at all times of the day and night. I had no intention of leaving my Mughal seed in the world of pigeons. I avoided the advances of even the most insistent females. In pigeon society, it was scandalous to have an adult pigeon without a partner, in spite of so many available options. I wished then that Anu had also turned into a pigeon. We could have lived happily ever after, without the impediment of religions at war with one another.

Knowing that my father was fond of pigeons, I looked for houses with pigeon lofts in Model Town. There was one huge bungalow with a big flock of Shirazi pigeons. I was certain this would be my father's house, and I was right. On the sixth day of my quest, I saw him standing on the terrace of the house, flying his pigeons with sounds similar to those used by Delhi's pigeon-flyers, not by Lahori kabootarbaaz. He had not changed much, except for a few strands of white hair in his sidelocks. Abba was surprised to see the strange golden Shirazi landing on his roof out of the blue. He threw some bajra seeds towards me and I obliged him by eagerly picking them up with my beak. Carefully, he moved towards me to catch me. I wanted to be held by him, to be hugged and loved by him, but not this way, not as a pigeon. Nonetheless, I let him hold me in his big hands. As an experienced pigeon lover, Azizuddin could see that I belonged to a unique breed of Shirazi pigeons, but how had I landed on his roof? He spread my wings gently to see if there were any markings that would tell him who my owners were. I wore no ring with my owner's name on my feet, as was usual with expensive pigeons.

'You golden Shirazi, where have you come from? You are a priceless bird, the first golden pigeon I have seen or even heard of. I must protect you,' Abba said, kissing me on my beak.

I wanted to tell him that I needed his protection, that I was a fugitive from the law and an alleged murderer. He tested me by releasing me into the air but I flew back and landed on his shoulder. He was pleased with this sign of affection from a strange pigeon, and ran his fingers lovingly down my back.

Abba was soon joined by my brother Aijaz. I was shocked to see him: he was the spitting image of me, except that he was wearing a Pathani suit, which I never wore. He had not only my face, eyes and height, but also my voice. I felt as if I were looking at myself in the mirror. Abba handed me over to him. It was obvious that Aijaz had also developed a love for pigeon-flying.

Aijaz was mesmerized by my beauty. 'Abba jaan, I have never seen such a perfect Shirazi. Where has it come from?' he exclaimed.

'I don't think this is a Lahori pigeon. It has come from far away, maybe from Shiraz in Iran, or Kabul, and seeing our flock of Shirazi, it has landed on our roof,' Abba said.

'Maybe from Delhi?' said Aijaz.

'No, in Delhi, no one has anything like this. I know every Shirazi there,' Abba said confidently.

How could he know that it was his own son, Shiraz, who had flown all the way from Delhi?

'Take care of this pigeon, Aijaz. I have to return to Islamabad, and from there I'll go to London for a week to see your sisters. When I return, I'll decide what to do with it. Till then, you train it and look after it.' Saying this, Abba disappeared into his vast mansion.

Aijaz fed me and put me in a cage, away from the other pigeons. I was already missing my friends at the Daata Sahib shrine, but was happy to be near my brother.

Gradually, I learned that Aijaz lived in this house with a distant aunt and an army of servants for company. My father's second wife Ayesha Begum now lived in London with her daughters, who were studying at the London School of Economics. Abba was away most of the time on his ministerial work and to be with Ayesha and their daughters. I used to envy Aijaz but now I pitied him because the poor boy had never known the love and care of women like our Ammi or Nani.

Aijaz came up to the terrace every morning and released me with the rest of the flock. I soon discovered that he was arrogant and ill-mannered and loved to boss over the servants. He lost his temper at the slightest provocation. He didn't have the courtesy of our father or the wisdom of our mother. I used to follow him around and watch him from the air. In the morning he went to Atchison College, where he had a number of girlfriends. He also had a few female friends outside his college. He used to take them to a guest house in a suburb of Lahore and make love to them. I would watch his sexual antics from the window of the guest house – that was the advantage of being a pigeon – but I decided not to disturb his privacy.

Aijaz played cricket and was the captain of the Lahore University team. He was surprised when he discovered me one day, following him to the cricket ground. No ordinary pigeon would do that. Pigeons, once released, embark on long flights with their flock, but here I was, following my master like a pet dog. Aijaz also loved fast cars and had a Harley Davidson motorcycle, the like of which I had never seen in India. In Pakistan, they imported their cars from Europe and America, unlike India, which manufactured only one car: the Ambassador. Aijaz, I found, was a careless driver who didn't bother about his safety or that of others on the road. I could see that my father's money and power had spoilt him. But the poor boy was on his own, without the love of a mother or the care of a father. My heart went out to him.

Azizuddin Khan returned after ten days. He came up with Aijaz to look at the pigeons. Tea was served to him on the terrace. He sat there talking to Aijaz. He was worried. He told Aijaz that he had received a phone call from Delhi.

'Your brother Shiraz is missing. He was supposed to come to Lahore to meet me, but I told them that he has not contacted me,' he said, sipping his tea. 'There is a warrant of arrest against him for the murder of my old friend Lala Brij Behari. I can't imagine him harming anybody, he is such a decent and caring boy. Did anyone try to contact you or come to the house?'

I was pleased to see that Aijaz was disturbed by the news of my disappearance. It meant that he cared for me.

'Where has he gone? I hope he is safe somewhere. I'll keep an eye out for him. If he comes here, everyone will recognize him since he resembles me,' he said now, in a worried tone of voice.

I wanted to say that I was already with them. I wanted to inform my mother that I was safe, but I could do nothing about it. It was deeply frustrating and I cursed Babur for it. Then and there, I decided to return to Delhi and meet my family and Anu, whom I missed so much.

Next day, as soon as all the pigeons were released, I separated from the flock and flew towards Amritsar. In fifteen minutes I was flying over the Wagah border. From up there, I couldn't tell where

India began and Pakistan ended. The same green fields, the same canals, the same wheat being sown in the same fashion. I could see no sense or logic in Partition. I met my old friends at the Golden Temple, had my fill of prasad and flew towards Delhi. Now I had the confidence to fly alone. I had fine-tuned my senses to hear the sound of falcons' wings from a distance and rush for the nearest hiding place.

It was an uneventful flight. By late evening I was back in Delhi. I flew to Ballimaran and landed in my Nani's house. I could see her sitting in her usual place in the courtyard, her paandan beside her, but my mother was nowhere to be seen. I hid myself in a small air passage in the courtyard from where I could watch all that went on in the house. Nani looked frail, and older. Nothing had changed but there was sadness and silence in the atmosphere. Happiness had flown from that house along with me.

Next morning I learned that my mother had gone with Bundu to Sunder Nagar, to stay at the house of Dr Hunter, who had since returned from London. I immediately flew there and found him having breakfast on the verandah with Ammi and Bundu. I was so excited that I landed directly on the breakfast table, overturning a few cups and saucers.

Ammi was taken aback to see the golden pigeon again. 'This is the pigeon I told you about. It came the day Shiraz disappeared and now suddenly it has landed here from nowhere,' she told James.

Bundu tried to catch me, but I flew up to the ceiling fan and sat there.

Ammi said, 'I have this strange feeling that my Shiraz has turned into this Shirazi pigeon.'

James laughed. 'I hope that's true, but I don't see any resemblance to our Shiraz in this strange pigeon, except for the name.'

'You know there is a belief among the Mughals that Babur's father turned into a pigeon to escape his enemies. Maybe the same has happened to our Shiraz. I didn't see him leaving Humayun's Tomb. We never found a body and since then he has vanished into thin air. Maybe the magic of our saints turned him into a ghost or a pigeon.'

I was happy that Bundu was speaking the truth, but was also afraid that he might try to catch me and confine me for my own safety. I decided to fly away and watched my mother secretly after that, without revealing myself.

I spent nearly a month in Delhi, flying from Nizamuddin to Chandni Chowk. My most painful discovery was that Anu had been married off in great haste, to the son of a rich diamond merchant of Jaipur. The news devastated me. I lost all hope, and the will to live. I wanted to become a falcon's prey and end my life. In my distress, I flew all over Delhi without eating or drinking anything, just looking for a falcon to finish me off. No falcon came to my rescue, though, and I had to accept the reality of my miserable existence.

On full moon night, I flew over the big white marble dome of Humayun's Tomb, searching for Babur. I wanted to tell him that I preferred to die than to live as a pigeon anymore. I saw no sign of Babur or any other ghost that night. I flew to the bench where I had gone to sleep and met Babur on that other fateful full moon night. I cursed him and all my Mughal ancestors for abandoning me like this when I needed them the most.

When morning came, I flew to the dargah of Sufi Hazrat Nizamuddin. Sitting there, I prayed to the Sufi to turn me back into a human.

'If you help me, Khwaja, I will feed all the pigeons that come to your dargah for the rest of my life,' I requested the saint in all sincerity, but to no avail. I prayed that at the very least I would get the chance to meet Anu and see with my own eyes that she was fine. I prayed for her happiness.

My prayers were answered on the third day. Anu came to visit her family for the first time after her marriage. I found her sitting on the terrace, crying silently. In her hand she had my picture and she was talking to it. She looked pale and forlorn. I wanted to hold her and kiss away her tears.

She looked up and saw me and a faint smile appeared on her lips. 'Golden pigeon, you are back. Have you brought any news of my Shiraz? Does he still love me?'

I wanted to reassure her that I loved her more than ever. I lived only to see her, touch her and love her. I perched on her hand, which was coloured with henna. She held me to her bosom and said, 'If you meet my love, tell him that only he resides in my heart. I wanted to soar with him into the skies but now I am confined to the four walls of a haveli in Jaipur. That man has a cold diamond in his chest instead of a heart, and thinks I am one of his precious pieces of jewellery to be kept in an iron safe.'

I was happy to be so close to my darling Anu, but miserable at her pain and loneliness. There was no denying the guilty pleasure, though, in knowing that she had been married against her wishes and was unhappy with her rich husband. I knew that no one could have married her off against her wishes, had it not been for the tragic turn of events on that Holi. Now she was lost to me forever, married to this diamond merchant.

I spent a greater part of the day on the terrace of Anu's house. Most of Lala Brij Behari's pigeons had gone. The few that were left were being looked after by the servants.

I also learnt to my dismay that my friend Vinod had been discovered. His parents had found out he was gay and sent him to London for further studies – and to save the family from the shame which came with this news. Naina Devi, their mother, had become very sick after these multiple shocks and was mostly confined to her bed.

Anu had to return to Jaipur after a few days. I decided to fly with her and find out where she lived and also to have a look at the man who was the master of my beloved's body, if not her heart and soul.

She left in an Ambassador, in the care of their family clerk, Munshi Chandu Prasad, an old man who loved Anu. The road to Jaipur was full of potholes, and they moved very slowly. As a pigeon I was used to flying at a speed of 120 to 140 kilometres per hour. I could reach Jaipur in a couple of hours, but now I had to fly at the speed of that miserable car.

I would have enjoyed looking at the Pink City but for the circumstances. I watched Anu's car enter the gateway of a splendid haveli. A curtain was put up on both sides and a covered passage was created for her to pass into the courtyard of the zenana, the female quarters. Anu, who had been a free bird in Delhi and never cared for any social bindings, was kept in strict purdah in this house.

The courtyard had a marble fountain and large rooms around it. There were a number of peacocks with long tails prancing in the courtyard but no sign of pigeons. Anu went straight to her room to rest after the long journey. I found an air passage in the room, from where I could watch her. Servants brought food for her but she refused to eat. Her mother-in-law, a matriarch in a brocade silk sari and lots of diamond jewellery, came to admonish her.

'You must eat, if not for yourself then for your husband, who will come to your bed soon. You must get ready to perform your wifely duties with a pleasant face and a smile,' said the woman in a cold voice.

'I have a headache. Tell your son to go elsewhere to perform his husbandly duties,' Anu said to her mother-in-law in an equally harsh voice.

'Where will he go, if not to his wife, you silly girl? Get ready, he will come in an hour's time and remember, I want a grandson from you soon.' She went out without waiting for a reply.

'I am not a vessel to receive his dirty seed. I am not a child-making machine for your family.' Anu was talking to herself.

Soon the servants came to prepare her for bed, but Anu refused to change or wash.

Ramesh Chandra, Anu's husband, was a big dark man with a protruding belly, over which he wore a long flowery Rajasthani jacket. He was drunk when he entered her room. He tried to seize her in a crude embrace. She pushed him away and got up from the bed. She stood before him like a cat ready to scratch his face. I wanted to laugh, but a pigeon can neither laugh nor cry. After a few clumsy attempts to grab her, the unfortunate man gave up and collapsed in a drunken slumber on the bed, snoring loudly. He was no match for Anu, who had always been more agile than any boy in Chandni Chowk.

Anu slept on the sofa, never allowing her husband to touch her. I was heartbroken at her plight. What a lively girl she had been, and what kind of married life was this that she was destined to suffer. I couldn't stand it anymore and decided to fly back to Delhi.

There I learned that Nani had had another heart attack. She was asking for her grandson Shiraz. She wanted to see him before she died.

The next full moon night, I waited at the tomb once again, for any sign of Babur. At midnight I saw the shadow of the emperor and flew over it. Babur looked up and said, 'You are doing well as a pigeon, Shiraz. I think you may prefer to remain a pigeon now.'

I knew he was pulling my leg, but I retorted nonethless. 'I would prefer to face the gallows than to remain a pigeon, you know that very well.'

'I know that, but I can't do anything about it. You have to go back to Lahore and wait for the right time.' Before I could respond, the shadow of the emperor vanished.

I went to see my mother in Sunder Nagar. Nani was staying there too, convalescing after the heart attack. I saw them having breakfast on the lawn. I sat on the branch of a tree and listened to them talking softly. Nani was in a wheelchair. From their conversation I gathered that Uncle James had proposed to Ammi again and this time Nani had agreed.

Qudsia Begum had wanted my mother to remarry, not an angrez but a wealthy aristocrat from Delhi. She had forced Azizuddin to send the divorce papers signed by a qazi. However, she had failed to convince her daughter to marry some handsome man of her choice. After my disappearance, Nani realized that Ammi had gone into a state of depression and only Uncle James could bring her out of it. And so she agreed to have the white Mughal as her son-in-law.

Uncle James wanted to take Nani and Ammi to London and get better treatment for her in his hospital. But Nani said to him in her frail but still clear voice, 'You go to London with Hina, and I will wait here for my Shiraz. I know he will come back one day and he should find me waiting for him.'

'What if he is already dead?' Ammi gave voice to her worst fear.

Uncle James put a hand on her shoulder and Ammi started sobbing. My heart went out to her. Uncle James hugged her and wiped her tears.

'You know, Hina, Shiraz didn't go to Lahore. He didn't go to London either. He is somewhere in India. He is a smart boy, I know he will come back.' Uncle James tried to give her the confidence he himself lacked.

'Then why doesn't he contact us?' Ammi put her head on his shoulder, uncaring of Nani's presence.

I wished that humans could communicate telepathically, as we pigeons did. I tried to send my thoughts to Ammi, but it didn't work. I decided to fly back to Lahore and find a way out, if not for Anu, then for Ammi and Nani. I didn't want Nani to die before she embraced me once more. I knew that nothing gave her more pleasure then feeding me biryani with her own hands. I wanted to come back for that biryani.

۱۲

There was not a trace of a cloud in the vast blue sky. I was flying as if I had flown all my life. Now I knew which route to take to Lahore. There were several flocks of pigeons out on their morning flight. They looked at me curiously but did not try to strike up a conversation. I saw a few falcons but they were more interested in attacking a big flock of pigeons then a lone bird like me. From this height, the world looked beautiful. The green fields of Punjab passed under me. I could see the Himalayan peaks in the distance. I knew that a pigeon could easily fly 800 kilometres in a day. All the knowledge I had gained from expert pigeon-racers like my father and Brij Uncle now came in use for me.

I flew straight to Daata Sahib, the abode of great saints and Sufis. I sat on a wall and prayed as I had never prayed for anything. I felt as if I heard a voice, the voice of Daata Sahib himself. 'Have patience, child, your time will come, but first you will have to make a sacrifice that you may later regret.'

I was not sure whether the voice was real or just a figment of my imagination. It left a big hole in my heart. Sacrifice? What sacrifice? I could think of no sacrifice that I could make in my present condition. As a pigeon, I had nothing to give. I sat there the whole night, neither eating nor sleeping. In the morning, I flew to my father's house. Aijaz was surprised to see me.

'You shaitan, you devil of a pigeon, where did you go? I

searched for you everywhere. I sent my spies to see if some bird dealer had caught you.' Aijaz lovingly patted my back and fed me with his hand. 'I will not put you in a cage, but don't disappear again. I know you have come back because you like me.' Saying this, Aijaz left for college on his Harley Davidson. I decided to follow him. I cursed my father for giving him the motorcycle, which he raced through the congested streets of Lahore recklessly, endangering his own and others' lives.

Instead of going to class, Aijaz picked up a beautiful girl and took her on a ride on his motorcycle. The girl was worse than him, egging him on to drive faster, with her hand on his fly and her large breasts pressing against his back. Aijaz didn't require any coaxing for his daredevil antics. My pigeon's heart couldn't take it after a while, so I decided to leave him to his girlfriend and fly over the city of Noorjahan.

I found old Lahore more beautiful than old Delhi. It was greener, cleaner and better organized. I took a few rounds over the city and then perched myself on the dome of the Badshahi mosque, which reminded me of Delhi's Jama Masjid. At night, the lighting was mesmerizing. I loved to fly over it and look at the sprawling structure from above. I wished that Delhi's Jama Masjid was as clean and attractive.

Sitting there, I thought of my brother, who was my carbon copy, yet so different from me. I felt sorry for both of us, for we never had the chance to play with each other or share the small things that make life so wonderful. Partition of our land, which was supposed to give everyone their due share, had robbed all of us of our happiness and peace of mind. India and Pakistan were twins but never at peace with each other, permanently suffering the pain of separation, desperate to reunite but always doubting each other's intentions. I reflected that if there had been no Partition, Aijaz and I would have been the best of friends, Abba would have lived in Delhi with us, I wouldn't have been involved with Brij Behari's murder, nor transformed into a pigeon. I held Jinnah and Nehru responsible for my becoming a pigeon, besides all the other problems faced by my country.

As a free bird, without a master, I had the advantage of sleeping anywhere. That night I made the mistake of resting at the mosque. At the shrine of Daata Sahib, no one touched the pigeons, but here the 'chirimaar', the birdcatchers, had put up their nets and being new to life as a pigeon, I got my foot entangled in one of them.

The birdcatcher was a ferocious man with a big moustache and a booming voice. He rightly thought that he had captured a bird worth thousands of rupees. He immediately put me in a dirty bag with some other pigeons. He took us to a house in the famous Hira Mandi, the mohalla of dancing girls. The man's name was Katta Khan. He was basically a seller and buyer of human flesh, a pimp and a procurer of young girls from the poor, remote areas of Punjab and Afghanistan. Bird-selling was his part-time business. He handed over the other two common pigeons to a fat woman, whom he addressed as Janu, to be cooked for his evening meal, and told her not to touch his golden Shirazi.

'Janu, this kabootar is more precious than your most beautiful Gulabo Jaanum. Don't even think of cooking it, I will get a big price for it,' he told the fat painted woman.

'Oye, are you mad? Who will give you good money for this kabootar?' the woman admonished Katta Khan in a loud voice. 'You bring a new gori-chitti young girl and I will easily sell her for the first night for five thousand rupees. But you, Kutta Khan, you bring a kabootar every day instead of a kabootri.'

'Haramzadi, my name means katta, the gun, and not kutta, how many times do I have to tell you. Next time I get a virgin flower, I will give her to Munni Bai and not to you,' Katta said angrily.

The woman laughed and crudely kissed the man on his dirty cheek, pulling his moustache. 'Hai hai, you don't like me calling you a kutta, but you are my darling dog. I will call you kutta a thousand times.'

I realized that I was in one of the famous kothas of Lahore. The woman put me in a cage, where I could hardly breathe. The two other pigeons, common rock doves, were immediately slaughtered and washed for cooking. I heard their painful cries as they were killed and realized that if Katta did not find a buyer for me soon, I would face the same fate. I had wanted to die, but now I wanted to live, even as a pigeon. You value life only when death looks you in the eye.

For the next twenty-four hours, I didn't get any water or food. Janu Bai had only one use for pigeons; she was waiting for an opportunity to slay and cook me. The following afternoon, someone opened my cage and pulled me out. It was a young girl. 'What a nice kabootar, give it to me, Amma Jaan,' she said to Janu Bai.

'That fool Kutta wants to sell it for thousands of rupees. Give it some water and bread crumbs, otherwise it will die and I won't hear the end of it from him.'

The girl, whose name was Shagufta, came like an angel to save me. She not only gave me water and food, but took me to her small room. She loved birds and talked to me constantly, telling me all about herself. She had been kidnapped from a small village in Afghanistan and brought to this kotha by Katta Khan. She was fifteen and had her initiation, or nathutrai, last year. She proudly told me that she had fetched three thousand rupees for her virginity, which was auctioned and bought by a very old landlord of Punjab. Like many men, he too believed that he could regain his virility by having sex with a young virgin. The normal rate for a young, fair girl like her was only fifty to hundred rupees per session. Shagufta told me all this as if I was an old friend. The good thing was that her room had a window, covered with wire netting, through which we got some fresh air.

In the evening, Shagufta got ready to receive her first customer. Normally, she disposed of seven to ten customers each night. He was a fat middle-aged shopkeeper, who it seemed had not had a bath for months. My chance to escape from the room and that horrible human smell came while they were busy going at it. I was trying to navigate my way out of the small passage of the kotha, when Janu Bai saw me and shouted, 'Catch it, catch it, Kutta will kill me if that kabootar escapes.'

Many hands moved to catch me. I nearly escaped but someone got hold of my tail and snatched away a handful of feathers from it. I was put back into that hellhole of a cage. I knew that it would not be possible for me to fly till my tail feathers grew back.

Katta Khan came in the morning with the good news that he had found a great connoisseur of pigeons who was ready to pay a handsome price for me. I was cleaned up and brushed, although he was not happy that I had lost a few feathers. He put me in a basket and got into a tonga to deliver me to the pigeon-racer.

I was happy to get out of that hellish place. I also knew that a connoisseur of pigeons would give me the freedom to fly and I would have a chance to escape and return to my father's house.

The tonga stopped and I was taken up many stairs. From the sounds I could make out that I was on a terrace with a big flock of pigeons. Katta Khan pulled me out of the basket and placed me before my buyer.

Azizuddin Khan looked dashing in a dark striped suit. He was looking at me and smiling like a child who had got back his favourite toy. Suddenly, there was the sound of something moving very fast in the air and then a loud crash. Kutta Khan had fallen from the chair he was sitting on, such was the force of my father's slap. The moustached pimp had been expecting praise for his effort, not a blow.

'Haramzade, bastard, you have brought my own pigeon to sell to me?' Azizuddin was livid with anger. 'How dare you? Get lost before I break your legs.'

The big burly Pathan was trembling like a leaf. With a great effort, he stood up and ran down the stairs with Aijaz and a few servants following him and throwing a few more punches at him.

Abba picked me and looked at my broken wings. 'Not much damage, you will be fine in a few days'. He paused and added, 'I think I'll call you Shiraz, the name I gave to my younger son.'

There was some strange force bringing me back to him again and again, and reminding him of me when he looked at the pigeon.

He handed me over to Aijaz. 'Take good care of this pigeon and make a video of it as soon as it recovers. I want to send the video to some of the European collectors to see if it is a new, improved version of a Shirazi and if they have seen a golden bird like it before.'

'Abba, this Shirazi doesn't behave like a pigeon, I have found him following me around like a dog, which a pigeon never does,' Aijaz complained to our father.

Azizuddin laughed. 'Maybe I have employed him to keep an eye on you. Pigeons have always been great spies, from the time of the pharaohs to the CIA and MI6.'

'Why do you want to keep an eye on me? What have I done?'

'You have not been attending college; you have been visiting cheap motels with cheap girls. I am getting reports from different quarters.' Azizuddin looked at Aijaz disapprovingly.

'You have been spying on your own son? And don't call my friends cheap.' Aijaz's voice rose in anger.

'Don't forget that you are the son of a well-known minister. The media and police informers see you and report on you from time to time,' Azizuddin said in a conciliatory tone. 'I want you to concentrate on your studies. You are my only son, and I want you to go to England for your higher studies.'

Abba went back to Islamabad the next day. He couldn't stay long in Lahore as he was in a political tussle with the foreign minister, Zulfiqar Ali Bhutto. At the breakfast table, I heard him tell Aijaz that Bhutto, with his populist ideas and mercurial nature, was pushing President Ayub Khan towards disaster. He had led Pakistan into a war with India in 1965, with disastrous results. Now he was looking for a new adventure.

Azizuddin was trying to educate his son about politics, but the latter was not interested in anything that required his attention for more than a few minutes.

Since I could not fly, I was not put in a cage and had a free run of the house. I spent most of the day on the window sill of Aijaz's room when he was at home, or in the kitchen, where the chief cook Samad mian, an eccentric old man, used to listen to All India Radio on his small transistor. He was from Lucknow and made wonderful kebabs. He hated Pakistan and abhorred the crude ways of the other Punjabi servants. He had worked at my Nani's house in Delhi and still talked about her all the time. And he cursed Pakistan to irritate the other servants. I loved to sit on the big kitchen window sill and listen to AIR and to Samad talking about the good life in Delhi and Lucknow. I wanted some news about Ammi and Nani, but the radio only informed me about Indira Gandhi, the prime minister, and her problems with Morarji Desai, her deputy and an adversary. AIR frequently played the songs of Lata Mangeshkar and Mohammed Rafi; it was a pleasure listening to them singing together and letting the Pakistanis know that Hindus and Muslims could still sing a duet together, in spite of the bitterness of Partition. The Punjabi servants hated Samad for praising Lata, India's melody queen, and criticizing Noorjahan, the nightingale of Pakistan. But the kitchen was Samad's domain and no one was allowed to listen to any Pakistani channel on his radio.

During this time, I became quite close to Aijaz. For the first time in my life I had the chance to be with my brother, and I wanted to learn as much about him as I could. In any case, I had nothing better to do than follow him around. I wished that I could communicate my thoughts to him. He had reformed a little after being admonished by Abba. He preferred to drive a car to college, instead of his monstrous motorbike, and had stopped taking his girlfriends to the guest house.

He had also got used to my presence and talked to me about his day in detail. 'You understand all that I tell you. I think you are some kind of a jinn and not a pigeon. Anyway, I like your company; you are the first pigeon to understand me. You are not dumb like the other birds.'

Aijaz wanted to play for Pakistan but more than that, he wanted to be a Hindi film star. He was a great fan of Dev Anand and used to argue with Samad, who thought that Dilip Kumar was the best actor in the world.

Aijaz had a vast wardrobe and loved to dress up. His suits and jackets came from London and Paris. I realized that Pakistanis manufactured hardly anything. Everything came from Europe or USA.

Sitting on the branch of a tree in the big lawn of his college, I used to watch Aijaz gossiping with his friends. All the girls of the college had a crush on him and he enjoyed the adulation. The only girl who never paid any attention to him was a Parsi girl, Scheherazade. She was from one of the richest families of Pakistan. She was beautiful, with an hourglass figure and a sharp mind, a serious girl who wore no make-up but still looked pretty. She was not impressed by Aijaz's good looks or by his cars. She lived in her own world, unmindful of her surroundings. In a way she was the biggest challenge in Aijaz's young life.

Occasionally, he talked to me about Scheherazade. He felt that she was too arrogant and thought too much of her rich parents. He said he didn't find her attractive. According to him, she was unsocial and a bookworm. I could see that he was infatuated by her. He was not used to being ignored by pretty girls, and his ego was hurt. If I was not a pigeon, I would have laughed at him.

His desire for Scheherazade often reminded me of my Anu. How was she, how was she being treated by her husband? Had he succeeded in forcing himself on her? I knew that no Indian wife could resist a husband's advances for too long.

One day I was happy to see that Aijaz had succeeded in persuading Scheherazade to have coffee with him at a restaurant on the Mall. I watched them from a distance and was surprised to find her laughing at Aijaz's jokes. She was no longer the serious, reserved girl she was in college, and was chattering away without any inhibitions. I could see that Aijaz had made a good impression on her and she let him drop her near her house.

I was happy for Aijaz but also worried that this could end in disaster like my affair with Anu. Parsis were conservative people and did not encourage their girls to marry outside the community. The only silver lining I could think of was that the founder of Pakistan, Mohammad Ali Jinnah, had also married a Parsi girl.

Abba came home after a month. He was happy to find that Aijaz had been attending his classes regularly, but he seemed to be upset about something. Later that day, he called Aijaz into the big garden behind the bungalow. With his hand on his shoulder, he told him that he had something important to tell him. I sat on a branch above them, trying to listen to their conversation.

'Your mother has remarried. She has married an English gentleman. I heard the news only yesterday.' Abba sat down on a bench under the tree. Now I could hear them more clearly.

Aijaz was quiet for some time, trying to absorb the news, and then he said, 'She is not my mother; I have no mother. In fact, I have no father, no brother. I am all alone in this world.'

'Don't say that, my son. I have always loved you. Maybe I have been too busy with politics. I should have given you more time, but I have always cared about you.' Abba tried to hug Aijaz, but he pushed him away.

'She left me and took Shiraz with her, she never loved me. Why did my mother choose Shiraz and leave me with you?'

I could hear the anguish in my brother's voice. I wanted to tell him that it was not true; she loved him as much as she loved me. It was just a coincidence that he went with Abba to Lahore and I remained with her in Delhi. It could just as easily have been the other way round. I wished I could embrace my brother and cry with him at this irony of fate.

'Aijaz, it is our fate, we are just pawns in its hand. Your mother loves you as much as she loves Shiraz. It was circumstances that separated us.' Abba was silent for a moment and then he said, 'We did not understand at that point what Partition meant. We thought we would travel between India and Pakistan at will. We never thought that it would divide our love for each other, that the two countries, born of the same womb, like twins, would become enemies. We were so naive in those days, my son. I am sorry. I have always missed Shiraz, as I know your mother has missed you every moment of her life.'

'What about Shiraz? Has he been found? Is he still alive?' asked Aijaz.

'No, your grandmother has been calling me. She thinks he is somewhere in Pakistan, but we have no information about him.

I wish he would come here, and then you two could be together. I would leave politics and we could all live together somewhere outside Pakistan, maybe in London or Dubai.'

They sat in silence for some time, lost in their thoughts, listening to the chirping of the sparrows and parrots. I wanted to join them and share my feelings with my brother and father. It was another irony of fate that I was so near and still so far away from them. I concentrated hard and tried to connect with my brother telepathically.

Suddenly, Aijaz spoke. 'I have this strange thought sometimes that my brother Shiraz has turned into a pigeon and has come to live with us. I feel a very peculiar connect with this golden Shirazi, as if it's telling me something.'

'Yes, it's very strange, my rational mind can't explain it either. You know why I named your brother Shiraz? He looked like a small pigeon at birth and I loved Shirazi pigeons, so I named him after my favourite pigeon.' Abba laughed.

'Do I look exactly like him, Abba?' asked Aijaz.

'You are identical twins. Even I could not distinguish between you two, only your mother could. Even when you were two years old, only she knew who was Aijaz and who Shiraz.' Abba was smiling, lost in his memories.

Sitting on the branch of that tree, I could feel a filial love for him for the first time in my life. I wished Ammi were here too, and we could once again unite as a family. I knew, of course, that it was not possible, She had married Uncle James and I was happy for both of them. I missed them and wanted to fly back to Delhi and see them. But Babur had told me that the solution to my problems lay in Lahore, at the dargah of Daata Sahib. I had to stay on here.

Abba stood up and said, 'The only silver lining is that your mother has gone to London. If you go to London for your studies, you can meet her there.'

Aijaz didn't reply. I knew that he was thinking about Scheherazade. He had no desire to go to London to study, leaving her here in Lahore.

⟡

Abba went back to Islamabad the next morning. I was happy to have had some information about Ammi from him. I knew that with Uncle James she had another chance at happiness, but it meant that she would divide her love between the two of us. All my life I had not had to share my mother even with my father or brother.

I felt emotionally connected with Aijaz for the first time. I could feel his pain, his loneliness, and his feeling of betrayal. He thought that Ammi had decided to abandon him and stay with his younger brother in Delhi. I realized that he hated me for monopolizing our mother. He did not understand the circumstances and compulsions that made her stay back in Delhi. Hindustan was an article of faith for her, it was her mother, her past, her culture, her history, her ancestors, her blood. How could she choose Pakistan over India? In fact, even in India there were very few people who understood the dilemma of Muslims like her.

Aijaz had started to behave quite responsibly and was taking an interest in his studies for the first time. He also experimented with sending messages to Scheherazade through me – the old pigeon mail. It was clearly quite exotic to do this in the age of telephones and Scheherazade was thrilled to receive his love letter on a Sunday morning, as soon as she woke up. I sat on the window sill of her room while she lay sleeping on her bed. When she awoke, she saw me and smiled. I had to virtually hang before her face to make her realize that I was carrying a message in a very tiny tube attached to my foot. I don't know what it said, but she laughed and jumped out of bed. She wrote a message on a small strip of paper and put it back in the tube attached to me. I then flew back to Aijaz. They became so enamoured of this means of communication that they made me fly to and fro the whole day. From that day they communicated more through me than directly, even on days when they met each other. And I must say I enjoyed it much more than anything I had done till then as a pigeon.

I used to fly over Aijaz's car every day when he went out. A couple of times I saw Katta Khan, the pimp, watching him from his big truck parked in a bylane near his house. I thought that he was looking for an opportunity to trap me again. So I kept a safe distance from him.

One day, Aijaz decided to take Scheherazade on a long ride on his Harley Davidson. As he zoomed out of the driveway, I flew overhead and saw a truck suddenly emerge from the bylane and move towards the bike. Aijaz tried to avert a head-on collision and rode his bike on to the unpaved footpath. It hit a lamp post and Aijaz was thrown up with great force. The truck drove away; I had a brief glimpse of Katta Khan at the wheel. There was no one on the road to witness what had happened. I wanted to fly after the truck but flew down to Aijaz instead, where he lay on the road, with injuries all over his body. His helmet had come off and his head was battered. Hearing the sound of the crash, the servants had come rushing out of the house. Someone called the ambulance and the police.

By afternoon, Abba had arrived in a special government helicopter. Aijaz was in a coma, with multiple fractures, and his left lung was damaged, but the worst was the injury to his head. I watched all the activity from the roof of Sir Ganga Ram Hospital. Scheherazade had arrived too, and was sitting alone in the hospital corridor. I went and sat next to her. She picked me up and hugged me; I could see the tears in her eyes. Everyone prayed for Aijaz, but by midnight the doctors had given up. He was announced dead by the morning. Azizuddin was desolate but silent. He had lost both his sons. And I had lost my brother just when I had found him.

I wanted to tell everyone that it was not an accident; Aijaz had been murdered by Katta Khan. The man had finally taken revenge for his humiliation by our father. Everyone thought Aijaz's reckless driving was responsible for the accident. Nobody had seen the truck that suddenly came in his path. The poor boy was being blamed for his own death.

Aijaz was cremated at the Miani Sahib graveyard after Zohar, the afternoon prayers at the Daata Sahib. Azizuddin was a powerful minister and a popular man in Lahore, and the crowd of mourners stretched for miles. Even Bhutto, his adversary, flew down from Islamabad for the funeral.

I could do nothing but fly in circles, first over the dargah, during the Namaz-e-Janaza, and then over the graveyard while Aijaz was being buried. My heart was bursting with sorrow. I didn't know if Ammi had been informed about the death of her first-born. I didn't even know whether she was in Delhi or London.

The Miani graveyard is a vast burial ground where thousands of people have been buried from the time of the Mughals. Many great generals and Mughal princes lie buried here. When everyone had departed after settling my brother in his last resting place, I came down from the gulmohar tree to pray at his grave. The sun had gone down and it was dark, except for a few oil lamps and candles burning on some of the fresh graves. Aijaz's grave was covered with rose petals. I sat on it silently, praying for the soul of my brother. I prayed for my father, who had lost his only son; I wept for my mother, who had lost everything she had lived for, in less than a year. I cried for Scheherazade, who had lost her love at such a vulnerable juncture of her life. I prayed for myself;

I had now lost my brother, with whom I had spent nine months in the close confines of our mother's womb. I wanted to die and be buried along with him.

I was sitting there on that grave, lost in my thoughts, when suddenly I heard the voice of Hazrat Daata Ganj Baksh. 'Shiraz, the time has come. The sacrifice that was required for you to live again has been made. Now go straight to Delhi and pray at the dargah of Hazrat Nizamuddin. You must not stay in Lahore even for a day.'

I trembled like a leaf, feeling the presence of a strong force near me. I tried to fly, but my wings were leaden. I tried to speak, but could make no sound. I fainted, drowning in a sea of darkness. I heard the voice of the saint again. 'One more thing. You are never to reveal to anyone that you, Shiraz, have entered the body of your brother Aijaz. If you break this trust, the curse of your ancestors will forever be upon you.'

It was still dark when I regained consciousness, but a faint light was emerging in the east. It was the sound of the azaan over a loudspeaker from the nearby mosque that brought me out of my slumber. I sat up and, to my surprise, realized that I was not a pigeon anymore. I was in human form but naked, without a stitch of clothing. I tried to stand up, dizzily holding on to a tree, and took a deep breath.

It dawned on me then that I had taken on the form of Aijaz. The great sacrifice that was necessary to bring me back to human form, was the death of my brother. My soul had now entered Aijaz's body and the two of us, divided by Partition, had once again rejoined to be one. I was devastated. I didn't want my human form back at this cost. But things were beyond my control. The moment I opened that golden box at Humayun's Tomb, the powerful spirits of Genghis, Timur and Babur had taken over. I was a mere puppet in the hands of unseen cosmic forces.

I looked around and saw a small house not far from where I stood naked. The front door opened and an old man emerged. He was probably going to the mosque for morning prayers. He left the door open behind him. Hiding behind the bushes, I slowly moved towards the house. The good thing was that there were no dogs in this graveyard – Muslims regard dogs as napak or impure. I peeped into the small courtyard cautiously. A few clothes had been hung out to dry on a string. I moved in quickly, picked up a pajama and kurta, and ran out. I hid behind a tree and pulled on the clothes. Then I sat by the grave of my brother. It seemed untouched, still covered with rose petals. I prayed once more for his soul. I cried for both of us. It was morning now. I stood up and looked for a way out. A number of shoes lay at the door of the mosque. I picked up a pair which seemed to be of my size, put them on, and walked out of the graveyard. I had no money, nowhere to go, and the saint had warned me not to stay in Lahore even for a day. I started walking towards the Wagah border, which I knew was about forty miles away.

۱۳

I wanted to go to Model Town and embrace my father and tell him that his son was alive. I wanted to share his loneliness and pain, but I was afraid of the cosmic forces that had warned me to go straight to Delhi. These forces had conspired to make ordinary mortals like Genghis, Timur and Babur into world conquerors. They rose like a storm from the deserts of cold mountains to build extraordinary empires because the cosmic forces had combined to make them invincible. Today, the same forces had conspired to play with me and the fate of my family. I didn't know what else they had in store for me. But I was terrified of them and was keen to follow their command to the last letter. I wanted to go back to my beloved Delhi and to Ammi and Nani. I had no passport, no identity and no money. It had been easy to fly into Pakistan as a pigeon; it was difficult to go back in human form. I decided to risk a visit to my father's house. Perhaps I could find something amidst Aijaz's belongings that would help me.

Silence hung over the house like a shroud. Abba had returned to Islamabad after the funeral. I entered through a side door and went up to Aijaz's room on the first floor. Opening his wardrobe, I picked out a smart woollen jacket, trousers and shoes. I changed from my kurta pajama into the Western clothes and looked at myself in the mirror. I saw a handsome and elegantly dressed gentleman. I searched the drawers and found not only Pakistani money but a few hundred pounds sterling. My brother's passport lay casually in a drawer.

I came down and peeped into the kitchen. There was nobody about, no servants either; everyone, it seemed, was mourning the death of the prince of the house. I was famished, as though I had not eaten for days. I opened the fridge and found a half-eaten tandoori chicken. I put it in a plastic bag along with a few naan, and an unopened box of sweets. Then I went out into the back lawn. It was still very early in the morning and since there was no one to attend to, the servants were taking it easy. I sat on a bench behind a bush and ate the cold food. I had to get out of Lahore quickly but, before doing that, I had an important task to perform.

I hired an autorickshaw and went to the shrine of Daata Sahib. After praying there, I felt a little lighter. I walked down to the infamous Hira Mandi then. It was not difficult to find Jaanu Bai's kotha. I was in luck; Katta Khan's truck was parked outside, and he was asleep in the back. The lane was deserted. In this locality, people slept in the day and celebrated the whole night.

I nudged Katta to get him to open his eyes. He was a light sleeper. He came awake immediately and looked at my face. His mouth opened but no sound emerged: he was looking at the ghost of the young man he had murdered only a day before. I smiled at him, enjoying the terror in his eyes. He was shivering, lying there on the floor of the truck, paralysed with fear. I took out the sharp knife I had picked up from the kitchen in my father's house and put it to his throat. He snapped out of his paralysis and sat up. That was enough for the blade to cut through his larynx. I left him bleeding with the knife still in his throat and walked away. I knew that if I had left Lahore without punishing my brother's killer, I would have never forgiven myself.

As a pigeon I had learned how to look for directions in Lahore. I went to the bus stand and took a bus to the Wagah border.

In the bus, a short, thin fellow who looked like an emaciated monkey came and sat next to me. His name was Akbar. In this part of the world, strangers start talking to each other without any introduction.

'Sahib, going to Wagah?' he asked me in a reedy voice.

'Yes,' I replied curtly.

'And from there, to India?' He laughed.

I kept quiet. He moved closer to me and said conspiratorially, 'Sahib, paar jaana hai? Do you have a visa? I go across every week for my business.' He smelled of cheap cigarettes.

'What is your business?' I asked.

He laughed and said, 'Sahib, my business is my business; tell me about your business. Are you escaping from Pakistan? I can help. It will cost you only a few hundred rupees.'

It was strange how this man sitting next to me knew exactly what I wanted. It was a narrow road full of potholes, and the rattling of the old bus caused my head to hit the ceiling every few minutes. There was a long row of trucks at the border, waiting to cross over into India. Akbar told me that I could hide in one of these trucks and get across. It would cost three hundred rupees each for the Pakistani and Indian customs police and a hundred for the truck driver.

'What will you get out of this?' I was still very suspicious of him.

He laughed like a child and clapped his hands. 'I will get across free, riding on your shoulder.'

I had no option. I wanted to get across at the earliest. So I decided to take the risk.

In the truck, I was made to hide behind some boxes which were carrying almonds from Peshawar for the Indian market. It was suffocating in the confined place. I was worried, not about getting caught, as I had already paid the money, but about getting my jacket spoiled. Once, I had hidden under the seat of a tonga to avoid going to Pakistan. Today, I was hiding again, while running away from Pakistan. That day, nearly two decades ago, my mother was there to give me comfort, but today I was all alone, escaping from an uncertain past to an unknown future.

The truck moved at a snail's pace, stopping after every two minutes. Then I heard some harsh voices. Someone moved the box behind which I was hiding. I looked into the face of a young Sikh. It was a policeman, looking at me with unsmiling eyes. I thought the game was up and I would be arrested or sent back into Pakistan. But the man smiled and winked at me. Putting back the box, he said in Punjabi, 'Everything okay, move.'

The visa had worked and our truck crossed over safely into India. Now we were moving at breakneck speed and I had to brace myself to make sure I wasn't crushed under the boxes. I was dropped at the Amritsar Mandi, the wholesale vegetable market.

I had mixed feelings after entering my beloved India. I felt relieved, but I missed Lahore, the city I had fallen in love with. Old Amritsar reminded me of Lahore and I walked around to get my bearings. I had flown into the city many times as a pigeon, but this was the first time I was walking down the streets of Amritsar. I went straight to the Golden Temple.

It was a Sunday afternoon and the temple was full of devotees. As a pigeon, I had sat on the walls of the sanctum sanctorum and listened to the kirtan. Now I found myself standing in a queue; it would take hours to get inside. I decided to sit beside the water tank in the courtyard and listen to the gurbani and watch the flocks of pigeons flying around. I looked around for my friends, my female pigeon admirers, but it was impossible to distinguish one bird from another.

I went to the big hall where langar was being served. It was always an amazing sight, thousands being served fresh, clean and tasty food in such a disciplined manner. I sat down and realized that the person who was serving me was a rich and famous industrialist. Sikhs have this great tradition of serving – what they call karseva. I ate like the hungry man I was. Emerging from the temple compound, I first got a few pounds changed into rupees, and then enjoyed a tall glass of Amritsari lassi at the corner of Jallianwala Bagh, where General Dyer had shot down hundreds of peaceful protestors, at point-blank range.

My train to Delhi was late in the evening. I decided to buy a few gifts for Ammi and Nani; I was going home after more than a year. I also bought a kurta pajama for myself: the Saville Row woollen jacket was making me rather conspicuous.

On the train, I found a seat next to a Sikh family, who offered to share their dinner with me, even though it was not enough for their family of four. Everyone slept, except me. Thoughts of the strange journey I'd undertaken in the last one and a half years crowded my mind. I remembered the words of Daata Sahib and swore that I would keep the secret in my heart forever.

Old Delhi railway station had probably not changed at all from the time when my mother had fled with me on that fateful morning in 1950. It was cold and foggy outside, with hardly any visibility. I took a cycle-rickshaw to Ballimaran. What I really wanted to do was drop in at Katra Neel to see Anu, but I knew she wouldn't be there and, besides, they would have had me arrested immediately. I was aware that an arrest warrant was still out for me, for the murder of Lala Brij Behari. I had bought a cheap muffler at the railway station and I now covered half my face with it, and pulled a cotton Gandhi cap over my head. I sat with my head bowed, not looking at anyone. Anybody looking at me would have thought I was a milkman from a village outside Delhi.

Ballimaran hadn't changed in the year I had been away – the same long line of shoe stores and leather shops, the same Bismillah Hotel, where I had met many great poets and writers. I could smell my favourite nahari. The tonga dropped me inside my mohalla. I was gripped by emotion as I walked towards Nani's house. I felt as if I were returning after decades. Luckily, there were very few people in the lane at that hour of the morning.

I knocked on the door. Someone called from inside, 'Who is there?'

What could I say – the son of the house, the pigeon that had turned into a human, a murderer escaping the law? I myself didn't know who I was: Shiraz, Aijaz, or a cold-blooded killer, a pawn in the hands of cosmic forces.

'Milkman.' I could think of nothing better.

A woman, probably a new servant, opened the door. She had a big pot in her hand, and held it out for me to pour milk in it from my bucket. But I had neither milk nor a bucket. She was annoyed and started closing the door. I immediately put a foot inside and said, 'Where is Nani, I want to speak to her.'

She pushed me back and tried to close the door. Suddenly, I heard Nani's voice. 'Who is there? Let him come in.'

Evidently, Nani still had sharp ears and could recognize a familiar voice. The servant let me in. I was standing in the courtyard of the house where I had spent most of my life. I stood there, looking at the harsinghar tree and Nani's colourful parrots in their cage, and the door of my mother's room, which was locked. The curtain of the sitting room moved and Nani walked in, frail but still erect. She looked searchingly at the familiar stranger with a muffler wrapped around his head.

'Who are you?' she asked.

I removed my cap and the muffler. Nani stood as though turned into stone. Her mouth opened but she could not utter a sound except for a faint sob. I moved towards her and embraced her, sobbing, 'Nani, Nani, I am back, your Sherry is back.' Nani hugged me with a strength I wouldn't have known she still possessed.

She pulled me inside the room, looking around fearfully, and shouted at the servant girl, 'Chunni, lock all the doors. Don't let anybody come in unless I say so.'

I put my head on Nani's shoulder, feeling safe and protected after a long time. She always had that effect on me.

Nani had so many questions for me, and so much to tell me. I didn't tell her the truth because the truth would have been difficult even for Nani, mistress of the jinns, to believe. I lied to her that I had gone to Nepal and had been hiding in a remote village from where I couldn't communicate with anyone.

'Where is Ammi?' I asked her.

'Beta, your mother has gone to London. She has married James. After your disappearance, she was so depressed that I thought it necessary to send her far away from here.'

'But you should have gone with them too,' I said.

Nani laughed. 'At my age, the only place I am comfortable in is my Dilli. I want to die here and not in a strange, cold place.'

'Where is Bundu?' I asked.

'He has become a big laat sahib in London,' Nani informed me happily. 'He has gone with them and is looking after James's race horses. He even goes to advise the queen on her horses. He is a big man in London, no more a mere tongawala.'

'How could everyone have left you all alone in Delhi, when you are so sick?' I said angrily.

I was longing to ask her about Anu, but Nani pushed me into the bathroom and said I must first wash and eat and then she would tell me everything.

After I had changed, Nani brought me a breakfast of halwa-paratha, which I loved. Once I had eaten, she asked me to sit next to her. Taking my hand, she said, 'I have some bad news for you, Shiraz.'

I was nervous. I knew that it must have something to do with Anu. 'Has something happened to Anu?' I inquired fearfully.

'Anu is fine. Aijaz, your brother, whom you never saw, has died in an accident. I got the terrible news only yesterday.' Nani was crying silently.

I couldn't tell Nani that I had seen Aijaz die. I couldn't tell her that I was very close to my brother before his death. I couldn't even tell her that this person sitting next to her was Aijaz with Shiraz's spirit and mind. I wanted to tell her so much but couldn't tell her anything. I behaved as if it was news to me. I hid my face in her lap and cried, both for myself and for my brother.

When I was young, Nani used to say, 'One day you two will be one. Like Hindustan and Pakistan will be one, you two brothers will be together and play with each other.'

How could I tell her that not figuratively but literally, we were one. It was my mind and spirit and Aijaz's body that sat before her.

There was a knock on the door. Nani was terrified that someone had seen me and informed the police, but it was just the real milkman this time.

Nani said there was still a warrant out for me. The real killers had not been arrested and the police still believed that I was the one who had killed Brij Uncle in cold blood. I couldn't stay in my house for long. I had to hide somewhere.

'Nani, I am fed up of this hide and seek,' I said. 'I don't want to run anymore. Let them arrest me. I have not committed any crime. I am sure I will be proven innocent.'

'Beta, things are not that simple. In the present communal atmosphere, after the war with Pakistan, people will believe anything about a Muslim, even when he is proven not guilty. This old woman knows that there is no justice in the world. You must hide till the real murderer is apprehended.'

'That may never happen,' I said. 'How long will I run from the law?'

'No, you will go to London. In fact, one reason I have sent Hina to England is to secure a safe place for you. She also believed that you would not be safe here anymore.'

'I won't be safe anywhere till I am proven innocent of this charge,' I said. 'Nani, tell me about Anu, where is she? Is everything all right with her?'

'That girl is the cause of all your troubles,' Nani said bitterly. 'She has left her husband and lives with her parents in Katra Neel. She has a daughter whom she keeps away from her father in Jaipur – which woman would do that?'

I was happy to hear that Anu had left her husband, but also sad that she was having a difficult time. I knew she hated the Jaipur jeweller; she couldn't have survived with him. How I wished I were a pigeon again. I could have flown to Anu's house unseen and watched her from close quarters, without being caught. I could see her child too. It was obvious that she had been raped by that brute. In India, once married, a woman's body is the property of her husband, for him to do as he likes.

Nani told me that my mother used to call from London every day at around noon. She didn't know as yet about the death of Aijaz. Nani didn't know how to break the news to her.

Exactly at noon, the phone rang. It was Ammi. Nani said, 'Hina, listen, someone would like to speak to you.' She gave the receiver to me.

My head was pounding. I listened to Ammi's voice without uttering a single word. 'Hello, hello, who is there? Please speak up.'

'Hello, Ammi, it's me,' I whispered.

Now it was my mother's turn to be silent. Then she said, 'Oh God, you are back. Allah has heard my prayers. You must come here immediately. I don't want you to stay there even for a moment. I am sending Bundu immediately; he will make all the arrangements to bring you here.'

Nani was worried that I might be arrested before I was able to make my escape to London. Through her underground connections, she had already had a false passport made for me. It had a picture of me with a beard. Now she wanted me to grow a beard as soon as possible so that I could travel to London on that passport. I told her that it would take at least a fortnight for me to grow a passable beard.

'We don't have so much time,' Nani said. 'I want you to go within a couple of days. You had better arrange for a false beard.'

'No, Nani, a false beard could easily expose me. I will wait for a fortnight for my own to grow.'

I couldn't tell her that I didn't want to leave Delhi without meeting Anu.

I didn't have the new phone number for Anu's house, and the telephone directory and inquiry gave me only the phone number of Lala Mukund Behari's jewellery shop, not his residence. Then an old memory floated to the surface of my mind.

When we were young, I used to fly my kite in such a way that it would fall on the terrace of Anu's house. I decided to try the same trick now. I had found some of my old kites in the cupboard in my room. Ammi must have stored them carefully. However, I found that it was no longer easy to do what I wanted. Many high-rise buildings had come up between Anu's house and mine. I couldn't see her roof from my house. There was also the chance that the message would fall into the wrong hands.

The longing to see Anu finally got the better of me, and I went up to our terrace with my kite before dusk. I wrote on the kite, 'Back home. Want to meet.' I knew that she would recognize my handwriting.

I didn't tell Nani what I was doing, otherwise she would have locked the door to the terrace and not let me step out. She had wanted me to hide in a secret underground room in the house till I was ready to go to London. I had convinced her that I would remain behind the high walls of our terrace, and no one would see me.

My red-and-white kite, with its message, soared into the sky. Another kite from some nearby roof tried to follow it for a duel. Normally I would have loved the challenge, but now I avoided it and soared high up in the sky. I aligned my kite in such a way that it would fall at a point where I thought Anu's house was. It was a huge risk, but love can make one blind. My kite fell, and then something pulled it and the string broke.

For hours that evening, I looked at every kite, hoping that one of them belonged to Anu. But no kite came my way. I went back into the house when it grew dark, losing all hope of receiving a message.

I did the same thing the next day, but was disappointed once again. There was no way for me to know if my messages were getting through to Anu. Nani had got it into her head that I should go to either Ajmer or Mehrauli, where she had a vast network of Sufi friends. But I couldn't leave Ballimaran until I had met Anu. I decided that I would take the risk of going to her house, dressed as a milkman.

Late in the evening, when Nani had gone to bed, I was sitting all alone in the courtyard, thinking about my future and what I would do if I was able to escape to England. Suddenly, there was a soft rap on the front door. Chunni went to the door and, without opening it, asked, 'Who is there?'

It was just eight in the evening, but no one visited Nani at that hour. A female voice said, 'Is Nani at home? I want to see her.'

Chunni said, 'Nani has gone to bed, she can't see anyone now.'

'Please tell her I am her niece, Anu. I want to see her urgently,' the voice I would recognize in a million answered softly. I jumped up and opened the door before Chunni could stop me. A woman clad in a black burqa, the kind that was fashionable in those days among young Muslim girls, stood there. I knew it was Anu behind the veil. I pulled her in and immediately closed the door, locked it, and led her towards the staircase. Before Nani could get up, I had taken her to my room on the first floor. She took off her burqa and I saw a beautiful smiling girl, trembling with fear and anxiety. I wanted to embrace her, if it was the last thing I did, but I was not sure if she would respond. She was married and the mother of a child. However, before I could say anything, she rushed forward and hugged me. I stood there, holding her with all my strength, afraid that she would vanish if I loosened my grip. She was touching my face, tracing every contour with her delicate fingers. Her closeness, her smell and her touch sent electric shocks through my body. Her presence was so overpowering that I feared I would faint if I did not move away from her. I pushed her back and took her face in my palms, looking into those enchanting golden eyes. Unlike me, she was smiling.

'Are you mad, Anu? You have put your life in danger by coming here.' I spoke in a whisper. 'Did anyone see you coming?'

Before Anu could reply, there was a knock on the door. Nani wanted to know who was with me. I told her that it was a friend, she need not worry, and asked her to go back to sleep.

'Why shouldn't I worry?' Nani said angrily. 'I worry even in my sleep. Let me meet your friend.'

'I am coming in a moment, Nani, please go to your room,' I replied equally harshly.

I took Anu in my arms, inhaling the intoxicating perfume that emanated from her body.

'I don't have much time. I got your kite, but now kite-flying is forbidden for me.' Anu couldn't resist touching my lips with her fingertips. 'One of my school friends is getting married and I am supposed to be spending the night at her place. I got this burqa from her maid and rushed to your house in the hope that I would be able to see you.'

I kissed her on the lips and, looking into her eyes, asked, 'Tell me about yourself and your child. How is your husband?'

'I have left him. I hate him as much as I love you.' Anu sat down on the only chair in the room. 'Shiraz, I can't be with another man ever, even if he is my husband. I chose you to be my man, the day I met you for the first time.'

I could see the tears in her eyes. 'What about your child? You can't keep her away from her father.'

'He is the only person who knows that he is not the father of that girl.'

'Then whose is she?' I asked, taken aback.

'I did not allow that husband of mine ever to touch me. The poor man was up against a Dilli ki billi, a Delhi cat.' Anu laughed for the first time. 'He knows that he is not the father of Shireen, but he will not tell anyone, to save his dignity and manhood.'

'You call the child Shireen – a Muslim name?'

'Because the father of the child is a bloody Muslim.' Anu was smiling again.

'No, I don't believe it. Don't tell me that Shireen is my ...'

'Yes, Mr Shiraz Khan, believe it or not, you are the father of my daughter. You are the only man I have ever been with.'

I was stunned. 'Do your parents know?'

'No, you are the first person I have told. I wanted to tell you that day, when you came to see me on Holi, that I had missed a period, but things took such a turn after Brij Uncle's murder that I could not tell anyone about it. After that I had terrible bouts of morning sickness and I am sure my mother guessed everything. She immediately got me engaged to that obnoxious jeweller from Jaipur. At first I resisted, but with you vanishing without a trace and me three months pregnant...'

I looked at Anu with wonder and admiration. I had thought it was I who had suffered, but now I saw that Anu had had a much more difficult time.

'Anu, you know I did not kill anyone. Do you have any idea who killed your uncle?' I had more reason now than ever before to prove my innocence. More than ever, I wanted to be free and to see my daughter.

'I have a good idea, but no proof. It has to be someone from my family. I know you are innocent. You couldn't even kill a fly, Sherry.' Anu was holding my hand and I could feel her inner turmoil and anxiety.

Suddenly, there was a rap on the door. I decided to go down before Nani became seriously worried.

Holding Anu by the hand, I led her towards Nani. 'You recognize this girl, Nani?'

'I knew it had to be a girl. You Mughal men have always been silly in love and war. How would I not know this kite-flying girl who has been desperately searching for you for the last one year, calling me every other day?' Nani looked at Anu with affection.

A storm had been building up since the evening and now it had started raining. I was worried about how Anu would return to her friend's house in Bazaar Sita Ram.

'Don't worry, I've told my friend that I might spend the night at Nani's house, if I found you here. She will make sure no one gets to know. In any case, there are so many people in her house that no one is likely to notice my absence.'

I was glad to hear this, but still tense and worried.

Nani kissed Anu on the forehead and said, 'Children, I know you have so much to talk about. Take her to your room, Shiraz. I'll send some food for you two.'

'Just a cup of tea for me, Nani. I am not hungry, I had dinner at my friend's house,' Anu replied.

I took Anu back to my room. She was fascinated by my childhood photographs, which my mother had covered one wall with. I wanted to ask her a thousand questions, but she was busy looking at my pictures and having great fun at my expense.

'You resembled a coconut when you were young. Your brother was a cutie-pie, what is his name?'

'We are identical twins, you silly girl.' How could I tell her that I now lived in the body of my brother Aijaz? 'Forget about my photographs and tell me about Shireen. Where is she right now?'

'So you think you are a father now and want to see your child? How can you be sure it's your child?' Anu was still in a mood to tease me.

'I don't give a damn who fathered the child. Any child of yours is my child too. Do you understand?' I wrapped my arms around her and brushed her lips with mine. Anu, I remembered, never hesitated in matters of sex, at least with me. She bit my lips gently, before embracing me passionately.

I hadn't locked the door and in Ballimaran there was no concept of privacy; no one knocked before entering. I knew I should push Anu away, but I didn't want to hurt her. Luckily, Chunni did knock on the door before entering. She saw what was happening and was all smiles. She had brought some vegetable pakoras and hot gaajar ka halwa. With the rain pouring outside, there could be no better sight than a plate of fresh hot pakoras. Anu hugged Chunni and said, 'I love pakoras, Chunni, but don't come again till I call you.' With that, she pushed the girl out of the room and shut the door.

'Girl, do you have no shame or fear? What will she think?' I said, embarrassed by her behaviour.

'She will be happy to know that I am serving her master much better than she ever could,' Anu replied, trying to speak with a hot pakora in her mouth.

Anu might be a mother, but she was still like a child, a girl of eighteen. I myself was hardly twenty, but circumstances had matured me beyond my years.

Taking a sip of hot, sweet masala tea, Anu said, 'You have changed, Shiraz. You taste different, you smell different, and you feel different. You are not my Shiraz, you are a different man.'

I was speechless for a moment, thinking that Anu had discovered my secret, but then I recovered and laughed at her. 'Who am I then? Am I the ghost of Shiraz? Or a ...'

'I am serious, I am not joking. Your mouth tastes very different,' Anu cut me short. 'I feel like I am kissing a different man. Your muscles under my fingers feel different too. Does this happen when one goes through a trauma, I wonder.'

I wanted to tell her that she was right, I was a different man. She was making love not to me, but to my brother Aijaz. But that was a secret I had to carry to my grave.

Anu finished her tea and came back to hug me. She kissed me passionately, then loosened the string of my pajama and said, 'Let me taste you there and then I'll tell you how different you are.'

In no time we were joined together, hungry for each other, wanting to forget all that we had gone through in the last eighteen months. It was more of a spiritual and emotional hunger we fed that night, than a physical one.

Once the hunger was quenched, we were at peace and ready to talk. It was still raining intermittently. I couldn't believe that I was lying next to my Anu, making love to her. She was running her fingers through my hair and it was making me extremely sleepy, but I resisted. We both knew that we would not get a chance to be together like this for a long time to come.

'Once or twice, when I was with my husband, I almost let him have his way, thinking that it would legitimize my pregnancy, but at the last moment I felt so revolted that I threw him off. Anyhow, within a few months, I came back to Delhi with the news that I was pregnant. Among the lalas, it's common for a girl to give birth in her mother's house. Since then I have not gone back. Ramesh, my husband, knows that Shireen is not his child, so he is not keen to take me back. Luckily I had a daughter, so his parents are not keen to have her either. If it had been a boy, they wouldn't have left me in Delhi even for a day. They would have claimed the ownership of their grandson.'

'How come your parents let you call the baby Shireen, didn't they object to a Muslim name?' I asked.

'Her official name is Sheila and my parents call her by that name, but I call her Shireen. You know the film *Shireen Farhad*? I watched it during my pregnancy and decided that if I had a boy, I would call him Farhad and if a girl, she would be named Shireen,' Anu explained.

'When can I see Shireen? Where is she right now?'

'I have a very nice servant girl, Shanti, who takes care of her much better than I ever could. You know I have rejoined college and am now in the second year, economics honours, at your old college,' Anu said. 'I leave Shireen with Shanti when I go to college. Sarla Didi, the communist leader, helped me join Delhi College.'

'You didn't answer me. When can I see my darling daughter, and can I tell Ammi and Nani about her?'

'No, don't tell them yet. Sunita's wedding is after three days, on Sunday. I'll be spending a lot of time at her house – my mother knows that she is my closest friend. I'll bring Shireen the day after and then sneak away in my burqa to your house. But don't tell Nani that it's your child,' Anu said.

We talked and made love the whole night. She left before the morning azaan, protected by her burqa. I wanted to escort her, but she said that would make her much more conspicuous and I might be seen by the neighbours.

In the West, I am frequently told that Indian women are shy and submissive. I, however, grew up surrounded by women who were fiercely independent – like Anu, Nani, my mother. I believe that if they had been born in any Western country, they would have been great social or political leaders. But even living where they were, their ability to stand up to society and not be treated like sheep was amazing. I think, in those years immediately after India's independence, there was an atmosphere of liberation and enlightenment. Ballimaran and Chandni Chowk were home to several visionaries, who spread the message of a new age of equality, rationality and freedom from dogma. Hasrat Mohani, the founding member of the Indian Communist Party, Aruna Asaf Ali, the star of the 1942 Quit India Movement, Sarla Gupta, the young trade union leader, and young poets and artists like Husain, Gulzar, Josh and Habib Tanvir, all used to gather here and thought of themselves as part of an enlightened age.

Ammi called from London the next morning. 'Bundu has got his tickets, he will reach Delhi on Sunday and then you may return with him in a few days. I am counting every minute till I see you, my dear boy.'

'Ammi, it will take at least ten days for my beard to match the photograph in the passport. I too am longing to see you, but there's no option. We'll have to wait.' I couldn't tell her I was also waiting to see my little daughter.

I sat at the window of the second-floor room of our house, from where I could see the lane. Watching from behind the curtain, every woman in a burqa, old or young, thin or fat, appeared to me like Anu on her way to meet me. In the evening, she called to say that she could not get out and would try to come the next day. I went to sleep after that and dreamt of my daughter the whole night.

Next morning, I didn't have to wait long. Soon after I awoke, I saw Anu walking down the lane. Even in her black burqa, covered from top to bottom, I could tell that it was my girl. I rushed down the stairs and asked the servant to open the door. Nani was having her morning bath. A moment later, Anu was standing in the courtyard, holding a little bundle of pink in her arms, looking at me with those golden-brown eyes. I rushed to her and took the little girl in my arms and kissed her on both cheeks. She looked just like Anu. I saw nothing of myself in that face, except perhaps the curve of the upper lip.

There was a peculiar glow in my chest, a dizzy feeling of happiness. I sat down in the cane chair, under the harsinghar tree, holding my daughter in my arms and looking at her face. She was getting irritated with all this kissing and cuddling by a stranger and her face was puckered up to cry.

Nani came out, looking curiously at me and the child. 'Who is this little doll?' she inquired with a smile.

'Oh, she is Anu's daughter, Shireen,' I said, a little embarrassed.

'Anu's daughter? Let me look at her, give her to me,' Nani said. Anu was still standing, wearing her burqa, looking at this scene of her daughter meeting her father and great-grandmother for the first time. Her eyes were wet with tears.

'She is the carbon copy of her mother. Shireen is indeed

shireen. You know that shireen in Persian means very sweet?' Nani took out a ten-rupee note and put it in Shireen's little hand, as the 'munh-dikhai'. I then went to my room and fetched a five-rupee note and put it in Shireen's hand.

'I don't see any likeness of the father in this child,' Nani said. She was smiling, but for a moment my heart stopped, thinking she had guessed the truth.

Anu didn't have much time; she had to return home with the child in an hour. I played with Shireen, trying to retain as much as possible of the child's image, because I knew that I would not be able to see her very soon again.

Bundu arrived from London the next day. He was wearing a smart suit, an overcoat and an expensive hat. He had learned fast and changed into a sahib, but for me he was still Bundu Chacha. He had booked our tickets for London on a British Airways flight for the following Sunday. I had seven days left in Delhi.

Before leaving, I had to meet Emperor Babur at Humayun's Tomb. He had not appeared in my dreams even once after I had returned. Luckily, the following Thursday was also the fourteenth night of the moon, when the ghosts of the Mughal kings roamed around Humayun's Tomb. Nani went as usual to Nizamuddin, with Bundu accompanying her. I went earlier in the day, unknown to her, disguised as a gardener. I took a seat-sharing tonga for one rupee from Delhi Gate to the dargah of Hazrat Nizamuddin. It was from here that the strange story of my metamorphosis had begun and now I was back in the same place, listening to the qawwali of Hazrat Amir Khusro. Sitting there in the courtyard in front of his mazar, I prayed to him and to all the Sufi saints to help me out of this ordeal so that I could unite with Anu and my daughter Shireen.

There were several flocks of pigeons in the courtyard of the shrine. They were believed to be the good spirits of human beings.

I fed them, wondering how many of them were humans like me, turned into pigeons. I could not look at any bird, especially pigeons, in the way I used to earlier.

I saw Nani enter the courtyard with Bundu, leaning on his shoulder, but watched them from a distance. Today, I was not dressed as a man from an affluent family but as a poor gardener, in a dirty old pajama kurta and a torn cap. I walked down to Humayun's Tomb, across the road from the shrine. I knew that the gardeners and watchmen there had been told that I might come by sometime and if they gave any information about me to the police, they would be rewarded. I went in from a side entrance in Nizamuddin East, keeping under cover of the bushes. I saw Nani enter the vast garden of the tomb from the main gate. A close watch was being kept on her movements too: the police thought she was the key to my arrest. They held her responsible for my escape but could not arrest her as she was very well connected. Even Indira Gandhi, like her father before her, was fond of her and the police knew Nani could seek her help if required.

Nani went up the huge red stone platform on which the tomb was placed. She prayed at the grave of Humayun and left only when it became dark and the full moon had emerged from behind the tomb. The guards were herding everyone out of the mausoleum. I hid myself in one of the secret alcoves. The good thing was that the guards were terrified of ghosts and stayed far away from the tomb on fullmoon night. As the darkness spread and the bright moon climbed the sky, there was total silence except for the sound of a few parrots flying overhead and jackals crying in the jungle behind the tomb. I went up to the grave of Humayun and his queen, Hamida Begum, to offer fatiha. I was afraid of humans but the fear of ghosts and jinns had totally evaporated from my mind.

I waited patiently for Babur to emerge and answer my

questions. Sitting there on the bench in front of the tomb, I gradually fell into a deep sleep. It was Emperor Babur who woke me up. 'Get up, young man, this is no time to sleep, you have to go very far.'

'You will not let me rest in peace anywhere. How long are you going to test my patience and endurance?' I said.

Babur laughed. 'Your trial has just begun. I had to endure the trials, defeats and betrayals for decades, before I could rest a moment. Those who are chosen to lead have no time to rest or complain. Today, you are the chosen one, but first you must prove yourself.'

'I have no desire to lead or to prove myself. I want to live a simple life. Because of you I have suffered for the last eighteen months. And it's back to square one. I'm still running from the law, still facing murder charges,' I said bitterly.

'But you had a great adventure in the last few months. You had a bird's-eye view of the world. You met your brother and were united with him. How many people get to enjoy the life of a bird?' Babur was speaking with a finger pointed at me.

'You call this an adventure? I was turned into a pigeon for no purpose. My brother is dead and I am forced to dwell in his body, and you call this getting united with my brother?'

'You and your brother were one. Your mother was supposed to give birth to one boy, but they were divided on the night of 14 August by some evil forces. You are two halves of one single whole. You were incomplete without each other. Neither is your brother died, nor have you vanished. The fact is that you have merged into each other. We Mughals are here to unite this land, not to divide it.' Babur spoke as if from a pulpit.

'I don't know what you are talking about – Aijaz and me, or India and Pakistan. Just tell me how I can help myself. Is my escape to England going to save me?' I asked the emperor.

'Nothing is going to save you. You have to pay the price for the sins of your ancestors.'

'Why should I pay for your sins? Why should we in the twentieth century be sacrificed for the real or imaginary sins of our ancestors?' I asked angrily.

'If you want a simple life, I can turn you back into a pigeon and you can lead the uncomplicated life of a bird. As a human being, you have to pay a price for everything, even your birth, which was not in your control. Tell me what you want, you will never get another chance like this,' Babur said in a challenging voice.

'As if I have a choice. You know very well that I want to live with my daughter and I can't do that as a bloody pigeon. I want a solution to my predicament as a human and not as a pigeon,' I said.

'Then pay the price. You will be punished for a murder you did not commit. Learn to face life as it comes and you will be a true successor to your Mughal ancestors.'

Saying this, Babur vanished, leaving me all alone in the cold winter night. I opened my eyes but could see nothing. There was fog all around. Even the massive tomb was swallowed up by the dark thick fog. Shivering, I walked out into the darkness, trying to find a way out of this mess I was trapped in. Babur had once again left me without an answer or a solution.

۱۴

I left for the airport on Sunday evening, two days after my encounter with Babur. Bundu had given the responsibility of driving me to Palam Airport to a reliable Sikh taxi driver, Sukhvinder Singh. He himself was travelling separately, to reduce the risk of being caught. We were to behave as complete strangers when we met at the airport. I was travelling as Tameez Ahmed, an electrician from Old Delhi, with an appointment letter from a hotel in London. Our flight was at 11.30 p.m., but I reached the airport by 8.30. A number of Sikh farmers were travelling on the same flight. They could not speak a word of English but were migrating to England to work in the factories there. Their presence gave me some confidence. I only had a small bag with a few clothes. The girl at the British Airways counter smiled at me and asked in Hindi if I was travelling by air for the first time. I told her that I would be seeing a plane for the first time in my life. She told me not to worry, there were many others like me and I would be helped by the Hindi-speaking airline staff. She handed me my boarding pass with a smile.

I was nervous about facing the immigration officer. He was the real test and the biggest hurdle. There were still a couple of hours for the flight to take off. I found myself a seat in the row of chairs in the lounge and waited for Bundu to show up. He arrived an hour later and went straight to the airline counter. He had travelled to London half a dozen times in the past year and a half, and was an expert by now. He filled up the immigration form and went to the immigration gate straight away. He had nothing to fear. I was not sure whether he had seen me, as he did not once glance in my direction. Once he had vanished behind the counter, I moved towards the immigration queue slowly and reluctantly. I stood behind an old Punjabi woman. She looked at me and said in Punjabi, 'Puttar, travelling for the first time?'

'Hahnji, mataji,' I said.

'Don't worry, I've lived in London for the last thirty years. These angrez are the biggest fools in the world. I can't speak a word of angrezi, still I do double job.'

I smiled at her, waiting for my turn.

The immigration officer was a tall Jat policeman with a surly voice. The old woman was cleared without any fuss. It was my turn now. I was sure that I would be caught. I placed my documents in the small window behind which the policeman sat looking at me with a fixed, accusing stare. He looked at my photograph, then asked me, 'Why are you going to London? Can't you get some work in Jama Masjid?'

'Jama Masjid?' At first I didn't understand what he meant, then remembered that the address given on my passport was an area near Jama Masjid. 'I ... I get more money in London,' I stammered an explanation.

'Money, money, money, you all want money. Okay, go and die in that cold country.' He stamped my passport and then looked at my face. I froze under his stare. 'Why is your beard so small, in the photo it is much bigger?'

'I trimmed it, I am sorry,' I replied.

'So that you look handsome, you want to impress those gori white girls?' He laughed at his own joke and handed me my passport.

Like a bird let out of a cage, I almost ran from there, fearing that he would call me back at any moment. In the immigration hall I saw Bundu sitting on a bench, sipping tea from a paper mug, and rushed towards him. I was so relieved that I forgot his instruction not to come anywhere near him till we were out of London's Heathrow Airport. He looked through me as if I did not exist. Realizing my mistake in the nick of time, I made an about turn and moved towards the farthest corner of the lounge.

My mouth felt dry, as if I had just run a marathon. I drank some cold water from a large cooler in the lounge, which provided free water to the passengers. In those days, to sell water to anybody, friend or foe, was regarded as a sin. There was still more than an hour for the flight to take off. I sat in a corner and watched the other passengers. I wanted to call Nani and Ammi and give them the good news that I had cleared immigration without any hitch and was ready to board the flight. There was a phone on one of the walls in the lounge and one could make a call free of cost, but there was a long queue of people already waiting to use it.

A British passenger who had vacated the seat next to mine had left behind his copy of the *London Times* and I picked it up idly. Uncle James used to get the *Times* regularly, although a week late, when he lived in Delhi. I read it occasionally to improve my English. I was soon absorbed in reading about the political crisis the Harold Wilson government was facing, and didn't notice the two men who came and sat on chairs next to me. One of them nudged me rudely and said, 'What's your name? Show me your passport.'

For a moment I didn't understand what he wanted, but one look at his face and I saw police written all over it. 'Why do you want to see my passport, who are you?' I asked. I tried to sound aggressive but couldn't keep the tremor out of my voice. 'Show me your passport,' he repeated in an authoritative voice. I handed over my passport without any further argument.

'So, an electrician reading the *London Times*,' he said mockingly. 'Come with me.' He literally pulled me to my feet.

I realized my mistake but it was too late now. An electrician from Jama Masjid reading the *Times* was obviously an object of suspicion for an Indian policeman. How could I have made such a silly mistake? I stood up and went with them. I looked around for Bundu but couldn't find him anywhere. I was escorted to a side room, where a few policemen in khaki sat around gossiping and drinking tea. My escort pointed to a chair and told me to sit down.

'Where is the list of fugitives for whom a lookout notice has been issued?' he asked the policeman sitting behind the small desk.

The other policeman handed him a file and he started flicking through some hazy black-and-white pictures. Suddenly, he slapped his partner on the back and said, 'Yes, my suspicion was correct. He resembles the boy who killed that rich jeweller in Chandni Chowk.'

I began to weep. One mistake had shattered my dream of escaping to England and meeting my mother.

'You are Shiraz?' the policeman shouted. I kept quiet but the tears rolling down my cheeks told him that he was right.

I was immediately arrested and confined in a small lock-up at the airport. All my efforts to escape the law in the last eighteen months had come to naught. I thought of Ammi, who would be waiting at the airport for me. I thought of Nani, who had promised all the saints that she would cover their graves with new expensive sheets if her Sherry got to England safely. I thought of Bundu, who would be worried sick, waiting for me to board the flight with him. Strangely, at that moment, I was not worried for myself, only my loved ones. I thought of Anu and my sweet little Shireen. What would Anu think when she heard of my arrest?

There was nothing to sit on, in that dirty lock-up. The floor was sticky and smelled of urine. The stench was nauseating and I had to try very hard to close my mind to it. I stood there the whole night, holding on to the bars. In the morning, the same dark, tall policeman who was called Dharam by his associates came with some other policemen. I was to be transferred to the Chandni Chowk kotwali, where the murder case had been originally registered.

I was handed over to the kotwal, who looked like a decent man. Inspector Ajit Singh let me go to the toilet and wash myself and then offered me a cup of sweet masala tea. He was a middle-aged man with a gentle manner. I requested him to make a phone call to Nani and inform her about my arrest. He pointed to the old black instrument on his table and said, 'Go ahead, make the call.'

I dialled the number with a shaking hand, not knowing what I would tell Nani. Chunni picked up the phone. Hearing my voice, she called out to Nani, who was getting her hair oiled by a masseur who came every Monday morning to give her a massage. Nani took the receiver and asked, 'Sherry, where are you? Have you reached London?"

'No, Nani, I am still in Delhi,' I told her hesitantly. 'I was arrested last night at the airport. I am at the Chandni Chowk kotwali.' I could hear Nani's laboured breathing at the other end; she had developed a mild asthma in the last few years.

'Don't worry, my dear boy. I will come there as soon as I can. I know the kotwal, he will be nice to you.'

Now I knew why Inspector Ajit Singh had been kind to me. Nani always maintained good relations with the police officers at the kotwali. She was one of the most respected women of Old Delhi, and often helped poor people in their dealings with the police. She had also helped the police on many occasions to control the mob when things got ugly, especially in a Hindu–Muslim confrontation.

Inspector Singh said, 'I know your Nani. You come from a

good family. I can't help you, but I'll see to it that you are treated well. Only, you will have to cooperate with me.'

'I will, as much as I can. I have not committed any crime and I have no hesitation in telling you the truth,' I told him honestly.

Nani came with some food and a flask of my favourite Darjeeling tea. The aroma raised my spirits a little and I was able to give her a weak smile.

Inspector Ajit Singh assured Nani that he would do his best to see that I was not beaten up or tortured.

'You ask him to tell me the truth and I will see to it that he is treated leniently,' he told Nani.

'My Sherry always speaks the truth. He has not killed anyone and he has nothing to fear.'

As soon as Nani left, I was handed over to a fierce-looking sub-inspector, Bholanath, who assured me that once I was given the 'treatment', I would sing like a canary. Bholanath was a six-foot tall Thakur, with a big black moustache, a pockmarked face and fierce red eyes. One look at him and it was clear that the man had no compassion in him.

'The most hardened criminals tell me the truth when I make love to them', he said, laughing crudely.

I looked around for Inspector Ajit Singh to save me from this brute, but he was nowhere to be seen. In that dark room, there were a few ropes and pulleys. I was made to sit on an iron chair and my hands were bound with rope to the hooks in the corners.

'You look rather soft for a murderer. Confess your crime and I will not touch you, but if you think you can impress me with these innocent looks, think again. Tell me why you killed the lala,' Bholanath said in a deceptively polite tone.

'I didn't kill the lala, I am telling you the truth.'

Bholanath laughed as if I had told him a joke. 'Tell me what you did with the jewellery you took from the house. Is it hidden somewhere or already disposed of?'

I sat silently, looking at him. Bholanath made a sign with his left hand and a rope was tightened around my chest, under my armpits. He pushed a button and I was suddenly hanging a few feet above the ground. Sitting in his chair, he kicked me in the groin with his heavy leather shoe and a wave of searing pain shot up to every part of my body. I screamed and the brute laughed with pleasure.

'Poor innocent boy. Give him an ice cream and he will confess to his own murder.' He stood up and went out, leaving me with his two, equally sadistic, colleagues. They were like Laurel and Hardy, one short and fat and the other thin and tall.

The short, fat one said, 'Oye chikne, are you still a virgin? How many men have fucked you?' The thin, tall one added, 'By the time I am finished with him, his back hole will be like Delhi Gate, open for all traffic.' They laughed at their own sick joke.

I was terrified. I had never been a very physical person and I didn't handle pain well, but now I was facing the sort of treatment that would make even hardened criminals confess to any crime on earth.

'Please let me go, I am telling you the truth, I did not kill anybody,' I pleaded, but they were busy taking off my clothes. A shiver went up my spine in the December chill. Except for my underwear, I was naked. Hardy was looking like a hungry vulture at my smooth naked body. They pulled in a big tub filled with ice and water. My hands and feet bound, I was placed in this tub. Now I understood what the 'ice-cream treatment' meant. They left me there to freeze. Soon, my back and legs, which were submerged in ice-cold water, became so stiff and the pain so unbearable that I could not stop myself from moaning in agony. At some point I fainted.

When I came to, I saw Inspector Ajit Singh standing above me. He smiled and said, 'I am sorry those idiots do not understand that you are not a hardened criminal, you are from a very important family and you cannot be treated like this.' My body was aching and I was shivering so badly that I could not utter a word. He offered me a cup of hot tea. I wanted to throw the steaming tea on the two-faced bastard's face, but I didn't have the strength to even hold the cup. With an understanding smile, he brought the cup to my lips and said, 'Sip some tea, it will help you to talk.' The slimeball wanted me to confess as soon as possible, to make his job easier. My body was still frozen but my mind was sharper than ever. I understood that they were playing the typical police game of good cop and bad cop. He left me with the cup of tea, waiting for me to recover.

Since court timings were over for the day, they were in no hurry; I was to be presented before a magistrate only the next morning. They had all day and night to torture me and make me confess. In the afternoon, I was taken to the comfortable office of the inspector. He was eating hot pakoras and jalebis from the famous shop of Dariba in Chandni Chowk. He offered me some and I accepted without hesitation. I knew I would have to preserve my strength to survive this ordeal.

'Shiraz beta, now that you have been caught, it is in your interest to give us all the details of your crime.' He spoke in his usual soft manner. 'Tell me, when did you plan this robbery? Where have you hidden the jewellery? Why did you murder Lala Brij Behari? Did you always plan to kill him?'

I smiled and, copying his manner, spoke very calmly. 'Inspector, you may torture me or kill me, but the truth is that I did not kill Brij Uncle, nor did I commit any robbery. Your whole investigation is misdirected.'

For the first time, he lost his cool and shouted at me. 'You idiot, you will know the truth only when you are hanged. I have all the evidence stacked up against you.'

'Then why are you torturing me to confess? Hang me if you have the evidence.' The last few hours had already toughened me considerably.

Before he could say anything, his peon came in to announce that H.R. Anand, the well-known criminal lawyer, was waiting outside to meet me. Inspector Singh jumped to his feet. No one could keep such an influential lawyer waiting.

Anand, who was also a close family friend and came to our house on Eid every year for kebab and sewain, walked in and embraced me.

'Don't worry, my son, I am here. Did they touch you?' Without waiting for a reply, he turned to the inspector and said coldly, 'If you lay a finger on this boy, I'll hit you so hard in the court that you will regret it all your life.'

'How can you even say such a thing, Anand Sahib? You know that we do not indulge in such practices anymore,' the cop said with an obsequious smile. 'Look, I had just got pakoras and jalebis for Shiraz.'

'Beta, I know you are trapped in a very ugly situation, but I will do my best. Don't answer any of their questions unless I am present.' Anand looked at the inspector. 'You may interrogate him only in my presence.'

'Sir, no need for interrogation, our case is all tied up. We only have to recover the stolen jewellery,' the inspector said, pouring some tea for the lawyer.

'There was no robbery, the lala is lying to get the insurance money. This boy has not stolen anything,' Anand said confidently.

I felt something approaching hope for the first time since my arrest. With a lawyer like Anand on my side, it would not be easy to convict me for a crime I had not committed.

I was presented before a magistrate, who gave a two-day judicial remand to the police to interrogate me. With my lawyer watching over me, the interrogation was much more civilized.

Nani's Sikh friends and followers, who lived across the wall in the famous Sisganj gurdwara, sent me delicious food from the langar. The Laurel and Hardy couple, who had been so eager to rape me, watched from a distance, taking out their frustration on other prisoners. They were addicted to torture, and couldn't sleep without hearing the painful cries of their victims.

Inspector Singh wanted to know who had helped me to escape. I told him that I had fled to Pokhra in Nepal and no one had helped me. He was not convinced and planned to send a police team there to verify my claim. How could I tell him that it was Emperor Babur who had helped me fly to Lahore as a Shirazi pigeon? He would have sent me to a lunatic asylum without further ado.

On the third day, I was dispatched to Tihar Jail, the largest prison in Delhi. My lawyer told me that they were charging me under Section 302 of the Indian Penal Code, under which punishment could be death by hanging or, at the least, life imprisonment. There were a number of reliable witnesses who had seen me running away after committing the crime.

Since childhood, I had had the ability to detach myself from all that was happening around me. Now, I watched everything as if it was happening to someone else and I was a mere spectator.

The police van was like a huge black box, dark and suffocating. The small openings, supposed to be windows, were covered with thick iron nets and glass blackened with soot and dust. I tried to peer outside to see my world passing by. We stopped briefly in front of Red Fort and tears came to my eyes at my pitiable condition, I who was one of the direct descendants of the last emperor, Bahadur Shah Zafar. But then I thought of the emperor himself, who had been kept in the basement of the same fort, all chained up, and this gave me some solace and strength.

We passed Chandni Chowk, where I had slept with Anu for

the first time and where she had probably conceived Shireen. There were a dozen other prisoners in the police van. One of them came and sat next to me and asked, 'First time?'

I answered abruptly, 'Yes.' He was a short, thin man in his mid-twenties, with a pockmarked face and long oily hair smelling of jasmine. He was smiling at some joke of his own, or perhaps he was in the habit of always smiling, even while travelling in a coffin-like black van to Tihar.

'Why are you going in?' he asked with a toothy smile.

'Section 302, for the murder of Lala Brij Behari of Chandni Chowk,' I replied brusquely.

For the first time, he stopped smiling and looked at me with respect. In the pecking order of prisoners, those who are charged with murder are at the top. Then recognition dawned on him.

'Okay, you are that Muslim boy who murdered the lala on Holi. Now I remember. I was also in Chandni Chowk, playing Holi and drinking bhang with my Hindu friends, when the riot started.' He spoke as if I was the hero of some great act which he had been privileged to witness. He extended his right hand towards me and said, 'My name is Salim Tota.'

I held his rough hand and asked, 'What is your crime, why are you going in?'

He laughed loudly. 'I go in every six months to sort out my accounts in the jail. You are very lucky that you met me in this van, otherwise tonight would have been the most colourful night of your life.'

'What sort of account, and why am I lucky?'

'Shiraz mian, I know your Bundu Chacha, he was a great friend of my father. You are under my protection now, no one will touch you, otherwise you would have been sodomized by half a dozen bastards.' He laughed again, irritatingly.

Salim looked at one of the prisoners and said, 'Oye Langde,

it's your duty to protect my younger brother here. If anybody touches him, tell them he is mine.'

'Why are you being sent to the prison?' I was still curious about this self-appointed guardian of mine.

'I supply everything inside the jail, from charas to opium to bhang, LSD and angrezi wine. I go in to settle my accounts every six months. If you need anything, tell me.' He laughed loudly and slapped me on my back. 'You are like my younger brother. You want any drug, a girl or a boy, ask me and I will get you anything inside the jail. Outside, I am nobody, but you will see that inside I am the raja. Even the jailor harami salutes me because he gets a hefty purse from me every month.'

Salim was right. I was lucky to have him as a protector. Inside Tihar, you were at the mercy of the powerful prisoners. Homosexuality was rampant, not only among the prisoners, but also among the prison guards. The first night was the worst, when you were kept in a common cell with around sixty prisoners. It was like no-man's land. You had not yet been assigned your barrack, you had not been categorized. You were at the mercy of hardened criminals who liked to choose from the fresh supply of men. Occasionally, there were fights as many laid claim to the same person. In their parlance, I was a new 'chikna', to be tasted by some of the most powerful ustads or bosses. I was terrified by the appearance of these men. They were staring at me as if I were a piece of tandoori chicken left on the street for hungry beggars.

We were first taken to a room where everyone had to take off their clothes and hand them over to the guards. From then on we were supposed to wear only loose, striped prison clothes. Everyone took off their clothes as soon as they entered the room, except me. They were laughing and comparing their dicks. The prison guards were also enjoying the show. I stood there paralysed, unable to get naked in front of this bunch of perverts. A guard hit me with a polished black stick. 'Oye, behanchod, take off your clothes, I can't wait the whole night for you.'

Immediately, Salim came to my rescue. 'Oye, don't touch him. He's my younger brother, he'll wear his own clothes.' Salim looked challengingly at the others in the room, but no one dared defy him.

'One more thing. He's not a gaandu like you bastards, so don't even try to touch him, otherwise I'll slice off your miserable pricks and force them into your own throats. Do you understand?' Salim was not smiling any longer, his voice was cold and commanding.

I realized the extent of perversion there that night. On the chilly December night, everyone was freezing. We were given dirty, smelly blankets full of lice, which I was afraid even to touch. However, most of the prisoners were busy forming partnerships and seducing or threatening the new prisoners. They looked at me with greedy eyes but left me alone. One of them, a big man with red bulging eyes, sat near me and whispered, 'How long will Salim Tota protect you? He will leave after a few days, then you will be mine. You like to suck, or you want my big pole in your tight little ass?'

I was petrified. It was the longest night of my life. Salim was whisked away by the prison officials. Only Langda remained to protect me. He took his job seriously and performed it with sincerity. 'Madarchod, go and suck your own dirty cock, don't come anywhere near this boy', he shouted when someone came too close to me.

After that no one touched me, but I could hear the horrible sounds of a sexual orgy taking place all around me. I tried to close my mind to the sounds and concentrate on what Langda was telling me. To my dismay, he was also known as Timur-Langda, after my famous warrior ancestor, Timur Lang, whom the Mughals had regarded as a greater conqueror than Alexander or even Genghis.

Timur told me that basically he was a thief who also assisted Salim in his business. He had forgotten how many times he had come to Tihar. It was like a second home for him. 'When I want rest, I come here. When my wife becomes a pain in the ass, I come here to relax. Bhai, these women, they are the worst enemies of men, but we love to be fucked by them.' He was very pleased with his comment.

Timur-Langda tried to tell me about burglary and even killing, hoping that one day I would be his worthy disciple. 'Sahib, the best time for burglary is in winter, when men hide between the warm legs of their women. The streets and lanes are empty, the chowkidars and guards also take refuge around a bonfire. I prefer to operate between 3 and 4 a.m., that's the time when sleep is deep and sweet. Even the dogs get tired and go to sleep by that time.'

He was in an expansive mood and wanted to tell me the story of his life. 'Bhai, I was the best thief in Delhi, even the police officers respected me. One winter morning, I entered the house of a doctor. While I was opening the safe in the house, his wife came into the room. She was a few years older than me, and beautiful. I ran away that night, but could not forget her face and her dreamy eyes. Sahib, the best source of information about any family is the street sweeper in the locality. From him I learnt that her husband used to travel a lot. They had no children and she lived alone. Anyway, I entered that house again, when the doctor was travelling. The lady was awake even at three in the morning. She was a sad and lonely woman. As she sat there drinking alone, she looked even more beautiful than I remembered. She got up and suddenly pulled aside the curtain behind which I was hiding. She smiled and said, "Are you the same burglar who came last week? Why do you just watch and not try to rob me of my jewellery?"

'I was speechless. The slur in her voice made it obvious that she'd had far too much to drink. Her big, dark, magical eyes had turned me into stone, unable to move or say anything.'

I listened to him, wondering at how love could change the most ferocious man into a vulnerable boy.

Langda continued, 'She smiled at me and finally I gathered the courage to tell her that her most precious jewellery was her beauty, which I could never take from her. She offered me a drink and I chatted with her the whole night. After that I became addicted to talking with her. I used to go to her house whenever her husband was out. She was a heavy drinker and hated her husband, his money and everything else in her life. She was like a bird in a cage; she wanted to fly away but did not have the courage to do so. I never touched her, nor did she ever encourage me to do so, but she loved to chat with me on those lonely nights. She thought I had a wonderful life, free of any chains or responsibilities. She enjoyed my stories about my adventures as a burglar. One night, I went there and her husband was not only present in the house, he was waiting for me with a gun. A bullet hit me on my leg; I was able to escape but became lame for life.'

I was fascinated by his story. 'What happened to the lady?' I asked.

'Poor girl, her husband divorced her and sent her back to her home town of Bangalore. He called her a whore and a sex maniac, but she never even touched me. Since then I have travelled to Bangalore half a dozen times, but I can't find her. Sahib, I used to visit the prostitutes of G.B. Road at least once a week, but since then I have lost interest in all women. I only want to find my Hema to speak to and worship.'

Timur-Langda proved to be a great teacher and advisor for me in the prison. I wouldn't have survived Tihar without him.

It is not that I did not have my share of problems and fights in the prison. Langda was a great blade-baaz, one who could use blades in a fight very effectively. He provided me with a spoon, with its handle sharpened like a knife. I had not even killed a mouse in my whole life, but I soon found out that jails can turn even the most innocent person into a seasoned criminal.

We were allowed to meet our family members once a week; in jail parlance, it was called 'milai' or meeting. Even this meeting was a farce because the prisoners and their relatives stood on either side of a double-wire mesh, separated by iron bars. There was a gap of a few feet between the two sides. More than a hundred prisoners spoke to a few hundred relatives on the other side, simultaneously. You could barely see the faces of those who had come to visit you, and had to shout to make even a few words audible. It was a frustrating experience, both physically and mentally.

No one came to see me on my first 'milai'. I waited for my name to be announced, and kept waiting till the meeting time was over. It was disheartening. I had waited for this day the whole week. Every prisoner had a fixed day in the week for his milai, so my turn would come again only after a week. I felt as if I would suffocate in those seven days. I thought my life was over, I was either to be hanged or given a life sentence to spend the rest of my days in this hellhole.

Three days later, a prison guard came searching for me; I was being summoned to the head jailor's office. As I entered the room, I saw my lawyer, Anand, and then I noticed Uncle James and Ammi. As soon as they saw me, they all jumped up from their chairs. I went straight to Ammi and she embraced me. We cried silently for a few moments but then she pushed me back and looked at me. 'Sherry, my child, how thin and dark you have become. Please take care of yourself . We will do all that is necessary to get you out of jail.'

Uncle James, who was now my stepfather, hugged me and said, 'We came on the first flight we could get. We are coming straight from the airport, thanks to Anand, who secured a special permission from the courts.'

Bundu had stayed back in London as there was an arrest warrant against him. The police had made him an accessory to the crime: he was supposed to have helped me dispose of the stolen jewellery.

Ammi had brought a box of chocolates for me from London. She handed it over to the prison superintendent, who assured her that I would get to eat one chocolate every day. Of course, I never got to see any.

The court had granted permission for me to be given a blanket, some clothes and books. The surprise gifts were the kites and plain string they had got for me, all due to the efforts of my lawyer. When we were allowed fifteen minutes alone, Anand told me that he had applied for bail and I could be out of jail in a few weeks. I also learned that Nani had been hospitalized after suffering a massive cardiac arrest. Uncle James said that he was taking her to London as soon as possible because she required a heart surgery, for which the newly established All India Institute of Medical Sciences was not fully equipped. I was very upset to hear this and told them to do whatever was necessary to help Nani. They were not to worry about me.

In the prison I was given two jobs that helped me make friends. One was that of a letter-writer for the illiterate prisoners, and the other was as the library assistant, who was also supposed to tutor and help those prisoners who were appearing for various examinations. Soon I was known as 'Chhote masterji', or young master, in my section of the prison, which housed more than 6000 prisoners. It was meant for 2000 men, but had to accommodate three times that number. The biggest problem was the toilets, which didn't have water; the flush system did not work. There were three toilets for 300 men and even these were not cleaned for days together. The stench was so powerful that I could not eat for days but then, humans adapt to all situations. Even now, when I think of it, I feel nauseous. I thought I would die if I didn't escape from the stench and filth soon. The toilet was full of human excreta; one could not sit there without vomiting. I was so terrified of going that I virtually stopped eating. The food, in any case, was not worth eating. The bread was full of small stones; the dal was so watery that you could hardly get anything onto your roti. Chicken was served once a week but it was a small piece of bone floating in watery yellow broth. Only those who were assigned to kitchen work managed to get some decent food.

In my first week there, Lalit Singh, the assistant jailor, offered me the job of his personal attendant, which would have allowed me to use his toilets, his kitchen and his servant's room. He was not only a bachelor but also an unashamed pervert who was always looking for new victims. He said, 'I'll make your life in prison so enjoyable that you'll never want to leave it.' Pinching me on my bottom, he tried to kiss me on the lips, but I pushed him away with such force that he left me alone for some time. This was one men from whom even my friend Langda could not save me. My friends in prison told me that he would be patient but he would get me in the end – even hardened criminals had not succeeded in escaping him, once he went after them. Luckily, some fresh young prisoners arrived and Lalit Singh got busy with them.

What made me popular among the prisoners was my kite-flying ability. I could fly dozens of kites simultaneously. Luckily, the prison superintendent, Mr Patel, a Gujarati, had a great passion for kite-flying. He told me that he had been the champion of Ahmedabad in his college days. Mr Patel got me some kite-making material and organized a kite-flying festival in the prison.

My kite workshop was in the garage of Mr Patel's bungalow. His whole family was passionate about kite-flying. His two children, aged eight and ten, became my fans and assisted me in my work. His wife, Jayanti Ben, also came from a family of kite-flyers and loved to discuss the finer points of kite-flying with me. I started spending a large part of my day in their house, which was adjacent to the prison. I used the toilets in their servants' quarters, which was a big relief, and had lunch in their house.

The kite-flying festival was held with great fanfare. I had made more than a hundred kites, but the problem was that prisoners were not allowed to use manjha, the strong, glass-coated string, for fear that someone might use it to kill another prisoner, or commit suicide with its help. The string provided to us was weak and could break at the slightest pressure. The challenge was to beat your opponent and capture his kite with the help of this fragile string.

My main opponent was a notorious killer and dacoit, Tyagi Pehalwan, who had been a national champion in his younger days. The other was, of course, the jail superintendent.

After the amateurs had had their fun, the professionals entered the field. I had a red-and-blue kite, with Anu written on it. Mr Patel had a green kite and Tyagi a black-and-white one. There were two other professional kite-flyers. They lost to duels with me in just a few minutes. Now began a duel in the skies between Mr Patel and Tyagi. All the prisoners supported Tyagi, while the prison staff and their families cheered their boss. Mr Patel danced around Tyagi expertly and did not allow him to trap his kite. Then, suddenly, his green kite fell on Tyagi's black-and-white one, like a hawk falls on its prey. I knew that Tyagi had lost the battle, but to my surprise it was Mr Patel's kite which got cut, and all the prisoners shouted in one voice, 'Bo kata.' Mr Patel was surprised, but graciously accepted defeat.

Tyagi could change his string and kite for the next duel, but he refused. I was wary of him. He was a man with a bloated ego and a well-organized gang within the prison. He had killed more than half a dozen men, including a police officer. He looked at me with contempt and said, 'Aaja, pilley, aaja. Come, you pup!' His supporters were clapping and jumping around. I had a large number of supporters too, but they were too afraid of the man to show their support openly.

My Anu was soaring into the sky beautifully. It had great balance and was using the air currents as expertly as a Shirazi pigeon. Tyagi did not attack me; he waited for me to come down on him. Suddenly, I saw something shining on his string. It dawned on me then that the bastard had cheated. He had made manjha by grinding glass pieces and mixing them with egg yolk and had polished his string with this mixture. I thought of exposing his trick but realized that it would only make him an even more dangerous opponent. I decided to use my understanding of air currents to my advantage. I had flown in these skies as a pigeon and knew that the air currents had the power to make a car fly if used correctly.

I allowed my kite to fly north of Tyagi's and waited for the right time. His supporters were shouting and taunting me to attack. I waited patiently, letting my kite float. When I felt the pressure of the wind on my fingers, I let my kite move from north to south, filling up all the wind in its wings. The air pressure pushed Tyagi's kite aside, and then Anu took the black-and-white kite in its grip, twisting itself around it and bringing it down, to shouts of 'Bo kata' from my supporters.

I looked at the string of Tyagi's kite, then picked it up and gave it to Mr Patel. Tyagi stood there, shouting at me and challenging me to a bout of wrestling; he was orginally a wrestler from Meerut. I had no intention of getting my bones crushed, so I declined his offer. Mr Patel hugged me and said, 'I realized that he had cheated and wanted to warn you, but you know how to take care of your kite. By the way, who is this Anu?'

I smiled shyly and he understood. Next day, he let me use his telephone to make a call to Nani and to Anu. I also spoke to Shireen, who uttered her first words for me: 'Baba, mama.'

۱۵

I used to read the newspapers every day, both in the library and at Mr Patel's house. The media soon lost interest in my case. There was nothing new to report as matters were moving at a snail's pace in court; nearly a year had passed and the charge sheet had not been filed, so the hearings could not begin. Not that this was surprising, because the whole legal system was based on denial of justice to the poor and the marginalized. Delay always acts against the innocent.

I was denied bail by both the sessions and the high court. The prosecution argued that I had escaped the law in the past and if I was released on bail, I would once again make a getaway to some other country. The judges concurred with this apprehension, so it looked as though I would have to remain in prison until the case was decided. I was, however, allowed to appear for my final-year exams – I had been studying for a BA in English Literature before Uncle Brij's murder – and I graduated with high marks. I wanted to study law, but no college was ready to give me admission. Finally, the court's intervention got me admission to a correspondence course at the law college in Agra University.

There is no better place to study law than a prison. Every prisoner understands the finer points of law better than a fresh law graduate. Every murderer knows the difference between Sections

302, 304 and 307 of the IPC. It was explained to me how one could murder an opponent without inviting action under any of these sections. In my own case, though, knowledge of the law was of no use as the legal system moved at its own slow pace, and I was helpless to do anything about it.

Then, suddenly, there was a flurry of reports in the media about my case. A major English daily carried a report that some of the heritage Mughal jewellery, reportedly stolen from Lala Mukund Behari's house, had made an appearance in some of the auction houses of Switzerland and London. The jewellery had been smuggled out of India and clandestinely put up for auction by some well-known auctioneers. Other articles followed, speculating that the jewellery had been smuggled out by me with the help of my family. Some of the papers went to town, calling us anti-national and hawkers of national treasure abroad. A couple of the more rabid communal papers demanded the arrest of my mother and Nani.

These reports sent me into a depression. I begged Ammi to take Nani for treatment to London, as my case was going nowhere and they were in danger of being arrested under media pressure. All the media reports were based on rumours, innuendoes and half-baked untruths. Every newspaper was trying to outdo the other by adding more masala to the previous story. This saddened me more than the fear of facing the hangman's noose. I thought of Nani, who was so passionate about India, her country. Ammi, who preferred to remain in her beloved India rather than go with her husband to Pakistan, was being labelled a traitor today. I, who was brought up to love this nation more than my own life, stood accused of being a thief and stealing from the national treasure. This so-called national treasure had been bought for peanuts by the lala's ancestors from the looters in 1857 and kept in his safe. The Mughals, whose treasure had been looted, who died and gave everything for this nation, were being labelled as traitors. Could there be a greater irony than this? I cried at night, cursing myself for going to Anu's house on Holi and bringing such shame and dishonour to my family.

I knew that if anybody had smuggled the jewellery out of the country, it was Lala Mukund Behari, Anu's father. He had killed his younger brother, put the blame on me, smuggled out the jewellery, and was now making millions by auctioning it. He had become the mayor of Delhi by exploiting all the sympathy generated on account of being the poor victim of a Muslim boy's murderous machinations. I had no proof against him, while he had the support of the media, society, law and even the judiciary. They were all highlighting the fact that my father was a minister in Pakistan and, by inference, I was unreliable and suspect. 1967 was an election year and every politician in Delhi was wooing the influential lala for his support. Nani tried to meet Indira Gandhi in spite of her bad health, but the prime minister was busy trying to save her government from the intrigues of Morarji Desai and Kamaraj. My family and I were caught in a quicksand of conspiracies, sinking deeper the more we struggled to get out.

Finally, charges were framed against me on the basis of the evidence provided by the police, to which I pleaded not guilty, and the hearing of the case began. The sessions judge was Justice Kapoor, who openly expressed biased opinions against Muslims in general and the Mughals in particular. He performed puja every morning in the court and openly said that India would have been a Hindu rashtra but for foolish secularists like Jawaharlal Nehru. My lawyer tried to get the case transferred to another court, but did not succeed. The attempt further infuriated Justice Kapoor and he showed his anger at every opportunity. There was no direct evidence against me. The iron rod which had been used to hit Brij Uncle had no fingerprints. Someone had obviously wiped it clean and the prosecution pointed the finger at me. No one had seen me committing the crime; there was no evidence that I had entered the bedroom of Lala Mukund Behari, where the iron safe was kept and where Brij Uncle was first attacked. All the evidence against me was based on the statement of Mukund Behari and some of his neighbours.

Lala Mukund Behari was the star witness for the prosecution. A big posse of media persons gathered outside the court the day he was called to give evidence. The Delhi government's legal department had deliberately chosen a well-known Muslim lawyer as the chief prosecutor. I.M. Khan was shrewd, but was also known to be corrupt. He was a tall, fair, handsome Pathan with a booming voice and the gift of the gab. He was known never to lose a case, however weak.

My lawyer, on the other hand, was an idealist who loved Urdu poetry and believed in the ideals of justice and fair play. He was known to help the poorest of the poor if he found injustice was being done to them by the system. He was also known to be a fearless crusader for human rights. He had a sharp mind and a firm but soft voice.

Lala Mukund Behari arrived in court with his friends and followers, wearing an expensive black achkan and the round black cap favoured by rich lalas. He took his place in the witness box without once looking at me. I knew he was hiding his guilt behind his confident smile and arrogance. He took oath on the Bhagvad Gita. Khan smiled at him and asked, 'You are the elder brother of the deceased, Mr Brij Behari?'

'Yes sir, he was fifteen years younger than me. When my father died, he was only ten and the responsibility for his upbringing and education fell on my shoulders. I brought him up as my own son.' Mukund Behari spoke in a deeply emotional voice.

'So you loved him like your own son and he preferred to stay in the same haveli with you, although he owned a number of houses?' Khan said.

'Yes, he had all the freedom he could have wanted in my house, without any responsibilities. He was very fond of pigeon-flying and the terrace of my haveli was reserved for his pigeons. Everyone in Chandni Chowk knows that I allowed him all the freedom to indulge his passion – even a parent would not have permitted as much.' It was obvious that he had rehearsed all the answers with the prosecution lawyer.

Justice Kapoor was looking at him with sympathy and respect.

'What did you see on the day of Holi?' asked Khan.

'I was playing Holi in the lane in front of my house. Brij was there too, with some of our neighbours. He told me that he wanted to go to the toilet and would return in a moment,' said Mukund Behari. 'Suddenly, I heard a commotion and shouting from inside the house. I went in, followed by some of our friends. We could hear shouts from the terrace, so I rushed up the stairs. There I saw my dear brother Brij lying on the floor next to the pigeons' net. This boy was standing over him. When he saw us, he ran down the stairs, pushing some of us aside.'

'Did he come frequently to your house?' asked Khan, pointing at me.

'Yes, he was a classmate of my son and used to come and play with him. We did not object, thinking that he belonged to a respectable family, but we soon realized that he was not a good influence on my son.'

'Was he invited by your son to come and play Holi with him?' asked the prosecution lawyer.

'No, Vinod had specifically told him not to come, as he planned to play Holi with his friends in Delhi University.'

'How did he enter your house? Did he inform any family member that he was there?'

'No, we were not aware of his presence in the house. No one saw him coming. He did not enter from the front door. It seems that he took advantage of the festival, when the doors of most houses are left open. He must have entered through a side door. We became aware of his presence only after the murderous attack on my brother.'

'Did Shiraz have any enmity with your younger brother?'

'I can't say, but Brij was very friendly with him and used to involve him in pigeon-rearing as his father, Aziz Khan, who is now a Pakistani minister and a rabid opponent of India, was also a pigeon-racer when he lived in Delhi.'

My lawyer immediately objected to this statement and it was withdrawn, but the lala had made his point: I was the son of a Pakistani who was anti-Indian, and therefore extremely unreliable. The newspapers had been belabouring this point from the day of my arrest, as if the fact of my being the son of a Pakistani minister was sufficient ground to convict me for the murder of Brij Behari.

'Do you think Shiraz had any reason to kill Brij Behari?' asked I.M. Khan.

'Brij once told me that the boy was upset and believed that we had taken advantage of the Mughals and acquired their precious jewellery for a pittance. He also believed that his father's jewellery shop in Dariba was looted by us during the riots that followed Partition. He wanted to take revenge for this. It seems that he befriended my son and entered our household with a devilish plan to rob us. He had been planning it for quite some time.'

My lawyer again objected to this statement as speculation and hearsay, but Justice Kapoor was in no mood to entertain any objection.

'When did you become aware of the robbery and how did he open the safe in your bedroom?' asked Khan.

'Sir, I don't know, but when I entered my bedroom, I saw that the safe was open and all the jewellery was missing. There was blood on the floor and the bed. It looked as if Brij had been attacked in that room.'

'Did anyone else have the keys to your safe?'

'Yes, my wife Naina Devi also had the keys. It seems that they were stolen from her a few days earlier.'

'What is your assessment of the value of jewellery stolen from you?' asked the prosecution lawyer.

'In the international market, the value has been assessed at a hundred and fifty million dollars, but historically, it's priceless.'

Khan said he had no more questions to ask. Before my lawyer could cross-examine the lala, Justice Kapoor adjourned the court for the day.

I hated Lala Mukund Behari more than ever. I was sure that it was he who had killed Brij Uncle, it was he who had smuggled all the heritage jewellery out of India, and it was he who had manipulated the evidence to get me convicted. In my eyes he was the devil incarnate, whose only morality and religion was to make more and more money.

It was Friday, so the courts were closed for the next two days, which meant that the judge had given Mukund Behari two days' time to prepare. The next day, Anand came to see me in prison. He was upset with the judge and said, 'There is no direct evidence to nail you but the attitude of the judge is enough to tell us that he has already made up his mind.'

'What can we do to counter this?' I asked.

'My boy, under our legal system, there is no jury, everything depends on the attitude and will of the judge. I wanted to call your friend Vinod and his mother Naina Devi to the witness box, but the crafty lala anticipated that and has sent his wife to America for treatment – she has been diagnosed with cancer. Vinod has accompanied her and they are not expected to return for nearly a year. Chances are she will never come back, as the cancer is in an advanced stage.'

I was devastated to hear this, for I was fond of Anu's mother. She had always been ill-treated by the lala, who cared little for her. I was also disturbed by the fact that Anu was all alone with her father, who had turned against her ever since he became aware of our relationship.

'I want to call his daughter and your friend, Anu, to the witness box,' said Anand.

'No, never! I will not let you to do that,' I said firmly.

Anand was taken aback by my reaction. He didn't know that Anu was also the mother of my daughter. I didn't want her to be exposed like this. Nobody must know that I had gone to her house secretly to meet her and it was she who had let me in.

'We have no alternative plan. In order to save you, I need her to come to the witness stand and tell the court that you were with her when the incident took place. It was she who invited you to her house that day.' Anand was insistent.

'You want the whole world to know that she was alone with a Muslim boy who came to meet her secretly. I would rather be convicted than inflict that upon her.'

'They are going to get half a dozen witnesses to question your character and activities, but you won't allow me to get one witness who may prove your innocence. She should come forward herself if she loves you,' Anand said, looking at me challengingly.

I didn't know what to say.

That night I met Babur in my dreams after a long time. I lashed out at him. 'Where were you, Sir Emperor, leaving me in this shithole? Why don't you help me get out of trouble, if you have the powers and blessings of all your so-called cosmic forces?'

'Shiraz, Alexander, Genghis and I, we all sacrificed a great deal to achieve what we did. We killed, maimed and destroyed whoever came in our path. We were ready to die every day, every moment, but you want to have your cake and eat it too.' Babur laughed. 'You don't want blood on your hands, but you want a victory. You want wealth, but also talk of socialism. You want to possess the world, but you also talk of human rights. You want democracy, but still want to be ruled by one family, the Nehru dynasty. You are just like all the others: a first-class hypocrite.'

'Are you talking to me or are you giving an election speech?'

'No, I am telling you some home truths. If you want to get out of this mess, you must be ready to sacrifice either your love, or your family, or your dignity. I am telling you an obvious fact that you can see but choose not to. You are not Shiraz anymore. You are Aijaz. Nobody knows this. If your fingerprints are taken today, they will be very different from the fingerprints found on the murdered man's body. They will not match those on the bloodstained clothes the police recovered and which they claim belonged to Shiraz. If your fingerprints don't match, no case can be made against you.'

I was stunned. It was true. If my fingerprints were matched today with the fingerprints taken from the murder scene and the body of Brij Behari, the case against me would be demolished. Why had I not thought of it earlier?

'That's a great idea. I'll tell my lawyer tomorrow.' I wanted to hug Babur.

'No, you can't do that. You have given your word to Daata Sahib that you will not let anyone know that you have entered the body of Aijaz. If you break your promise, everyone you love will have to pay the price for it, a price so high that you will wish to die rather than live.'

'That means I can't save myself. I will have to spend the rest of my life in this hellhole.' I was exhausted by the mind games Babur was playing with me.

'No, your beloved Anu can come and save you. She can tell the truth, that when her Brij Uncle was being murdered, she was kissing you. You went to her house on her invitation. My dear boy, one has to sacrifice something to get something else. That is the law of nature. You sacrificed your brother to get the body of a human, now sacrifice the honour of your beloved to get your freedom.' Babur's tone was annoyingly condescending.

'I will have to talk to Anu about it. She will have to find a way to come and see me in the court when I go for my next hearing,' I said.

'That is for your silly, time-wasting, corrupt courts to work out. If it was my court, a decision would have been taken a long time back. There is another way, though.' I was getting tired by now, talking to Babur instead of sleeping peacefully, but I asked him what the other option was.

'Well, if your lawyer, or the police themselves, discover that your fingerprints don't match those found on the body of the murdered person, you will be free without inviting the curse of the saints.' Saying this, Babur vanished, leaving me with my dilemma.

Monday was a heavily overcast day. It rained incessantly and the road from Tihar Jail to Tees Hazari court was flooded, but we reached in time. The building was new, but the court of Justice Kapoor was flooded with all the water coming in from the balcony. He adjourned the hearing for Thursday, as the next two days were national holidays and the courts were closed. In India, we have more holidays than any other country in the world. We celebrate all the Hindu, Muslim, Sikh, Christian and Buddhist festivals, the birthdays of dozens of gods and prophets, and the birth anniversaries of political leaders and former prime ministers. All these holidays further slow down the creaking wheels of justice.

The next day, it continued to rain heavily; I started a fever and did not get up from my bed, which was just a blanket on the hard cement floor. Since it was a holiday, the prison dispensary was also closed. One of the other prisoners gave me an Aspirin, but by evening, my condition had worsened. I continued to shiver even after several men had put their blankets over me. It was clear that I was suffering from malaria. When the doors to the cells opened in the morning, the prisoners informed the jail guards. Most of the officers had gone on leave as they had two consecutive holidays. The jail superintendent had gone to Ahmedabad with his family. Except for a few Aspirins from the prisoners, I got no medical treatment. I lay there, drenched in my own sweat, shivering and semi-conscious. My head was aching so badly that I feared I would die.

Suddenly, I saw my mother by my side. She kissed me on my forehead and said that there was nothing to worry about as she was there to take care of me. She hugged me and I felt well again, my fever and pain gone. I felt so light that I started floating in the air like a kite. If my mother had not caught me, I would have floated high in the sky and gone somewhere far away with the birds. That was when I decided to be a pigeon again. It was the perfect solution to my predicament. I could fly out of the prison, visit Anu whenever I wanted to see her, play with my daughter Shireen, fly across the border to visit my father in Lahore.

I heard my mother's voice saying, 'Shiraz, will you be able to visit us in London, when you become a pigeon?'

'Of course. Pigeons can fly thousands of kilometres and, anyway, London is a more pigeon-friendly city than Delhi. I've heard that the queen loves pigeon racing too. I'll join her flock in Buckingham Palace,' I said, jumping around my mother like a small boy. Suddenly, I felt a sharp pain in my leg and my eyes opened. I was disoriented and didn't know where I was, but could feel a sharp needle entering my body.

I was in Delhi's Wellington Hospital in a state of delirium. My mother was nowhere to be seen. Instead, there was a rude nurse who loved to shout and insult the poor patients in that government hospital. Luckily, my bed was in a corner, where I could have some peace. The general ward was full to overflowing because of a malaria epidemic in the city. Patients were crying and shouting, their relatives chatting and disturbing everyone around them. Stray dogs roamed freely in the wards, snatching away the food of the patients lying on the floors, and sometime even gnawing at the limbs of an unconscious patient. As an undertrial, my ankle was chained to the iron bed. A doctor came to examine me and told me that I had been brought there in an unconscious state and had been in a delirium for the last forty-eight hours, but there was no need to worry as the worst phase was over and I was out of danger. In my conscious state, I thought the hospital was even worse than Tihar Jail. The treatment provided to the poor people was shabby and insensitive. It was not surprising that every day there were half a dozen deaths in the hospital. People were catching diseases and infections from each other. I wanted to get out of there at any cost.

In the evening, Nani came with a basket of fruits. Accompanying her was a burqa-clad girl. Instantly, I forgot all my troubles. It was Anu. The first thing I asked her was, 'Where is Shireen?'

'At home. I couldn't bring her here, could I?' Anu said, brushing my hair back with her fingers. In her black burqa, she looked even more beautiful than usual. Surrounded by black satin, her face was like the full moon emerging from dark clouds. Nani hugged me and said that she had been coming to the hospital for the last two days, was found me conscious and in my senses for the first time. 'Tomorrow, your mother is also arriving, she will take care of you. I am too old to take care of anyone now. Tonight, this girl will be with you; she has managed to get out of her house for a night.'

I was on cloud nine upon hearing this. I had desperately wanted to talk to Anu ever since I was arrested. Already, I had spent more than a year in jail. Nani left us after a while. Anu cleaned my body with a sponge and before I knew it, I was fast asleep.

When my eyes opened, I found Anu sleeping next to me under my blanket, her arm around me. I felt so blessed to have this girl. She must have felt me stir, because she opened her eyes just then, kissed me on my nose and sat up.

'I have to speak to you before it's morning and time to go,' Anu whispered in my ear. 'I have decided to appear in court, Sherry. I will be a witness, because I know the truth. I know you have not killed anybody. My word against my father's will demolish the prosecution's case'.

'How can you do that, how can you publicly admit your relationship with me, how can you call your own father a liar and a murderer?' My voice was loud, causing many of the patients' attendants to look up in our direction.

'I don't care anymore. If I can't save you, what is the point of all this "izzat" and family honour? And even more than me, your daughter needs you. I have to tell the world that you are Shireen's father.'

'That would make our daughter a bastard in the eyes of society – born of a Muslim father who is charged with the murder of her grand-uncle.' I spoke passionately.

'You worry too much about society, while society doesn't give a damn about you. Don't you worry, I'll take care of everything.' Anu said she was going to get in touch with my lawyer and would discuss the matter with my mother, who was due to arrive the next morning.

Hina Begum came with Bundu, with a packet of the butter cookies and chocolates I loved. She looked tired and old. She hugged me and started sobbing. 'My Sherry, I had so many dreams for you but now I have lost both my sons, one to an accident and the other to fate. You have to get out soon and come with me to London. James is a very good man; he will give you a good life.'

'Ammi, I love you and have always wanted you to be happy. Don't worry. I will be released, if not today, then tomorrow. But I want you to stop Anu from appearing as a defence witness. She can't tell the truth about our relationship in an open court. I can't let her be shamed for my sake.'

Ammi had a sad smile on her face. 'You men will never understand. Women think from the heart and not from the mind alone. If I was in her place, I would do the same. But I will try and speak to her.'

Ammi saw the iron chain on my leg and was furious. She rushed to the hospital director's office. There she created such a ruckus that the director, an old Bengali gentleman, had to come to my ward and apologize to me personally. My chains were immediately removed and a policeman was posted outside my ward to keep an eye on me.

By the next day my fever was gone and, as the bed was required for other patients, I was sent back to prison. It was like a homecoming when I entered my barrack. Mr Patel, who had returned from Ahmedabad, was kind enough to come and see me. He gave instructions that I was to be sent food from his kitchen until I was well again. His wife made khichdi for me, which reminded me of Nani, who always insisted on making it for me with her own hands when I was unwell.

In the prison, I met some of the most compassionate men as well as some of the most ruthless bastards. Unlike in the world outside, jails are genuinely secular places. There are no differences of religion or caste. The hierarchy is based on the kind of punishment one is facing. Those who have been given the death penalty are segregated from the rest. Those given life imprisonment are treated as permanent settlers and are at the top of the hierarchy. Then there are those who have got ten years or more for homicide or dacoity. At the lowest rung are those who have committed sex crimes or white-collar criminals who have cheated the poor. Those accused of rape are treated as free game for everyone. Even the jail authorities do not try to protect them.

Some of the prisoners preferred being inside the prison to being outside. After their release, they committed a crime just to get back to the comfort of the prison. One such man was Billu, who was nearly seventy and had spent more than fifty years inside various jails. He was a one-man Mother Teresa inside Tihar. He would help everyone, without any discrimination. Even the most ferocious criminals respected him and listened to him. He knew criminal law better than any lawyer. Billu was a self-taught man who had mastered the English language and prepared applications and legal documents for prisoners who could not afford a lawyer. He now took upon himself the task of looking after me, as I was still very weak.

Billu was philosophical about life. 'Shiraz mian, look at this moon,' he said, pointing at the full moon outside our cell. 'It is a prisoner of its own path. It cannot move even a single millimetre from the path assigned to it. There are crows which can fly anywhere. There are butterflies, so pretty but so transient. Everything perishes, except those who love the path of their prison, like the moon and the sun. I am free as a bird in my mind, but I follow a given path like the moon; therefore, I survive. Once you learn to love and enjoy what fate has assigned to you, there can be no pain, no regrets and no separation. If your love is not selfish, if you don't want to possess your loved ones, you learn to love everything around you. To possess is to lose; therefore, learn to give and life will be beautiful. Freedom and slavery are all in the mind. You can be free in chains and behind bars, and you can be a slave with wings and a sky to fly in.'

I listened to the philosophy of this seventy-year-old man, who had spent most of his life within the four walls of a prison but knew the world better than most of us.

My trial continued to proceed at a very slow pace. Lala Mukund Behari was cross-examined by my lawyer, but the wily lala could not be trapped and he was able to answer most of Anand's questions with ease. He came across as a compassionate, caring elder brother, who had no differences or enmity with the deceased. The prosecution also called a few neighbours, who testified that they had seen me escaping from the scene of the crime with blood all over my clothes. They also testified that they had warned the family earlier about allowing me to enter their house and befriending their children. They all had praise for the elder lala, as a concerned and loving brother, and a pious man who donated generously to charities and religious causes.

Now it was for the defence to present its witnesses. Anand called some of my teachers, who all sang my praises as a young man of character. Neither Naina Devi nor Vinod could come to the witness box as they were still not back in India. Naina Devi's condition had worsened and it seemed unlikely that she would be able to testify. Anand requested the court to call Anu, the niece of the deceased, to the witness stand. Anu had become incommunicado since her last visit to me in the hospital. Her phone number at home had changed and she had not contacted either my lawyer or my mother. It was clear that her father had heard of her intentions and had virtually imprisoned her. The court summoned her to appear before it, but she did not come on the given date. The hearing was postponed three times, more than a month passed, but still she did not appear, so the court issued a warrant against her. On the day in question, a lawyer appeared on behalf of Anu and informed the court that she'd had to fly to America, as her mother was in a critical condition. The court was to close for the summer vacations, so Anu was given sixty days' time to testify.

I was worried about Anu and Shireen. It was unlike Anu to leave at this critical juncture, without informing anybody. Especially as she herself was keen to testify. I prayed to Allah and all the cosmic forces to protect her. For the first time in my life I was praying five times a day, like any pious Muslim. I also participated in all the pujas organized by the prisoners.

Ammi tried to get some information about the whereabouts of Naina Devi, but failed. Uncle James used his contacts in American cancer hospitals to get information about her, but to no avail. Lala Mukund Behari had also disappeared, probably to be with his family, but I believed that he had gone to take account of his stolen Mughal jewellery.

While we were busy with the trial, something terrible happened inside the jail. A prisoner escaped and Mr Patel was held responsible for it. He was transferred with immediate effect and I could not even say goodbye to him. The worst part was that Lalit Singh, his assistant, was given temporary charge of the prison. Lalit Singh had hated me since the day I had rejected his advances, and had promised that one day he would teach me a lesson I would never forget. My proximity to Mr Patel had saved me so far, but it was clear that now I would have to remain alert every moment. The first thing the new jailor did was to take me off library duty and send me to the kitchen. However, all the prisoners in the kitchen were sympathetic to me, so they gave me the lighter job of packing the food. Next, Lalit Singh took away all my books and my writing material. He wanted me to plead with him for small favours, but I decided to remain silent. This was not to his liking. All the scum of the prison owed him loyalty; now they began to behave as if they owned the prison. One day, I was attacked while I was sleeping. It was only Billu's timely intervention that saved me. My problem was compounded by the fact that Timur-Langda was no longer around to protect me. Soon I was shifted to the barrack next to the toilets. The smell was so overpowering that it was impossible to sleep or eat anything. Even my clothes began smelling of shit. Lalit Singh knew that I would not be able to stand it for long.

I went to his office, seeking an appointment. He immediately invited me in and said, 'Shiraz Sahib, you don't need an appointment, you may come to my office any time of the day or night.' He winked at me lewdly. 'Tell me, how can I be of service to you?'

'I want my barrack to be changed, I can't stay in that shithole.'

'I am sorry, but someone has to stay there. This is Tihar, not your Taj Mahal, Excellency, the last prince of the Mughal empire,' he said.

I ignored the sarcasm and said, 'Look, Mr Singh, I have no quarrel with you. Don't do this, otherwise I will have to fight back.'

He laughed. 'Who wants to fight you? I just want to love you, only once, and then you will have all your privileges. I had promised myself that the Mughal prince will suck me off at least once. Your ancestors sucked our country for centuries, why can't you suck my cock for a few moments?'

Saying this, he stood up and pulled down his zip, then started moving towards me. I pushed a chair between us and shouted at him to stop. He was a strong man. He grappled the chair from my hand and hit me with it. I fell down and he stood over me with his cock hanging out and a smirk on his face. He was so used to having his way with the prisoners that he was not even worried about somebody entering his office. I turned around and hit him on his balls with my foot, with all the strength I could muster. He shrieked and doubled up with pain; I stood up, opened the door and ran out to the kitchen.

Tyagi, my other enemy, whom I had defeated in the kite-flying contest, was in the kitchen. He never ate with the other prisoners. Special food was prepared for him in desi ghee, supplied from outside by his gang members. Even the jailor was terrified of him, as he could get anybody killed or kidnapped, sitting in the comfort of Tihar Jail. When he saw me, he laughed and said, 'Oye, patangbaaz, what happened, have you seen a ghost?'

I didn't have to answer him as Lalit Singh came rushing after me and started hitting me with a rod. He hit me non-stop, as if possessed. I fell down and covered my head with my hands, trying to save myself from the blows. No one had the guts to stop the jailor. I felt the bones in my left hand crack and screamed in pain. Suddenly, Tyagi stood up and shouted at him. 'Kutte, you want to kill this boy. Why?' He caught hold of the rod in Lalit Singh's hand and wrested it away.

The jailor's eyes were red, he was trembling with anger. 'This bastard thinks he is the prince of India, the son of Babur. He has insulted Hindus by murdering Lala Brij Behari. I have to teach him a lesson.'

Tyagi threw away the rod and shouted back, 'You gaandu, you're lying. You wanted to have sex with him, don't talk of Babur and Muslims. I have a fight with Shiraz, but I respect him because he is an honest man. If you want to fight, come, I'll teach you how to fuck a real man. I'll show you what it feels like when you invade an asshole. If you ever raise a finger against Shiraz again, I'll get your balls roasted in the tandoor and have them for breakfast.'

The jail guards and the prisoners in the kitchen were watching, but the jailor could do nothing. He stood up quietly and went out. Tyagi smiled at me and said, 'From today you are under my wing. If anyone creates any problems for you, just let me know.'

I can only think that Tyagi had been sent by the saints to save me, otherwise I would have died that day. I had multiple fractures in my left hand and bruises all over my body. I was immediately taken to the prison hospital by the guards, all of whom hated the new jailor. We didn't talk about the incident again. When my lawyer and mother came to see me, I told them that I had fallen in the bathroom and broken my hand. They didn't believe me, but kept quiet as they had more pressing problems to confront.

There was no news of Anu and her mother. The court date was nearing and we had no witnesses to present in our defence. I had to make a statement and was then to be cross-examined by the prosecution. I had nothing new to add to what I had already said. The situation was grim.

The courts opened after the summer vacation, but our witnesses were nowhere to be seen. There was no trace of Anu's family. Even the summons could not be served. Justice Kapoor was losing patience. He fixed the next date for my cross-examination for just a few days later. I prepared myself, but I knew I could only tell the partial truth. I didn't want to tell the court that I had gone to the house on Anu's invitation. In India, people kill and die for the sake of family honour; how could I dishonour the girl I loved so much?

The day of the hearing dawned hot and sultry. Even at eleven in the morning, the court room felt like an oven. We were sweating profusely. As Justice Kapoor made his entry, two women wearing black burqas entered the court and moved towards the bench. When the guard tried to stop them, one of the women raised her naqab and revealed her face. My lawyer stood up and moved towards them. He was talking to both the women when Justice Kapoor shouted, 'Order, order,' banging his mallet down on the table.

Anand walked up to the judge and whispered something to him. The judge immediately adjourned the court and asked both the lawyers to come to his chamber. As the women turned towards me, I was astonished to see the face of Anu, smiling at me. But who was the frail, old lady with her? To my shock I realized that it was her mother, Naina Devi. They came towards me and the old lady hugged me and kissed me on the forehead. 'I have come back, Shiraz, I will save you,' she said in a trembling voice. I could see that she was very sick.

Anu caught my hands and squeezed them. 'Sherry, I have persuaded Ma to come back and tell the truth. She is an eyewitness to the crime.'

The judge returned and announced that in the changed circumstances, he would first call the defence witnesses. He looked at the two ladies, who had by now removed their burqas. Naina Devi was the first witness.

Naina Devi's head was covered with a silk scarf as she had lost most of her hair to chemotherapy. She was wearing a plain cotton sari. Her fair skin had turned sickly white, and her sharp-featured face looked as if it was made of porcelain. She looked fragile, as if she would shatter into small pieces at any moment. She took oath on the Bhagvad Gita and sat down on the chair placed for her in the witness stand.

'What is your name?' Anand asked softly.

'Naina Devi.'

'Husband's name?'

'Lala Mukund Behari.'

'How were you related to the murdered person, Lala Brij Behari?'

'He was my brother-in-law, but I looked after him like he was my own son.'

'How were his relations with his elder brother, your husband?' Anand said.

Naina Devi was quiet for some time. Then she said softly, 'They had very good relations, but in the last few years, they also had many arguments. My husband did not believe in spending too much money, but Brij Behari had very expensive hobbies. He also wanted a share of the Mughal jewellery hidden in our house. Towards the end, they fought quite frequently. Brij wanted a division of all their properties and wealth.'

'Did they ever threaten each other?' asked my lawyer.

'I stopped them from attacking each other on many occasions. Brij used to lose his temper very easily.'

'What happened on the morning of 27 March, the day of Holi?'

Naina Devi asked for a glass of water. She looked exhausted and Justice Kapoor asked her if she wanted to rest. Naina Devi declined. She said that she did not have much time and wanted to fulfil her duty to her conscience.

'Tell me what you saw and heard on that day?' Anand asked gently.

'Everyone was playing Holi outside in the lane. I was supervising the preparation of thandai and sweets in the kitchen. At some point

I needed some saffron, which was kept in my bedroom. As I walked towards my room, I saw Brij stealthily enter it. He went straight to the big safe hidden behind the picture of Radha–Krishna. To my surprise, he had the key to the safe. It was then that I realized that my key, which used to be hanging from my petticoat, was missing. The other key was with Lalaji. I saw Brij opening the safe. I immediately went looking for my husband. He was playing Holi with his friends in front of our house. I called out to him and informed him that Brij was opening the safe in our bedroom.'

She took another sip of water and continued, 'Lalaji was already in an inebriated state after a few glasses of bhang. He picked up an iron rod lying in the courtyard. I tried to snatch the rod from his hand, but he pushed me and went straight to the bedroom. I ran after him. He pushed the door open. Brij was bent over, filling a canvas bag with jewellery. My husband raised the iron rod and hit him with full force on his head. Before he could hit him again, I caught hold of him from behind. Brij ran up the stairs, bleeding profusely from a wound in his head.'

Naina Devi was exhausted. She closed her eyes and sat silently. The judge asked if she wanted the court to be adjourned, but she just sought his permission to take her medicine.

After swallowing the tablets, she said, 'Lalaji wanted to rush after Brij Behari, but I didn't let him go. He was pacified by the fact that Brij had left the bag of jewellery in the room. Suddenly, we heard a commotion outside. I ran out and saw Shiraz come down the stairs in a rush.' She looked at me.

'Were you aware of his presence in the house?' asked Anand.

'Yes, I had seen him going up the stairs. I knew my daughter and he were childhood friends and always celebrated Holi together. I love Shiraz as much as I love my son Vinod. He is one of the most cultured and honest boys I have met in my entire life.' She looked towards me again and smiled.

There was pindrop silence in the courtroom. Many lawyers from the adjacent courts had come in to hear what Naina Devi had to say. A few court reporters had also heard that she was testifying and had gravitated towards our court.

'Did you see a bag in his hand?'

'No. He was empty-handed and people were shouting after him, "Thief, catch him, catch him." The truth is that when Lala Mukund Behari realized that his brother was dead, he asked me to keep quiet and cleaned the iron rod of his fingerprints and hid the jewellery, blaming this poor boy for robbery and murder.'

'Why didn't you tell the truth to the police earlier?' asked the lawyer.

'At that point I thought my first duty was to my family and my husband. I went along with my husband and told the police lies to save him. I was also worried about the honour of my daughter. I didn't want people to know that she had secretly invited Shiraz to the house.' She looked towards Anu, who was listening to her mother, tears shining in her eyes.

'When did you discover that you were suffering from cancer?'

'I was already sick, but a few days after this incident, I fainted a couple of times. The tests told us that the cancer was in an advanced stage. My husband was advised to send me to America. He took advantage of the situation to send me out of the country so that I could not testify.'

'Why did you decide to come back and testify now?' asked Anand.

'My daughter came to America and told me how an innocent man was suffering for a crime he had not committed. I know my days are numbered. The doctors have told me that I may survive a few years or die in a few months. When you see death so close at hand, you want to pay the debts of your loved ones before you die.

You want to live life on your own terms, even if it is just for a few days. So I decided to come back and testify. Hearing of this, my husband flew down to Boston, where I was undergoing treatment. He hid our passports somewhere and went away to Switzerland, to organize the auction of the stolen jewellery. My daughter, Anu, ran from pillar to post to get duplicate passports for us. It is only due to her efforts that we are here in your court.'

Justice Kapoor could see that the case against me had been demolished by this one witness. For the first time, he spoke. 'Where is Lala Mukund Behari now?'

'I think he is in Switzerland. He has not been in touch with us for the last two months.'

Justice Kapoor looked completely befuddled and at a loss as to how to proceed. He adjourned the court till the following day. Before I went back to prison, I went up to Naina Devi and hugged her. I wished my mother or Nani had been present in the court to hear her testify. But Nani was once again in hospital and Ammi was with her.

Anu said, 'Don't worry, Sherry, we are going straight to the hospital from here. My mother has been admitted there too, and she needs rest. We'll meet your mother and Nani. Now I am here to take care of everyone.'

I laughed and said, 'Yes, boss. I know you can take care of everyone, but what about Shireen, where is she?'

'I have left her in Boston, with my aunt; she is going to a school there. She is safe in America.'

Anu was amazing. I wanted to hug her, kiss her, make love to her. I had to remind myself that I was still a jailbird. I had to go back to the prison.

I could not sleep that night. Until that morning I had been looking at a bleak future, years of darkness behind bars. Now I was already planning what I would do once I was out of prison. In prison you learn to appreciate the importance of the small things in life. I wanted to have an ice cream at India Gate; I wanted to eat kebabs sitting on the steps of Jama Masjid. I wanted to watch a movie at Odeon cinema in Connaught Place. I didn't think of wealth or travelling or good clothes. These small pleasures were what I used to dream about every day, sitting in my prison cell.

I didn't tell anyone what had transpired in the court that day. I just kept quiet and went to bed early. But the anxiety of an uncertain future kept sleep at bay. What would I do once I was released, where would I go? Would I leave the country as my mother wanted me to do? The biggest question in my mind was what would happen to my relationship with Anu. She was still married to the jeweller from Jaipur.

I don't know when Babur entered my cell, if I was still awake or had gone to sleep, but there he was, smiling at me as if it was his personal victory. 'So, Shiraz, everything is working out, didn't I tell you? You have passed your "agni parikhsha", your ordeal by fire, with flying colours. We Mughals are proud of you. I told you that the cosmic forces test us and then bless us. Now you are the blessed one. Go and conquer the world.'

'I am not a conqueror like you, nor do I have the armies to become one.'

'These days, who needs an army? You conquer the world with your corporations and firms. Money is the sword of modern times, with which you defend or conquer. Go, Shiraz, the world is waiting for you.' With those words, Babur vanished.

When morning came, I got up, shaved and put on the clean kurta pajama the jail authorities had given me to wear. I was ready to face the judge again, maybe for the last time.

The court was overflowing, with the media present in large numbers. The morning papers had been full of the testimony of Naina Devi, which had turned the case upside down. My mother had also come with Anu and Naina Devi. Anand came up to me and said, 'Shiraz, the worst is over. Now you may be punished only for possessing a false passport.'

Justice Kapoor looked grim. His best case was slipping out of his hand. He asked Naina Devi to take the witness stand again. Now it was for the prosecution lawyer, Khan, to cross-examine her. Khan looked nervous and was busy whispering to the police officers. He stood up and said, 'Your honour, we have no questions to ask. In fact, the police want to withdraw all murder charges against Shiraz. It's a case of mistrial and we want to move an application for his immediate release.'

Nobody had expected the administration to give in so quickly, without a fight. It was obvious that they were already embarrassed about having built up a false case against me; they did not want any further trouble. The police officers informed the court that they wanted to reopen and reinvestigate the case in the light of the new evidence available and therefore wanted to withdraw the charges against me.

It was a difficult moment for Justice Kapoor. He was convinced that being a Muslim and the son of a Pakistani, I was responsible for most of the ills of society. However, he had no option but to release me. After a meeting with the lawyers and the police officials, he reconvened the court and announced my discharge and immediate release.

I had been dreaming of this day, but now I suddenly felt sad, as if there was a void in my life. I knew I would miss my friends and enemies behind the walls of Tihar Jail.

My mother, Naina Devi and Anu came up to me and embraced me. Next day, every paper had this picture of me surrounded by these three women, young and old, Hindu and Muslim, joined together in love and honest human emotion. Suddenly, Shiraz was not a dangerous murderer but an innocent victim of circumstances, whom every newspaper wanted to interview.

We went straight to Wellington Hospital, to give the good news to Nani. She was overwhelmed and kept holding on to me as if I would fly away if she released me. She asked the doctors to let her go home immediately, but they refused as her sugar levels and blood pressure were still very high. That did not stop her from ordering boxes of sweets from the nearby Gole Market and distributing them in the hospital.

From the hospital I went straight to the dargah of Hazrat Nizamuddin Auliya and Humayun's Tomb, to pray and offer thanks to all the spiritual and cosmic forces. I promised to come back again, but now I was eager to go to our house in Ballimaran. I wanted to sit in the cane chair under the harsinghar tree in our courtyard and sip the tea made by my mother.

The news of my release had already spread in Ballimaran and when I reached there, a huge crowd had assembled outside our house. I wanted some quiet moments with Anu and my mother, but that was not to be. I was surrounded by well-wishers, family friends and media persons till late in the evening. Every house in the mohalla was celebrating my release. It was not just the acquittal of an individual but of the whole community, which had been put in the dock for the alleged crime of one person. Every house had prepared something special for me and the food and sweets kept arriving throughout the day.

I wanted to talk to my mother about my very uncertain future. I wanted to tell her about my daughter Shireen. I wanted to make plans with Anu. One thing was clear to me, that I could not survive without her anymore. But Anu had to go back to the hospital to look after her mother. My own mother was so exhausted that she went to sleep as soon as her head touched the pillow. I lay awake, thinking of Aijaz, who was dead yet alive in me. I wished that we had not been separated. I wished there had been no Partition, no Pakistan, no migration. More than anything else, I wished that Anu was not married and we could be together with our daughter. Suddenly, I realized how ungrateful we human beings are. Till yesterday, all I had thought of was freedom from prison and an opportunity to begin my life anew, but here I was, already thinking of what I did not have, rather than being thankful for what I did have.

Nani came home from the hospital the next day and immediately got busy in organizing a party to celebrate my return. Anu and I decided the time had come to tell her and my mother the truth about Shireen. Nani was lying on her diwan in the courtyard under the harsinghar tree, shouting instructions at the servants. Ammi was sitting next to her in a chair, giving the final touches to my new sherwani. We thought this was an opportune moment to break the news. Anu sat on the diwan and started oiling Nani's long white hair. I sat next to my mother and started pressing her legs.

Ammi smiled and said, 'Yes, Sherry, tell me, what do you want?' She knew that whenever I wanted something, I used to press her legs to soften her up.

'Ammi, I want to tell you something important about me and Anu,' I said hesitantly. I was suddenly nervous about how they would react to the news, especially about having been kept in the dark for so long.

'I know what you want to tell me,' Ammi laughed.

'What?' I inquired

Nani said, 'We all know that you two are Laila Majnu – madly in love with each other.'

'But you also know that it's impossible,' she said.

Now Anu couldn't resist jumping in. 'What is impossible, our love?'

'No, your marriage,' Ammi said calmly. 'You are a Hindu and already married. Anyway, I don't want Sherry to get into more trouble. He is going to London the day after tomorrow.'

We were all shocked by Anu's reaction. She had been so strong throughout this ordeal but now she started crying like a child.

Nani embraced her and said, 'Don't make my little girl cry.'

'Anu, we all understand, but we don't want another Hindu–Muslim riot in Delhi,' Ammi said in a gentler tone.

I couldn't believe it. I had lived for the day when I could marry Anu, but here were my own people calling it an impossibility.

'I am not leaving Delhi without Anu and Shireen. I would prefer to die here than live in London without them.' I spoke with the cold confidence of a grown man.

'Beta, we understand your feelings, but you know you can't marry Anu. She is already married and there is no divorce in their culture,' Nani tried to reason with me.

Suddenly, Anu said angrily, 'Do you know who Shireen's father is?'

'Who?' Nani and Ammi said together.

'Shiraz Khan, your son, who else,' Anu whispered.

Nani and Ammi had probably guessed by now, but they still looked stunned. Both turned to me for confirmation.

I looked down and said, 'It happened accidentally, before Holi and before my escape. Anu was already pregnant when she was married.'

Nani and Ammi were far more progressive than most women of their time, but this was scandalous.

'I will get a divorce from that lala. He knows Shireen is not his daughter because the poor bastard never got an opportunity to touch me. He has already demanded a divorce, but my father refused to consider it. But now he is nowhere in the picture and my mother has agreed. Before she dies, she wants to see me happy. I have already told her everything. In fact, that is the reason she travelled back in her condition. She wants me to marry Shireen's real father,' Anu said, anger and anguish in her voice.

Everyone was quiet. The silence was broken by the voice of Bundu, who had come to inform us that Aruna Asaf Ali, the former mayor of Delhi and one of the most respected women in the country, had agreed to be the chief guest at the evening function. He looked at us and immediately realized that something was wrong.

Ammi said, 'Sherry wants to marry Anu. What do you think, Bundu?'

Bundu laughed, 'If it was in my hands, I would have married them off yesterday. I want to play with my grandchildren before I die.'

'You know Aruna had the courage to marry barrister Asaf Ali at a time when communal hatred was at its peak,' Nani informed us as if we didn't know.

'Where is my granddaughter? In America? I want to see her.' Ammi was now impatient to see Shireen. She stood up and embraced Anu, wiping away her tears. 'If you can get a divorce and your mother agrees, I would love to have a brave and beautiful girl like you as my bahu.'

Nani was angry. 'Nobody is seeking my permission. I am not dead yet. I am still the head of this family.'

Ammi said soothingly, 'Of course, Amma Jaan, nothing can be done without your blessings. But now we have to make preparations for the evening. Anu, you go to the hospital to your mother and see if she is well enough to attend the party.'

Anu laughed. 'Of course, sasu-ma, I'll leave immediately.'

But she did not leave before pulling me into my room and

giving me her favourite French kisses. Bundu had to shout for me to separate us and send her to the hospital.

Nani and Ammi had agreed to our marriage, but they were still perturbed, as it was not easy to get a divorce in a traditional Hindu family. There was also the fear of communal trouble. Although Indira Gandhi had won the elections, the Congress party had been weakened. Right-wing organizations like the RSS and the Hindu Mahasabha had become much more active.

We decided that once Anu got her divorce papers, we would all travel to London, where my father would join us, and the wedding would take place in a simple ceremony. We didn't want any religious conversion, so it had to be a civil marriage.

Naina Devi returned to her haveli in Katra Neel as she wanted to spend her last days in her own home. Vinod also returned home to be with his mother. Naina Devi had eventually accepted her gay son and his partner, a French fashion designer, with whom he was living in Paris. It was not easy for her, but she had learned to accept almost anything in the changed circumstances.

There was still no communication from Mukund Behari, although a warrant for arrest had been issued against him. The news was that he had made his millions from the sale of the Mughal jewellery and now lived in a small village in Switzerland with a German woman. Anu got a divorce without much difficulty as her husband Lala Ramesh Chandra was already sick of all the news about her and wanted to disassociate himself from her as soon as possible. As she had made no financial demands, he was happy to give the divorce in the civil court.

Uncle James and Bundu arrived from London the day after my release. Everyone I loved was around me except my father, who could not travel to India as relations between the two countries were still sour. He had ceased to be a minister after the ouster of Ayub Khan and was spending more time in England these days.

We talked on the phone and he promised that he would come to London for the wedding ceremony next month.

◈

On the next full moon night, I went to Humayun's Tomb to meet Babur. Anu came with me, as I wanted my ancestors to meet my beloved and the mother of my daughter. We entered the tomb around midnight from a small side entrance in East Nizamuddin and sat on the bench in the deserted garden, facing the tomb, as if waiting for the curtains to rise and the play to begin.

Soon dark clouds came and hid the moon, and it began to drizzle. I took Anu into the monument, within which the tomb was placed on a large platform. We sat near the graves of Humayun and Hamida Begum. The candles and earthen oil lamps which had been placed there the previous evening were still burning. The tomb, surrounded by the intricate, cut-stone windows of the monument, looked magical in the flickering candlelight. The shadows on the high walls, the sound of the wind and the rain were enough to make even a hardened man like me shiver with an unknown fear. Anu clung to me as we sat there waiting for the moon to emerge. They say that sleep comes even on the gallows. I don't know when the two of us, holding each other, fell into a deep sleep.

It was the light from the full moon that woke me. I was astonished to see the whole Mughal durbar in front of me. The tomb had turned into a grand palace, with red-and-gold silk curtains, Persian carpets on the floor and exquisite golden chairs inlaid with precious stones. Sitting at the centre was my old friend Babur. On his left was his son Humayun and on the right was Akbar. Jahangir, Shahjahan, Aurangzeb, Bahadur Shah Zafar and a dozen other emperors, whom I did not recognize, were present as well. On a higher pedestal, behind them, sat all the queens, including Hamida

Bano, Noorjahan and Mumtaz Mahal. It was a sight I could not have imagined even in my wildest dreams. Anu and I in our simple cotton clothes looked like beggars in the midst of such grandeur and opulence.

Babur smiled at us and said, 'Come, my children, we are all here to welcome you. You have passed your ordeal of blood, fire and death with dignity and patience. You have earned the right to carry our name and our traditions to the new age and the new world. Shiraz, you are fortunate to have the blessings of the Sufi saints who dwell in this ancient land. In the great Mughal tradition, you have brought Hindu and Muslim blood together, and it is this unity that will allow Hindustan to dominate the world in the future. We bless your daughter Shireen as a worthy successor to the blood of Genghis and Tamerlane, two of the greatest conquerors the world has seen. Go and conquer the world now, but learn to serve with compassion and love, rising above religion, caste, creed, colour and race. Our empire survived as long as we followed this dictum but crumbled the day we adopted a bigoted and narrow religious approach.' Babur looked at Aurangzeb as he said this.

'Where shall we go from here, tell us, great Mughal? Shall we stay here in India, the land of our ancestors, or go to England, the land of the angrez, who destroyed our empire with their deceit and machinations?' I asked Babur.

'Go to the land of the angrez and conquer them as they conquered us, through trade, business, money, and by playing on human greed. And remember your competitors, who are also from the ancient lands of the East, across the Himalayan mountains. Beware of them, as they will divide you as the angrez did.' Babur smiled and motioned to us to come forward. He kissed both of us on the forehead and then, one by one, each of the emperors blessed us.

Suddenly, I felt a splash of water on my face. A strong wind had brought rain water through the open stone windows, to where Anu and I lay on the bare marble floor of the tomb.

Anu said, 'Shiraz, I saw a beautiful dream. All your great ancestors were present here in this tomb.' I smiled and hugged her. If it was a dream, we had seen it together, and if it was reality, we were in it together. I knew that now nobody could separate us. We were blessed to conquer the world together; my Anu would be part of my life, wherever I went.

It was morning and the rain had stopped. We stepped out into the beautiful garden outside the tomb and looked at the bright new morning, redolent with the smell of fresh roses and the chirping of birds. With no one around to see us, I took Anu in my arms and kissed her on the lips.